THE PURSUIT

THE PURSUIT

Christopher Nicole

This first world edition published in Great Britain 2002 by
SEVERN HOUSE PUBLISHERS LTD of
9–15 High Street, Sutton, Surrey SM1 1DF.
This first world edition published in the USA 2003 by
SEVERN HOUSE PUBLISHERS INC of
595 Madison Avenue, New York, N.Y. 10022.

British Library Cataloguing in Publication Data

Nicole, Christopher
    The pursuit
    1. Narcotics dealers - Fiction
    2. Witnesses - Protection - Fiction
    3. Suspense fiction
    I. Title
    823.9'14 [F]

ISBN 0-7278-5806-8

Nicole, Christo
The pursuit /
Christopher
Nicole

F

1578952

Except where actual historical events and characters are being
described for the storyline of this novel, all situations in this
publication are fictitious and any resemblance to living persons
is purely coincidental.

Typeset by Palimpsest Book Production Ltd.,
Polmont, Stirlingshire, Scotland.
Printed and bound in Great Britain by
MPG Books Ltd., Bodmin, Cornwall.

The herded wolves, bold only to pursue;
The obscene ravens, clamorous o'er the dead.

Percy Bysshe Shelley

The Bride

'But that is simply marvellous!' Miranda cried, her voice rising above even the roar of the helicopter's engine. 'It looks so . . . so primeval.'

'That is because it *is* primeval,' Ramon said.

Miranda gave him a quick glance, suddenly anxious, and was reassured by his fingers closing on hers for a gentle squeeze. The pressure made her aware of her wedding ring. This man was her husband, and the sweetest, most romantic man she had ever met. That he lived in such a remote place was part of the adventure.

'But while we are primeval, we are not necessarily primitive,' he told her, and pointed. 'Your new home.'

For the last half-hour they had been flying over thick jungle and large areas of partly dry swamp – it was the dry season – the virtually impenetrable green and brown mass that carpeted so much of central South America. The only suggestion of civilization had been the thin ribbon of road winding its way between the trees, along which, at wide intervals, tiny villages were studded. But suddenly the trees had ended at a small river, and beyond it was an enormous area of open land, much of it under cultivation, but an equal amount of pasture, containing a considerable herd of cattle.

In what seemed to be the very centre of this gigantic farm there was a small town, dominated at one end by the spire of the church and at the other – some distance away from the rest of the houses – by a huge mansion, set in a fenced compound and surrounded by trees, fronted by a porch raised on colonial pillars, the roof of which rose to the third floor. Behind the compound, at a distance, were rows of warehouses, and stables with a corral for the horses, and further off yet an airstrip beside which were parked several aircraft of various sizes, from single-seaters to a couple of turbo-props, as well as an executive jet. In front of the house was a large, very green lawn, and to one side, a helicopter pad.

'Tremendous!' Miranda remarked. 'All that cultivation. What do you grow on such a scale?'

'We endeavour to be self-sustaining as regards food,' Ramon explained, watching her. 'Fasten your belt.'

Miranda obeyed, as she had so rapidly got into the habit of obeying him in everything – even before he had displayed his wealth to her.

Before today she had only ever known him in a civilized environment. Her first glimpse of him, at a hunt ball, had taken her breath away; he had worn white tie and tails, which had superbly set off his dark complexion and sleek black hair, making him the most striking man in the room. But then, she knew, he had been no less taken with his first sight of her, because she equally was the most striking woman in the room. Tall and slender – she was actually slightly taller than him – with long, smooth black hair which framed her quite beautiful features, she was always the most striking woman in any room, especially when wearing evening dress. It had been love at first sight – on both sides, she was certain.

Not everyone had approved. In fact, very few of her family and friends had done so. Her older sister, Yolanda, fortunately was married and lived in Scotland, so was not on hand to offer a personal opinion. She did, however, write a very critical letter.

Meanwhile Tom had said, 'My dear Mira, the fellow is a dago!' Younger brothers are no doubt entitled to make that sort of remark. But then, younger brothers also run the risk of being slapped; Miranda had burst his lip.

2

Mumsy had been no less aghast, but more tactful. 'Are you sure?' she had asked. 'Sure, sure, sure? I mean . . . well, he's so *different.*'

'Because he has Indian blood?' Miranda challenged. 'Ramon is descended from the Incas.'

'Ah . . .' Mumsy, for all her education, had clearly not been quite sure where the Incas would have stood on the social scale. 'I was actually thinking of cultural differences. I mean, he is a Roman Catholic . . .'

'I may well become one, too.'

'My dear, no Lichton has ever been a Roman Catholic.'

'Times change, Mumsy.'

'Well, he may want you to live in Bolivia.'

'He does. That's where he lives. Well, most of the time.'

'Darling, that is in the jungle. Mosquitoes and bed bugs, crocodiles and pythons.'

'They don't have pythons in South America. They have boa constrictors.'

'That sounds even worse.'

'And they don't have crocodiles, either. They have alligators.'

'Is there a difference? I do think that you need to consider this very carefully. There'll be no balls and no polo and no banquets, and no . . . well, *anything.* You'll be thousands of miles from Harrods!'

'I'm sure there'll be polo. But don't you see, Mumsy, it's all going to be a great adventure. That's what I want, a great adventure.'

'You cannot look upon marriage as a great adventure,' the countess pointed out.

And you should know, Miranda thought. 'Isn't that what's wrong with modern marriage?' she inquired.

The Countess of Clandine took refuge in the ultimate sanction. 'You will have to speak with your father,' she had determined.

*　　*　　*

3

The helicopter settled on to the pad. This was made of concrete, but still a cloud of dust rose around the machine, and it was some seconds before the rotors had stopped turning and one of the waiting men opened the door. Ramon stepped down first, and then held up his arms for her. Miranda decided that she had made a sound decision in accepting his recommendation that she should wear jeans rather than a skirt, and equally that ankle boots were preferable to high heels, even if she would not have liked to appear this way on Regent Street. With her hair tied back in a luxuriant ponytail and a broad-brimmed hat on her head, she felt like someone out of the Wild West, and reflected further that the interior of Bolivia was probably wilder than the West had ever been.

The waiting men bowed, and the waiting women curtsied. *They* wore skirts, voluminous garments that stretched to their ankles and swirled in the wind. Miranda would have acknowledged their greeting, even if her Spanish was limited, but before she could do so found herself facing a tall, dark, quite handsome man with lank black hair and a thin moustache.

'This is Duarte, my right-hand man,' Ramon explained. 'What you would call my manager.'

'*Bienvenida, señora*,' the manager said.

Still being held in Ramon's arms, Miranda felt at a disadvantage even had she been fluent in the language. '*Gracias, señor.*'

To her surprise Ramon did not even now set her down, but marched off towards the house still carrying her, while four Irish wolfhounds frisked about them.

'It's an awfully long way,' she protested.

'Not really. And a husband must carry his wife over their threshold.'

She sighed, and rested her head on his shoulder. In everything he did, he was the epitome of romantic love. She had gone to his bed – before the wedding – half afraid and half defiant, quite uncertain as to what such a man would look like and how he would behave, almost wishing to put him off by confessing, 'You understand that I am not a virgin.'

'Are there any virgins in England over the age of sixteen?' he had countered.

She had bridled. 'And I suppose there are in Bolivia.'

'Oh, indeed. Bolivian women take their premarital chastity very seriously. And even more when they are married. So do their husbands. It is a terrible bore.'

'Does that mean you won't marry me?'

'I would marry you if you were the biggest whore in Europe.'

She couldn't be sure how to take remarks like that, whether to be offended or treat it as a somewhat different sense of humour. The important thing was that he *had* married her. Now he paused in the shade of the porch to allow her to look up at the huge, jalousied windows and then down at the horde of white-clad servants waiting to greet her.

'Do you think your papa would approve?'

She wondered.

'Now, look here,' the earl had said when, having been commanded to his presence, she had seated herself before his desk. 'What's all this rubbish about you marrying some South American Indian?'

'Ramon has some Indian blood,' Miranda had conceded. 'Very aristocratic Indian blood. But his main ancestors are Spanish. Also very aristocratic. If you go back far enough there are dukes and things.'

'Two a penny,' the earl had remarked.

'One of his ancestors commanded the Spanish army that fought beside Wellington, at the battle of . . . well, somewhere.'

'Talavera.' One of the earl's – and therefore Miranda's – ancestors had also served with Wellington. 'And if my memory

5

serves me right, the fellow ran away. Anyway, you have only your boyfriend's word that they were related at all. Having the same name is no guarantee of that. What does he do for a living?'

'He's a rancher.'

'Ha!'

'A big rancher.'

'Who like all farmers is in debt, I presume, and wants an English heiress to bail him out.'

'That is not true, Daddy. Ramon is a millionaire. A multi-millionaire.'

'He has told you this, has he?'

'Yes.'

'And you believe him. I really thought you were a sensible girl, Mira. How old is this chap?'

'Thirty-one.'

'He has told you that as well, I imagine. And you are twenty-five.'

'Yes, Daddy,' Miranda said meaningfully. 'I am twenty-five.'

'Not much of a gap,' the earl acknowledged. 'But that is not important. What is important is that men of thirty-one do not become multimillionaires by farming and ranching.'

'Neither did he. He inherited his money from his father, who inherited it from his grandfather. Just like you, Daddy. The difference is that there are no death duties in Bolivia – at least, none that can't be gotten around by good lawyers and accountants – so he has managed to hang on to more of his inheritance than you.'

'I dislike that word "gotten",' the earl declared. 'All right, young lady, if your mestizo beau is so completely on the up and up, I assume you have no objection to my having him investigated?'

'You can have him investigated all you like, Daddy dear.'

*   *   *

Ramon carried Miranda across the threshold while his staff applauded. Then he set her on her feet in the entry hall, and she very nearly fell down. Born and bred in Clandine Hall she was no stranger to large and luxurious houses. But the Hall was a cottage compared to the Cuesta Ranch House. The initial difference was one of space and light. Clandine was necessarily a business of small rooms, hallways and staircases, except for the long gallery and the grand drawing room, and both of these were relatively low-ceilinged. It had been built some three hundred years ago, and had been designed for warmth more than comfort; even today only six of its fourteen bedrooms were en suite.

Here she gazed at a ceiling which actually did not exist; she realized when she raised her head that she was looking at the roof of the house, a matter of forty feet above her. And although she was being set down in the entry hall she might just as well have been set down in the drawing room or the dining room or any of several other rooms, because there were no walls – only gigantic marble pillars rising to either the roof or the galleries which surrounded the ground floor. To her left, some fifty feet away from where she stood, there were some chairs and sofas cosily arranged. Presumably this was the drawing room. To her right she was a further fifty feet away from a huge mahogany dining table surrounded by upholstered chairs. Behind the dining table there was at last an inside wall, against which there stood various sideboards laden with cutlery and silver-capped decanters, amidst which several doors led to the pantries and kitchens. And out of which there emanated the most mouth-watering odours; it was just coming up to noon.

To what a pilot might have described as ten o'clock from where she stood there were more groups of chairs and coffee tables, no doubt small sitting rooms, and beyond them she could make out, against the far exterior wall, an office with a huge desk and various banks of computers together with television sets and radios, but even this was as open-plan as the rest of the house. Immediately in front of her a curving grand staircase led up to the mezzanine first floor.

'You built this?' she asked.

'No, no,' Ramon said. 'This was built by my grandfather, in 1930. He also built the family fortune.'

'By farming?'

Ramon kissed her on the nose. 'He was an entrepreneur. All my family have been entrepreneurs. And now I am the last. But you will give me sons, and we will start the family all over again.'

When he spoke like that she loved him more than ever – despite what Daddy had had to say.

'I have had your friend investigated,' the earl had said. 'And he does appear to be a genuine millionaire.'

'There, you see,' Miranda said. 'I think you owe me an apology.'

'In that direction, you have it. However, Bower has also come up with some suggestions which are not so acceptable. You are aware, I suppose, that your boyfriend lives in a remote part of Bolivia?'

'I can hardly wait to see it.'

'Are you also aware that Bolivia is the home of the plant erythroxylon coca?'

'I have no idea what you are talking about.'

'I am talking about cocaine, Mira.'

'Are you suggesting that Ramon sniffs?'

'Don't you?'

'Well . . .' She made a moue. 'I've tried it. But I didn't like it. And I can assure you that Ramon doesn't.'

'I'm sure he has more sense. He knows too much about it. What it can do to people.'

'Now you are suggesting he is a drug dealer.'

'I have no evidence on that.'

8

'Well, then . . .'

'However, as I say, the fact that he lives in a place where cocaine grows naturally is suggestive. To cultivate and market cocaine is one of the quickest ways to become a millionaire, providing you can get away with it.'

'Oh, Daddy, are you seriously supposing that three generations of Cuestas have lived and become rich by growing and selling cocaine, and no one has ever found out about it?'

'I am quite sure a great number of people know about it, including the American DEA. The problem is that the growing and marketing of cocaine is not a crime in Bolivia. The government recognizes that it is not the most acceptable pursuit, so they try to control it by offering grants to farmers to grow something else, but there is no attempt to legislate against it. And the offer of a grant to people like the Cuestas does not cut much ice in view of the size of the world market they have tapped into. But they have been very successful at keeping their activities secret outside of the country. I believe some Bolivian drug-carrying planes have been caught and impounded, but their pilots and crews have never once betrayed their sources, even when faced with long prison sentences.'

'Which shows that Ramon can have had nothing to do with it.'

'It shows nothing of the kind. The suggestion is that everyone who works for him and people like him are so terrified of their employers they would never dare betray them.'

'Terrified? Of Ramon? You have got to be joking. Anyway, that is all supposition and, in my opinion, prejudice. You have just admitted that there is absolutely no evidence that Ramon deals in drugs, or ever has done. All you have is that he is rich and lives in a place where drugs grow wild. Really!'

The earl sighed. 'And you have got to be the most stubborn young woman in the world. I can forbid this wedding, you know.'

'You can't. I am an adult and can marry whoever I please.'

'I could have you made a ward of the court.'

'Oh, really, Daddy. At my age?'

'On the grounds of diminished responsibility.'

'Do that and I will never speak to you again. And I will escape from England at the very first opportunity, and join Ramon. Without being married to him.'

'But why? Why, why, *why*?' The earl's normally deep voice had become almost a wail. 'You have got to be about the most eligible young woman in all England, and you wish to go off and live in the bush with . . . well . . .'

'Please don't say it, Daddy. I happen to love him. I am in love. Weren't you in love with Mumsy, once?'

'Of course I was. I still am.'

Miranda raised her eyebrows; her father really had to suppose she was an idiot if he did not realize that she, and everyone else – including Mumsy – knew all about the pied-à-terre he maintained in Hammersmith. 'All right then. She turned you on, didn't she?'

'Yes, she did.'

'Well, Ramon turns me on. Every time he touches me I get goose pimples.'

'Do I interpret that to mean that you have been sleeping together?'

'Well, really, Daddy. Do you suppose I'd contemplate marrying a man I hadn't slept with? Suppose our foreplay didn't jell?'

The earl scratched his head. 'As I said . . .'

'I'm the stubbornest woman you have ever met. I prefer to think that I know my own mind. And as it happens, our foreplay does jell. Very satisfactorily. Ramon is a real *man*. He inherited an estate in the jungle, and he has made it even bigger and better than his father did. When you compare him with the lager louts with whom I am surrounded, who can only think of their Porsches or the money market, well . . . It's a choice between reality and a make-believe world. I prefer reality. It would be so very nice if you'd accept that and give us your blessing.'

The earl sighed again. 'Well, if you're that determined, I'll go along with it. But listen, I am going to give you something.'

'Oh, you darling.'

'I'm not talking about a wedding present. I happen to have a friend who has a business in La Paz; we were at Cambridge together. I am going to give you his address and telephone number.' He handed her a card. 'I'm not suggesting you look him up. From what I remember of Joe Smart he wouldn't go much for your Ramon. But if you ever need help, give him a ring.'

'Why should I ever need help?'

'You never know. Look, I'm not asking the earth. I'm just giving you an out. Just . . . well, this Ramon might have some hidden vices you don't like.'

'Oh, really, Daddy. You really are clutching at straws. If, by the remotest chance, Ramon turns out not to be the man I know he is, I'll just call it a day and get a divorce.'

'That may not be so easy. Bolivia is a Catholic country, even if they no longer accept it as a state religion. They won't recognize divorce.'

'Do you really suppose that will matter to me? I'll come home and get a divorce here.'

'That also may not be easy to do, either. You'll be on his territory, miles from anywhere. I'm trying to look after you, my dearest girl.'

'Oh, well . . .' She placed the card in her wallet.

'Voila!' Ramon threw open the double doors to the master bedroom. There were obviously several rooms on the first floor, all opening on to the wide, deep mezzanine gallery that surrounded the downstairs of the house. But it was impossible to suppose any of the others could compare with this huge expanse, the softly-carpeted wooden floor, the enormous divan bed, the open doors on to a balcony overlooking the rear of the house – where she discovered there was a huge swimming pool – while doors in the other wall led to two bathrooms.

'One each,' Ramon explained. 'I believe that bathrooms should be the most private places on earth.'

Away went her breath again, and with it, her resolutions. After what Daddy had suggested, she had fully intended to raise the subject of drugs before the wedding. But she had never got around to it, afraid of offending Ramon. Then she had intended to raise it on their honeymoon in Rome. But there simply hadn't been time between sightseeing and making love, and besides, when he had taken her to the Vatican there had actually been an audience with a senior cardinal – apparently the Cuestas had for years been staunch and valuable supporters of the Catholic Church in Bolivia. That visit had definitely put any apprehension Daddy might have induced on the back burner. How could a friend of a cardinal have any criminal connections?

She had in fact left that meeting filled with guilt that she was not herself a Roman Catholic. She had almost resolved to convert, despite the family tradition of staunch Protestantism – and indeed, in historical times, equally staunch and sometimes violent opposition to Catholicism. Something else to be discussed. But again there had simply never been time. And it was not something that Ramon had ever pressed, bless his heart.

But now, suddenly, she saw an aircraft taking off, a small two-seater. 'Where is he going?' she asked.

Ramon stood behind her. 'Just round in a circle, and then he will land again. He has a pupil with him. It is a flying school.'

'Here in the jungle?'

He smiled. 'Here on my ranch. I have a passion for flying myself. So do many young men. But in Bolivia there is no money . . . well, for a great many people. So my instructors give flying lessons free to any aspiring pilots. That is why I keep that little jet, even though I prefer the helicopter for getting around South America. Some of my pupils even get to be airline pilots.'

'You are so generous.'

He shrugged. 'I have more than I need, so why not share a little of it around? Do you approve of your bedroom?'

'I think it is magnificent. I think the ranch is magnificent. I think you are magnificent. I am so happy to be here.' For the first time she felt she really meant that.

He took her in his arms to kiss her. 'And I shall see that you stay happy.'

'Can I explore?'

'Of course. Tomorrow I shall take you on a guided tour.'

'Do we have to worry about snakes and things? Alligators?'

'No snakes. They were all killed or driven off when the property was cleared, seventy years ago. Sometimes one or two venture back, but my people kill them on sight. Even snakes have enough sense to know when they're on to a bad thing. Alligators, now . . . well, yes, there are alligators in the river. Actually, they are caiman.'

'What are they?'

'A species of alligator. Some of them grow quite large.'

'How large?'

'Well, we have at least one fifteen-footer.'

'Fifteen . . . Gosh! Aren't they dangerous? Don't they attack your cows?'

'They are dangerous, given the opportunity. And they would attack my cattle, given the opportunity. But the river is securely fenced. They have enough space to lie on the bank, as they like to do, but they can't get through the fence. Just remember never to go swimming in the river. We have the pool for that.' He kissed her. 'Let's have lunch.'

*   *   *

13

The meal was as superb as everything else, mainly steak, but served with a variety of vegetables – eddoes, yams, sweet potatoes, okras – that Miranda had never tasted before. The dessert was a fruit called soursop, which certainly had a tart taste, but a most sensuous texture. 'It is called the fruit of love,' Ramon explained. 'But that really means the fruit of sex.'

As he spoke English she wasn't embarrassed. The servants did not seem to understand the language, with the exception of the housekeeper, Felicity, a strikingly handsome mestiza woman to whom she was introduced before the meal. 'Felicity will teach you Spanish,' Ramon had said.

The housekeeper gave her a reassuring smile. Miranda had intended to pick up the language as she went along – preferably from Ramon – rather than go back to school, as it were. But she would have to learn fairly rapidly, she realized. After she had drunk her cup of delicious Brazilian coffee and sipped her ice-cold crème de menthe, Ramon announced, 'Siesta time. I will be with you in a moment.'

Miranda went upstairs to find two maids waiting for her. 'Hello,' she said.

They simpered, obviously not understanding her.

'It's all right,' she said. 'You may go. I am going to lie down.'

Another simper.

'Bed,' she said. 'Lie down.'

They understood when she actually patted the bed, and giggled happily as they undressed her – a new experience – and saw her beneath the covers. They did not seem to expect her to wear anything, and she did not wish to; the house was cool, thanks to the air-conditioning, but by no means cold.

The air-conditioning! She sat up as Ramon came in. 'All this electricity! Aren't you a hundred miles from the nearest generating plant?'

'We are two hundred miles from the nearest town,' he

corrected. 'But we have our own generating plant. It is situated far enough away from the house not to be a nuisance.'

'But what about fuel?'

'That is brought in by truck. We use a lot of it. Now, my darling' – he sat beside her on the bed – 'would you believe that on my first day back business has reared its ugly head? Although I suppose it is not so very strange: I have been away for three months.'

'Don't tell me you have to go away again?'

'No, no. But there is a man on his way here to see me. We will have to entertain him to dinner. Or rather, I will.'

'There's no trouble?'

'Trouble?' He gave one of his easy smiles. 'I do not have trouble, my dearest girl. I occasionally have a problem to solve. But I always do this. However, I think it would be best for you to dine up here tonight.'

'But . . . can't I meet this man?'

'You would be bored stiff. He is a most boring man. And we will be talking nothing but the most boring business. Believe me. Now, you see, over there is a forty-inch television screen. It is connected to a satellite receiving dish, and that remote gives you access to five hundred channels, worldwide. You can also call up any film you might wish to see by going to the index. The range covers from this year's releases to silents. So there is no need for *you* to be bored.'

'Sounds terrific,' she agreed. She had not come several thousand miles with the most exciting man she had ever met to watch old movies. Or even new movies.

But then he began to make love to her, and her discontent disappeared. After all, she was here for the rest of her life, on and off. What difference could one night make? But . . .

'Do you often have guests?' she asked when Ramon emerged from his shower.

'Guests? Sadly, no. Business partners, yes. And I accept tourists from time to time.'

'Tourists?'

'Well, you see, various holiday firms operate tours to Peru and Bolivia, and they contacted me some time ago with a request to be allowed to bring their parties up here to see a genuine Bolivian ranch set in the middle of nowhere. I saw no reason to object. Do you mind this?'

'Good lord, no. Daddy has open days at Clandine Hall. Do we charge these people?'

'The cost is included in their tour tickets, but the firms pay us a retainer, yes. It is not very much, but I never turn away money.'

'I should think not. But . . . coming all this way. We don't have to entertain them, do we?'

'Only to lunch. They fly up from La Paz early in the morning, look at the ranch, and fly back in the evening.'

'I'm glad of that. Or do you think I am being antisocial?'

'Not at all. It would be a dreadful bore to have to entertain the hoi polloi overnight. But, you know, you will find yourself glad to see them, after a few months. This is not a place where you can pop next door for a cup of tea, or even throw the occasional cocktail party.'

'Can't we have guests? Of our own choosing?'

'You mean friends of yours? I don't see why not. If they would be prepared to travel this far.'

'I was thinking of my brother.'

'Not Tom?' He was well aware of Tom's dislike for him.

'No, no, not Tom. He'd have a nervous breakdown at the sight of an alligator in the wild. Especially if it was fifteen feet long and called a caiman. But Adrian would love it.'

'I liked Adrian. By all means invite him to visit.'

A visit from Adrian would go a long way towards reassuring the family, Miranda was sure. He was eight years older than she, and was most certainly the outdoor type; he had a Blue for rugby, and was now a captain in the Royal Horse Guards.

He had even seen action, in some remote part of the Middle East. He was also the only member of the family who had taken to Ramon – who was also a superb horseman – and had recognized in the Bolivian an equal.

At the same time, he was totally pragmatic. 'If you really love the fellow, Mira,' he had told his younger sister, 'then go for it. But if he ever lets you down, I will personally twist his head right off his neck and shove it up his ass. And you can tell him I said that.' As Adrian Lichton was six feet four and weighed two hundred and three pounds without an inch of fat to be found anywhere, Miranda did not for a moment doubt that he was capable of carrying out his promise.

'If he is the ogre you suggest,' she pointed out, 'he will undoubtedly lock me up. So how will I let you know?'

'Ah, but he'll have to let you write home, to keep up appearances.'

'Ah, but, as a Bluebeard he will undoubtedly read my letters before he posts them.'

'Ah, but you will use a code. Don't you remember, when we were kids we played at spies? Don't you remember the code?'

'Hardly. I was very small when you and Yolanda were playing your games.'

'Well, then, listen. "The sky is a soft blue" means all is well. "The sky is a hard blue" means you have trouble. "There is no wind" means you have no information. "The wind is blowing" means you have something urgent to convey. "The wind is strong" means what you have to say is a matter of life or death. "I love you" means there is no crisis. "I love you so much" means I need help. "I love you so *very* much" means my life is in danger.'

'I had forgotten how melodramatic we were. Anyway, I shall never remember all of that.'

'Yes, you will. Just remember that if I ever get a letter from you saying "I love you so very much", I shall be on the next plane.'

17

'How will you let me know you're coming? I mean, wouldn't he read my incoming mail as well?'

'Back to the code. My letter will contain, somewhere, the word "wizard". Just to prevent mistakes, the word will be used twice, in consecutive sentences. That's all you need to know.'

She had not of course told Ramon what Adrian had said, but she felt that he of all the family would be capable of appreciating the ranch and the little empire the Cuestas had carved for themselves, and therefore be able to put Mumsy's and Daddy's minds at rest. Meanwhile his visit, or even the prospect of his visit, would be very reassuring for her as well.

So, what do I fear? she wondered as she watched Ramon dress. What did she *have* to fear? Here was unimaginable wealth and luxury, and unimaginable love as well. It was only Daddy and his suggestions that lay at the back of her mind, a constant irritant.

Ramon leaned over the bed to kiss her. 'I shall try not to be too late. But do not stay up for me if you feel tired.'

'I'll stay up for you,' she promised, and squeezed his hand. 'Will this businessman be staying?'

'Well, I'm afraid he will have to stay at least for tonight.'

'So I'll meet him at breakfast.'

'Ah . . . I suppose you will. I will make sure that he does not bore you.' He chucked her under the chin and went downstairs.

Feeling thoroughly frustrated Miranda got out of bed, put on a dressing gown, and prowled around the room. She was very tempted to go out on to the balcony and at least oversee the arrival of the unwelcome businessman, but decided against it, as she did not wish to upset Ramon on her first night in her new home. Instead she tried to watch a movie, without great success, and when just before dusk she heard the roar of an airplane, she could not suppress her curiosity and ran on to the balcony to watch the twin-engined aircraft dip down out of the clear blue sky and land on the strip. A jeep was waiting, and the three men who came out of the plane got into it and were driven towards the house. But long before she could make out their faces they were lost behind the trees, and although she went to the huge windows at the front of the bedroom she again could hardly make them out. They were welcomed on the porch by Ramon, and ushered inside. They all seemed to be in a very good humour.

She went back to her movie, and jumped when there was a knock on her door. 'Yes?' she called.

It was two waiters and a maid, wheeling a vast trolley on which was her dinner and a choice of several bottles of wine. They served her, and then stood around, apparently intending to stay. 'That's all right,' she said. 'I'll call you when I've finished.'

They looked at each other, uncertain what she had said, then gave brief bows and left the room. The food was delicious, as was the wine, and her discontent began to wear off. But the wine also had the effect of making her realize how tired she was after the seemingly endless travel of the past few days: from Paris to Miami, and thence airport-hopping down Central and South America to La Paz – which had included such mind-boggling events as flying over Lake Titicaca – before the final, long helicopter trip to the ranch. She had had to absorb so many changes of scenery and people that it was no wonder her brain was in a whirl.

She rang the bell and had the trolley removed, then was in bed and asleep by midnight – to wake with a start as a resounding crash echoed through the house.

Miranda sat up suddenly, for a moment unsure where she was. Then she scrambled out of bed, put on her dressing gown and ran to the door – and discovered that it was locked on the outside. Of all the goddamned cheek, she thought, banging on it, and then pausing to listen to raised voices, at least one shouting, but as they were speaking Spanish and very quickly she could not make out what was being said. Then they faded for a moment before becoming loud again from another direction. Whoever was doing the shouting was now outside the house.

She went to the balcony doors, opened them, and the heat of the night entered the cool bedroom like a physical force. It was some seconds before she got her breath back, and then she realized that with the heat there had entered a swarm of bugs. Slapping her shoulders and scratching her face, she went outside. Now the shouting was quite distinct, and she thought she could make out several men, all close together, laughing as well as shouting. Whether they were fighting or indulging in some horseplay she couldn't be sure. As for the crash that had awakened her, she had to suppose they had knocked something over.

She went back inside, closed the doors, and slapped a few more bugs. She had to pull the sheet to her throat to stop the remainder from getting at her body, and she was in any event still seething at being locked in like some delinquent schoolgirl, so it was half an hour before she got back to sleep. Only to be awakened – a few minutes later, it seemed – by the bedroom door opening.

She reached out of bed and switched on her lamp. 'Ah,' Ramon said. 'I did not wish to awaken you.'

'I wasn't asleep,' she lied, and sat up. 'Did you have a satisfactory meeting?'

He shrugged. 'As satisfactory as these things ever are.'

'There was an awful lot of noise.'

'Did we disturb you? I do apologize. These people like nothing better than getting drunk.'

'I heard a terrible crash.'

'I know. Again I can only apologize. One of those idiots knocked over an entire table laden with glasses.'

'Oh! What a bore. Do I have to do something about that?'

'You?'

'Well, if I am to be mistress of the house . . .'

'Oh, you don't have to worry your head about a few broken glasses. Felicity will order replacements, if they are necessary.'

'And has your guest now gone to bed?'

'I have no idea. I left him with some of my people, still drinking.'

'Then he at least must feel the meeting was satisfactory.'

'One must presume so, yes. Now, where did all these bugs come from?'

'Oh . . . when I heard the noise I tried to open the door, but it was locked. So I opened the balcony door instead. They must have been lining up.'

He frowned at her. 'And what did you discover out there? Apart from being eaten alive?'

'I saw a lot of men, shouting and laughing. They seemed to be playing a game. Were you one of them?'

'Not on your life. Horseplay has never attracted me. Again, I am sorry you were disturbed.'

'What really disturbed me was the fact that I had been locked in. Did you tell the servants to do that?'

'Of course I did not. Someone was being officious, I suppose because at these meetings there is always a lot of bad language.'

'I'm not afraid of bad language. I use it myself.'

'And you wouldn't have known what was being said, anyway, as you don't know Spanish. I shall give them a good talking-to in the morning. It will not happen again.'

As always, when she lay in his arms, all her fears disappeared. She slept heavily, and only awoke when the breakfast trolley was wheeled in.

Ramon was already up, had showered and shaved, and was

21

seated in a chair, wearing a dressing gown. 'My dearest girl,' he said when, the waiters having left, she got out of bed. 'You look simply ravishing. Welcome to your first morning on Cuesta.'

She bent over him for a kiss and was rewarded with a quick caress of her breasts and bottom. 'What's the program?'

'Well, I promised to take you on a tour of the estate. We will do this as soon as you are dressed. Before it gets too hot, eh? You have brought riding gear?'

'Of course I have. What about your guest? Isn't he breakfasting with us?'

'Good lord! I'd forgotten all about him. But I imagine we can fit him out.' He picked up the house phone and spoke in rapid Spanish, mentioning the name 'Sprightly' several times. 'I have suggested that our friend be awakened and invited to accompany us. I promise we shall not talk business.'

'Is his name Sprightly? That's not Spanish, is it?'

'No, no. He is an American.'

'And he came all this way to see you?'

'Oh, he is based in South America. He represents a packing firm which buys my beef, and is always trying to renegotiate the terms of our agreement – in their favour, of course. Do you know America?'

'New England. We have relatives in Connecticut.'

'A lovely place. Well, my dear, if you'd like to get dressed, we can get the day started.'

'I'll hurry.' Miranda bustled into her bathroom, had a luxurious shower, and returned into the bedroom, still towelling herself, to find Ramon on the phone again. He looked quite upset. 'What's the matter?' she asked as he replaced the phone.

'Sprightly is not in his room. And none of the servants have seen him this morning, so he can't have gone out early.'

'Where do you think he can be?'

'I have absolutely no idea. I know he was very drunk last night. And as you saw, he went outside with some of my people after dinner. They don't know where he is, either. I suppose he's lying somewhere with a hangover. I've ordered a thorough search to be made for him. But I don't think we'll wait for him to be found and recover. As soon as you're ready . . .'

Miranda had never been very good at dressing quickly, and it took even longer with three of them doing it – her two maids had now appeared on the scene. Ramon left them to it and went downstairs, and was seated at his desk when she followed half an hour later wearing jodhpurs and riding boots and a silk shirt, and carrying her hard hat. 'I'm sorry to have kept you waiting.'

'It was worth it. You look divine. But we do not wear those funny little hats. That would attract rather than repel the sun. I have a Stetson for you. Well . . .' He got up, and one of the phones on his desk rang. He picked it up. '*Dígame.*' Then he listened, a frown slowly gathering between his eyes. Next he issued a stream of orders before putting down the phone. 'We will have to postpone our ride.'

'What's happened?'

'They've found that crazy fool Sprightly.'

'Oh, dear. Has he hurt himself?'

'He has killed himself.'

'Killed himself?' Her voice rose an octave. 'But why?'

'Oh, I don't mean that he committed suicide. Although he virtually did just that. Apparently, drunk as he was, staggering about the place, he climbed over the protective fence and went for a bathe in the river. Can you believe it?'

Miranda clasped both hands to her neck. 'Oh, my God! You mean . . .'

'Yes. I must get down there. Listen, stay in the house. I will be back as soon as I can.'

'Can't I come with you?'

'Definitely not. You'd be sick for days.' He blew her a kiss and hurried from the room.

*   *   *

Miranda strolled through the vast cavern of a house, being anxiously smiled at by the various maids who were dusting and cleaning; presumably none of them knew as yet of the tragedy. But to have such a tragedy, on her very first night in her new home . . .

She wondered what was going to be involved. Presumably La Paz would have to be informed, and there would be a visit from the police.

She stood at the edge of the dining area watching two of the footmen scrubbing the floor, supervised by Felicity, who gave a hasty curtsey as she saw her new mistress.

'Is this where the table was overturned?' Miranda asked.

'Ah . . . yes, señora.'

Señora, she thought. She had never been called 'señora' before. She rather liked that. 'Was there a lot of damage done?'

'Damage, señora?'

'All those glasses. Were they all full?' She gestured at the footmen, who had stopped their work to gaze at her. The water in their pails was tinged with red.

'Ah . . . yes, señora.'

'Were they expensive glasses?'

Once again the hesitation. 'All our crockery is expensive, señora.'

'Where will you – *we* get the replacements? La Paz?'

'Ah . . . I expect so, señora.'

'Señor Cuesta said you would attend to it.'

'I am attending to it, señora.'

Miranda felt like scratching her head; this woman and she might have been talking about entirely different subjects. Instead she went outside, where she was greeted vociferously by the wolfhounds. There were several gardeners tending the flower beds and working on the lawn, supervised by a short, middle-aged man who hurried towards her, displaying a pronounced limp. He raised his straw hat. 'They no harm you, señora.'

'I didn't think they would,' Miranda said. 'I didn't know anyone here spoke English, apart from Felicity.'

'I have learned English,' he explained proudly. 'I am Pedro. I learned English when I was travelling for Señor Cuesta.'

'You travelled for him?' A gardener? Even if he appeared to be a head gardener. 'You mean, buying plants?'

'Señora?'

'This travelling you did. Was it to do with the garden?'

'No, no, señora. I have only been in the garden since I got hit.'

'Hit?' Here was someone else who seemed to be on a completely different wavelength.

'In the leg, señora. It was a forty-five. It broke my leg in four places. So the *patron* says, now that I am so slow, I must do the garden. He takes good care of his people.'

'Let me get this straight. You were hit in the leg, by a *bullet*? How did that happen?'

'I was, how do you say, the *patron*'s bodyguard. One of them.'

'The *patron* travels with a bodyguard?' Ramon had certainly not had one on his visit to Europe.

'When on business, oh, yes. One can never tell what may happen. Like last night, eh?'

Miranda experienced a great heat that seemed to spread right through her body. 'You know about last night?'

'Everyone knows about last night, señora. But not to worry. The *patron* will take care of it. He takes care of every-thing.'

'I'm sure you're right.' She so wanted to ask some more questions, but her instincts told her that would be a mistake. Besides, she equally wanted to sit down and think about what she had learned.

She went back into the house, and Felicity hurried up to her. 'Are you all right, señora?'

'Why shouldn't I be all right?'

'You look pale. Would you like me to bring you something to drink?'

'No, thank you. You know about last night?'

'Well . . .'

'Everyone knows about last night. But you did not mention it to me. A man died last night. Did it happen here? Is that blood those men are cleaning off the floor?'

Felicity's face seemed to close. 'You must ask the master, señora. He will tell you.'

'But you know what happened.'

'I only know what I am told to know, señora.'

Miranda felt like slapping her face, but her instincts warned her that Felicity's reaction might not be as passive as Tom's. Instead she went up to her room, to the consternation of the maids, who were still sweeping and dusting and making the bed.

'Out!' she commanded, and when they stared at her, tried, 'Vamoose!'

They got the message and hurried from the room, muttering at each other. Miranda threw her hat on to the floor, and then threw herself across the bed and lay there on her stomach, fists clenched.

What *had* happened? She didn't know. But she knew a man had died – and it did not seem to have upset the servants in the least. And she knew that Ramon usually travelled with a bodyguard, when on business. For protection, or . . .? She knew that Pedro had been shot. Had that been guarding Ramon, or shooting at somebody else? Killing somebody else? All this for an ordinary cattle rancher, even if a very rich one?

That didn't make sense. Everything Daddy had suggested came back to her, everything that she had so carelessly dismissed. Because she had loved Ramon. And she still loved him. He was the only man she had ever found who was totally satisfying. Even if he was some kind of gangster?

But he couldn't be. When he came home, he would explain everything.

She had no idea how long she lay there; she simply didn't want to move, to have to face any of the servants, while they knew so much more than she did.

She was still sprawled across the bed when the door opened. 'My dearest girl,' Ramon said. 'Felicity told me you were not feeling well. I am so wretched that such a thing should have happened on your first day here. How can I make it up to you?'

Miranda rolled over and sat up. 'By telling me the truth.'

'The truth about what?'

'About last night. That man was killed in this house.'

'That is absurd. His body, or what is left of it, was found in the river. It was not very pleasant, I can tell you. Contrary to what a lot of people suppose, you know, an alligator does not use its jaws to bite people in half. It merely grasps its victim and holds it under water until it – or in this case, he – drowns. Then the carcass is allowed to float to the surface and the 'gator tears pieces of flesh from it with its very front teeth. Nibbles, you might say. This can take a long time, so when the body was spotted just after dawn this morning, it had only been half consumed.'

'Ugh!'

'Absolutely. But there can be no doubt that he was alive when he fell in.'

'Did he fall? Or was he thrown, or pushed?'

'Whatever do you mean?'

'Ramon, that Mr Sprightly might not have died in this house, but he was certainly beaten up sufficiently to lose a lot of blood. I found your servants cleaning up what I thought was spilled red wine, but which I now know was blood. And when I saw those men outside last night, they weren't playing a game. They were carrying Sprightly towards the river, to throw him in. And what is more, he knew exactly what was going to happen to him; he was screaming for help.'

'You have been doing a lot of thinking,' Ramon said. 'Do you intend to publish this absurd theory of yours? That is no way for a wife to behave.'

'I wish to be your wife, Ramon. I just wish you to tell me the truth.'

He got off the bed and took a turn around the room.

'Like that man Pedro, the head gardener,' she said. 'He told me he was shot protecting you. Protecting you from what? Or who?'

He stood above her. 'I'm afraid I lead an occasionally dangerous life. Oh, there is nothing for you to worry about. There is no danger here on the ranch. But when I am away on business . . .'

'Nothing to worry about?' she shouted. 'What about this Sprightly? Did he come here to kill you?'

'No, no. I told you. He came here to renegotiate a business arrangement. I was unable to agree to his terms, and he became abusive, and even threatening.'

'And so you had him killed? You had him *murdered*? All because of some beef shipment?'

'Ah, no. As you seem to have deduced so much, you may as well know: it was to do with a drugs shipment.'

Miranda stared at him. 'You are a drug dealer? You *are* a drug dealer!'

'My family have dealt in drugs for ninety years. That is how we became rich. Most of those fields under cultivation that you saw from the helicopter yesterday are coca. I probably produce more coca than anyone else in the world.'

'Oh, my God! Oh, my *God*! Daddy was right.'

'He knows about this?'

'He suspected. He had you investigated.'

'And?' His tone was sharp.

'They couldn't find any proof. But he was sure of it. And I told him he had to be wrong.'

'I think that was very loyal of you. I appreciate it.'

'I told him he had to be wrong because I didn't believe it. I couldn't believe it, because I loved you. But if he was right . . .'

'You would suddenly stop loving me? Just like that?'

Miranda bit her lip. 'You are also a murderer. As soon as the news reaches La Paz, you will be arrested.'

'The only news that will reach La Paz is whatever I wish to tell them, which will be that there was an unfortunate accident.'

'But when the police arrive and start asking questions . . .'

'No policeman will ever set foot on my estate without my permission. I am a substantial contributor to the pension funds of several senior officers, and they are content to allow me to run my plantation as I see fit.'

'When the relatives see the remains . . .'

'There will be no remains for them to see. Dead bodies cannot be kept in this climate for more than a very few hours. Sprightly's remains will be cremated this afternoon.'

'You speak of it so lightly.'

'That rhymes: lightly and Sprightly. My dearest girl, when one has been brought up in a jungle, life – and death – takes on a much more commonplace aspect than in a so-called civilized community, where it is vastly overvalued. There are far too many people alive who should be dead, for a variety of reasons.'

'That is an impossible point of view. You are an impossible person.'

'But you love me.'

'I'm not sure that I can. I never thought you were a drug dealer, much less a murderer. I need to think about it.'

'Take all the time you wish.'

'I can't do it here. With you. I need to be away from

here, to get things in perspective. I want to go home. Just for a while.'

Ramon smiled at her. 'And I don't think I could permit that, my dearest girl. Certainly not until I can be sure you will not go rushing off to your father with all of my secrets.'

The Job

Detective-Sergeant Jessica Jones unlocked the door of her flat, and then banged it shut behind her. She did this deliberately, because she knew Tom was in – the television was playing very loudly. But there was no indication that he had heard her entry.

She took off her coat, hung it on the stand behind the door, and went along the corridor to the living room. He was, predictably, sprawled on the settee in his vest and underpants, drinking beer from a can and watching golf. He waved the can. 'How'd it go?'

'Bloody awful.' Even when feeling out of sorts Jessica spoke in low and husky tones; her mother had once remarked that she had a bedroom voice – not that she had ever put it to a great deal of use in that direction.

'Score?'

'Seven bulls, eight inners, six outers and four misses.'

'And you are just about the division's crack shot? You weren't concentrating.'

'You could be right.'

'Mind you, any normal human being would be over the moon with seven bulls out of twenty-five. But I don't suppose you classify yourself as a normal human being.'

'If I was a normal human being,' Jessica pointed out, 'I wouldn't be doing this shitty job in the first place. Are there any more of those in the fridge?'

'A dozen. Help yourself.'

Jessica did so, carried the beer and her shoulder bag into the bedroom, and sat on the bed. On the floor was a pile of Tom's discarded clothing, waiting to be loaded into the washing machine.

She thought that life was an unfair business. She and Tom were exactly equal career-wise. They were both detective-sergeants, both employed in the protection division of the Special Branch. They both earned the same pay, and to a large extent they shared the same interests. The only visible difference between them was their size: Tom was six feet two inches tall and heavily built, with craggy features and lank black hair; she was a slim five feet four, with straight yellow hair – which, when not in uniform, she wore just past her shoulders – and attractively clipped features. Her combination of fitness and slenderness made her look much younger than she was: she had recently celebrated her thirty-sixth birthday.

The other and perhaps most important difference was that she was divorced, whereas Tom had never married. Marriage was a commitment, and Tom's only commitment was to his job. Marriage could also mean children, and he was well aware that she was becoming more broody with every birthday; he regarded children as an even greater commitment. But despite all of that, she thought with some bitterness, she was still expected to wash his clothes.

However, first things came first. She stripped off her own shirt and jeans, socks and sweat-soaked underwear to add to the pile, then opened her shoulder bag and took out her Skorpion machine pistol to clean. A Czech-made blow-back, it weighed just over a kilo, and carried either a ten- or twenty-round magazine. Equipped with an extendable butt for extra accuracy, it would stop a man at seventy-five metres – if aimed with total concentration. And at this morning's practice she had only shot dead seven of the twenty-five targets presented to her. In her book that was D minus. But it was a reflection of her general mood of dissatisfaction with her lot. For all her condemnation of it, she actually loved her job, the excitement of it, even if there was also a considerable element of danger, and even if it had involved, on more than one occasion, the taking of human life.

That was not something that she ever allowed herself to dwell upon. Whenever she had shot to kill it had been in defence of either herself or her principal, the person she had been assigned to protect. She enjoyed the reputation she had gained over the years of calm and, where necessary, deadly efficiency. But she also knew that, if only by the law of averages, her luck, or skill, had to run out some time, and she could well wind up dead, or a cripple – she wasn't sure which was a worse prospect.

And when that happened, what would be left? Simply a hole in the ground. Which was why she dreamed, more and more, of getting out and raising a family. But to accomplish that, she needed a man who would be as committed to such an idea as herself. Tom simply wasn't that man. And he was the only man she had, as well as being the only man she wanted – when they were in bed together.

So life had to go on. She finished cleaning the gun, replaced it in her bag, making a mental note that she needed to replenish the magazine tomorrow – there was a reserve box in her drawer but she always liked to have a spare as well as the one in the pistol – and then stooped over the pile of clothes, scooped them up into her arms, and frowned, nostrils dilating as she sniffed. She was sufficiently familiar with Tom's deodorant, but here it was overlaid with another scent, strong as well as subtle and attractive. Someone wearing a most compelling perfume had very recently got very close to this shirt!

Jessica sat on the bed while she considered. She had an overwhelming sense of déjà vu. Her marriage had ended, eight years before, on a similar note. But on that occasion she had been a lot younger, less experienced, more impetuous . . . and the owner of that perfume had actually been in her bed, naked, with her husband. Having never cheated on Brian in her life, she had blown her top.

Now she was more mature and less inclined to explode. But she could still feel extremely angry, because she had never cheated on Tom, either. In fact, she had only ever shared a bed with three men in her entire life: her husband, Tom, and an almost forgotten youth who had been her first sexual experience. She supposed that made her old-fashioned. It certainly made her very square. The truth of the matter was that sex had never played a vital part in her life. It had loomed often enough. She knew she was very good-looking, and she had received sufficient advances. She had even twice come near to being raped by the various villains who had got their hands on her, however temporarily; she was willing to accept the occasional manhandling as part of her job. But what she really wanted from a relationship was possession, possession of her by her partner, and possession by her of her partner. That went way beyond sex. It required sharing on a wholesale scale, of every aspect of life. One could not share one's all with a man who was sharing at least a part of his all with someone else.

Of course, she reflected with her normal sense of perspective, it could just have been a kiss and a cuddle, strictly one-off, with some man-hungry bit. He would have to prove that. But even if he did, she was realizing with a sense of shock that she actually did want to call it a day. For all the fun they had together, the moments of mutual passion, the relationship had become sterile, futureless.

And here was the perfect cause.

Jessica carried the shirt into the lounge, where Tom was still watching golf. 'Ah,' he said, not looking at her. 'Mrs Norton called. The boss wants to see you. Mrs Norton said it's important.'

'It's always important. When?'

'She said as soon as you came in from the range.'

'Then I'd better get down there.'

'Eh?' He sat up. 'What about lunch?'

'Cook yourself something. And while you're doing that, think up a good cover story for this.' She dropped the shirt on his lap, returned to the bedroom, and had a shower. The time was a quarter past twelve, and however important might be Commander Adams' reason for wishing to see her, as his habits never changed, he would now be going out for a pre-lunch drink and then lunch itself, and would hardly be returning before three. But she didn't feel like eating, anyway, and she wanted to get out of the flat to think about things.

Tom was waiting for her when she stepped out of the shower. 'Where will you eat?'

'I'll get something in the canteen.' She pulled up her knickers, strapped her bra into place.

He was carrying the shirt. 'I can explain this.'

'I never doubted that you could. The question is whether I'll believe the explanation.'

'You know, you really can be a bitch.'

'And you qualify as a bastard.'

'Listen, about this shirt . . .'

'We'll talk about it later, after I've had a chance to think about it – and you've had a chance to get your story straight.' She put on her blue trouser suit over a white shirt – her favourite working outfit when uniform was not required – and slung her shoulder bag.

'No kiss?' he asked as she brushed past him.

'Not right now,' she told him.

'Well, JJ,' Commander Adams said, using the office nickname based on her initials. 'You're looking well.'

'Thank you, sir.' As she had anticipated, it was past three. Thus she had been waiting for three hours. She had actually had a sandwich in the canteen, but her mood had not improved.

Now she glanced from the commander to the other man in

the room. Here she liked what she was looking at. In contrast to the police officer, who, if tall and powerfully built, was also lantern-jawed and grey-haired, this fellow was approximately her own age, taller than Tom, she estimated, fair-haired and good-looking in a classical manner, and immaculately dressed in a blazer, grey flannels and an MCC tie.

'This is Captain Lord Adrian Lichton,' Adams explained. 'Detective-Sergeant Jones.'

'My pleasure.' Adrian Lichton shook hands. He had a firm, dry grasp.

'Lord Lichton is the Earl of Clandine's heir,' Adams further explained. 'Sit down, JJ.'

Jessica seated herself in one of the leather armchairs before the commander's desk; Adrian Lichton sat beside her.

'Let's see,' Adams said. 'Your last assignment has just been completed, has it not?'

'The crown prince returned home the day before yesterday, sir.'

'Sergeant Jones only deals with the best,' Adams explained to Adrian.

'Sounds impressive.'

'That is because she herself is just about the best we have.'

Adrian smiled at Jessica; he clearly did not entirely accept such praise. 'I'm sure of it, Commander. But . . .'

'You shouldn't be misled by either her size or her femininity. She punches more than her weight.'

'If you say so.' He was clearly still doubtful.

Jessica waited, vaguely amused.

'So, now . . . do you speak Spanish, JJ?'

'Only the odd word, sir.'

'Well, I don't suppose it's very important. Everyone speaks English nowadays. Have you ever been to South America?'

'No, sir.'

'Would you like to go?'

'As a holiday, or on duty, sir?'

'I'm afraid it would be duty. We wish you to go to a place called Bolivia. Have you heard of it?'

'Yes, sir. It is a land-locked country up against Brazil.'

'Absolutely. The Matto Grosso, eh?'

'Ah . . .' Jessica couldn't be sure about that as she tried to visualize the map.

'We wish you to go there, pick up a witness, and bring her back to England.'

Jessica looked at Adrian; she had known her boss for too long to suppose it was quite as straightforward as that.

'I'm afraid it isn't quite as straightforward as that,' Adrian said.

Jessica waited.

'The witness in question is my sister,' Adrian said.

'Lady Miranda Lichton, the Earl of Clandine's daughter,' Adams explained, to make absolutely sure Jessica understood who they were dealing with.

'Actually, she is now Mrs Cuesta. She married this Bolivian rancher chap, about six months ago,' Adrian said. 'Perhaps you remember it. St James's, Piccadilly?'

'I'm afraid not, sir.' Six months ago she had been recovering from protecting Princess Karina of Kharram.

'Well, the business wasn't really approved by my parents,' Adrian said. 'But Mira— Miranda is a grown woman and also a determined one, and this fellow is a millionaire, so they went along with it. So off she went to Bolivia.'

'Now she wants to come home,' Adams said. 'And this blighter won't let her.'

'And this is a police matter, sir?'

'Well, yes, it is. Or has become so. It seems likely that this Cuesta is a drug smuggler, on a very big scale. The DEA would very much like to nail him, but up till now they have had nothing to go on but suspicion. Now, Lady Lichton – or as you say, my lord, Mrs Cuesta – was unaware of this when she married him, but she seems to have become aware of it since, and also that he is, for all his charm and his money, a pretty unpleasant character, and possibly a murderer into the bargain. If we could get her to testify against him, the Americans might well be able to nab him the next time he leaves Bolivia, and lock him up.'

'And she is willing to do this?'

'Yes. We believe that she will testify. That's why he refuses to let her leave his ranch.'

Jessica considered. 'May I ask how we know this?'

'She wrote her brother and told him so.'

'Forgive me, sir, but you are saying that although her husband keeps her locked up on his ranch to prevent her from testifying against him, he allows her to write her family and tell them what is going on? Isn't that a testament in itself?'

'It's not quite like that,' Adrian said. 'There can be no doubt that Ramon censors her letters. But she and I have a means of communicating in secret, something we used to play with as kids. Here is a letter she wrote soon after arriving on the ranch.'

He took it from his breast pocket and handed it to Jessica, who unfolded it and looked at the heading. 'This is five months old.'

'As I said, it was written soon after her arrival in Bolivia. There have been two more since, all with the same message.'

Jessica scanned the writing. 'You must forgive me, Lord Lichton, but she comes across as perfectly content with her lot.'

'Ah, but it's the code, don't you see.' He leaned across her to point out the words. 'She writes that the sky where she is is a hard blue; that's our code for she is in trouble. Then she writes that the wind is blowing; that means she has urgent information to convey. When she adds that the wind is now very strong, she means what she has to say is a matter of life and death. And when she finishes, I love you so very much, she means that she considers her life to be in danger.'

'How very ingenious,' Jessica commented, a trifle sceptically. There was absolutely nothing in the letter which could possibly assist any prosecutor in nailing Ramon Cuesta, or convince any possible jury or judge to convict him. And they had only this handsome hunk's say-so that the code existed. She looked at her boss. 'And you are prepared to act on the basis of this letter, sir? With respect, Lord Lichton, you may know the code between your sister and yourself, but there is no evidence of it that anyone else could gather. Thus there is no evidence of any crime having been committed, or that Señora Cuesta is under any kind of restraint.'

'I agree that the evidence is circumstantial, JJ,' Adams said. 'But it is there. My lord?'

'Well, you see,' Adrian explained, 'when I received this letter, I immediately wrote back asking if I could come for a visit. She replied that it would not be at all convenient at this time.'

Jessica pulled her nose.

'Oh, quite,' he agreed. 'Although I have no doubt that that second letter was written under Ramon's direction. But that second letter again used the code, especially the farewell, I love you so very much. Well, when I received that second letter, I got in touch with a fellow called Smart, an old friend of the pater's – they were at Cambridge together – who runs a business in La Paz, and asked him to give me some information on the set-up there. He replied that while there are some suspicions regarding Cuesta, there has never been anything concrete; he is of course protected from the law by a system of bribery and corruption. However, he was able to tell me that something rather odd, and tragic, occurred on Cuesta's ranch just about the time Miranda arrived there. Seems that an American named Sprightly went up there to see Cuesta on business, got drunk during dinner, went for a walk following the meal, and fell into the local river, which is full of some rare species of alligators, who promptly chomped him up.'

'Good lord! What a way to go. But does that implicate Cuesta? If the police are happy . . .'

'The police aren't allowed on Cuesta's ranch. He is virtually a king up there. He informed La Paz of what had happened, and they accepted his story. The point is, the Sprightly tragedy is dated 12 March, and Mira's letter, as you can see, is dated 17 March, yet she does not mention it. This man came to dinner at her house only five days before – and in fact the day she arrived – and wandered off and got himself eaten by an alligator, virtually under her nose, and she doesn't mention it. That is not credible.'

'I see what you mean,' Jessica said thoughtfully, at last beginning to get interested.

'In addition, I made some inquiries through a friend of mine in the DEA, and he tells me that Sprightly is, or was, well known to them as a negotiator for the mob, someone who sets up deals and trading places and that sort of thing. That makes it seem very likely that he visited Cuesta to set up some kind of deal, they fell out, and Cuesta had him executed.'

'Most unpleasantly,' Jessica observed. 'What exactly is it you wish me to do?'

'We wish you to go to Bolivia,' Adams said. 'Find your way into this ranch, extract Mrs Cuesta, and take her to La Paz.'

'Where I will be waiting,' Adrian said. 'I can't come with you to the ranch, much as I would like to, because I don't think I would be allowed entry, and my very appearance would arouse suspicion.'

'And you think that an English police officer will be allowed in.'

'You will not be travelling as an English police officer,' Adams pointed out. 'You will be a tourist.'

'Cuesta allows escorted visitors on to his ranch,' Adrian

40

explained. 'They go in groups of a dozen or so, are shown everything he wishes them to see, and then are escorted back to La Paz.'

'That is your way in,' the commander said. 'Once you're in, you will have to play it by ear. But I have the highest confidence in your judgement.'

'Thank you, sir,' Jessica said, more thoughtfully yet.

'I have to say, Sergeant,' Adrian said, 'that when I went to the Foreign Office looking for assistance, and they recommended Commander Adams, I had no idea . . . well . . .'

'That he would be using a woman?'

'Well, the point is, all the evidence suggests that my brother-in-law can be quite a dangerous fellow.'

'I should think he is, if he feeds unwanted guests to an alligator.'

'Well . . .'

'Sergeant Jones is very capable of handling dangerous fellows, my lord,' Adams said.

'Ah. Well, if you feel sure . . .'

'There are some things I will need to know,' Jessica said.

'Of course.'

'Firstly, my lord, may I ask how Lady Lichton and this drug smuggler became acquainted? Was it in Bolivia?'

'No. At a hunt ball here in England.'

'You mean he was moving in your – *her* social circle.'

'Well, yes, he was. I'm afraid that doesn't mean a thing nowadays. If you have money, you can buy your way into anything. I mean to say, there is even a pop star who is a member of my club.'

'That is absolutely shocking, sir.' Jessica began to wonder just what she was being thrown into. She turned to Adams. 'You say I am to link up with a group of tourists.'

'It is a tour of Peru and Bolivia organized by an English firm. I'm afraid for the sake of your cover you will have to go along with them until you get to the Cuesta Ranch.'

'I've always wanted to tour Bolivia,' Jessica said unconvincingly, and turned back to Lichton. 'Would I be right in assuming that this ranch is some distance from La Paz?'

'Some distance, yes. It is over a hundred miles from the nearest other ranch.'

'A hundred miles of . . .?'

'Mainly swamp and jungle.'

'I see. Is there a road?'

'There is. But it isn't very good. And it's even worse in the wet season, which is what it is now. The tourists are flown in by plane.'

'And spend the night?'

'No. They fly up at the crack of dawn, have their look around and are given lunch, and then fly back in the evening.'

'I see. Now, is there any way of letting your sister know that I am coming? I mean, time would appear to be at a premium. I may not have the time to explain to her who I am and that I am working for her family.'

'That is not a problem. I'll tell her to expect you.'

'Bearing in mind the fact that her husband reads her mail?'

'Back to the code, don't you see? If Mira ever receives a letter from me in which the word "wizard" is used twice in consecutive sentences, she'll know that I, or an agent of mine, is on his way. Or hers.'

'I see. Now, I presume there are a lot of people on the ranch.'

'Oh, indeed. A whole township.'

'All of whom work for Cuesta, and therefore are loyal to him.'

'I'm afraid that is probably correct.'

'And you reckon there is absolutely no prospect of any official backing.'

'In Bolivia, no.'

Jessica looked at the commander.

'I'm afraid there isn't going to be any from here either. The

FO was quite definite about this. They have been in contact with our man in La Paz, and he says no way. Lady Lichton married in good faith and of her own free will. By doing so she became a Bolivian citizen, subject to Bolivian law – and more especially, to Bolivian marriage law. For us to attempt to interfere without cast-iron proof that Cuesta is a thug would be to cause an international incident. Thus anything we do has to be definitely covert. Once she is out, and gives her evidence, that will be a different matter.'

'And you are quite certain that she wants to come out.' Now she looked at Adrian.

'I would stake my life on it.'

'It happens to be *my* life you are staking on it, Lord Lichton.'

'Do you really feel that, JJ?' Adams asked.

'My experience of drug dealers, sir, is that they believe in protecting themselves to the limit. In the case of this man Cuesta, he appears to have proved that by his treatment of Sprightly.'

'There's a good point,' Adrian Lichton said. 'Well, if you really feel it will be too dangerous, I can try something else.'

'There is nothing else you can try, my lord,' Adams pointed out. 'You are a peer of the realm, heir to an earldom, and an officer in the British army. If you were to attempt anything on your own – or even more, with the support of any of your colleagues – and it were to go wrong, the scandal could bring down the government.'

'While if I get fed to an alligator, nobody will give a damn,' Jessica said brightly. Nobody at all, she thought, less happily.

'That makes me feel an utter shit,' Adrian said. 'If you'll excuse me.'

'I'm on your side, my lord.' She turned to Adams. 'Right, sir, I am to go in and contact Mrs Cuesta and bring her out, relying entirely on me and mine.'

'Ah . . . yes. Mine?'

'I will need a back-up.'

'Ah. You're thinking of Lawson. Yes, that might be an idea. You could travel as a married couple.'

'I was not thinking of Sergeant Lawson, sir.' While she knew there could hardly be a better partner if the going got rough, at this moment she had no desire to go off on a fortnight's jaunt with Tom in constant attendance. 'I'd rather round up my usual team, if you would make them available.'

'How many?' he asked suspiciously.

'I think two. If they are the best two.'

'You're not talking about that crazy pair of . . .' He flushed, and glanced at Adrian.

'Yes, sir. Whatever their personal inclinations, there are no two people I would rather have beside me at a shoot-out.'

'A shoot-out?'

'Well, if everything you have been telling me is correct, it may well come to that.'

'Oh . . . well, I suppose you could be right.'

Adrian produced a handkerchief to wipe his brow.

'Therefore, we will need to carry weapons.'

'Hm. Won't be easy, flying in and out of several countries, especially as part of a tour group.'

'If you are talking about hand guns,' Adrian said, 'my father's friend in La Paz could possibly arrange to obtain some for you. Guns are two a penny in Bolivia.'

'They'd have to be in very good nick.'

'They will be.'

'I should point out, JJ, that it is not our intention for you to start a war,' the commander remarked.

'I am thinking purely of self-defence, sir.'

He looked sceptical; he was well aware of her propensity for getting herself into situations from which only lethal force could extract her. 'Very well, sign up your team. If there is any difficulty with releasing them from current duties, refer to me.

Mrs Norton will arrange your bookings with this tour group, and will inform you when you will be leaving. Obviously it will be on the first available date.'

'Very good, sir. It would also be most helpful, my lord, if your friend could provide me with as much information as possible about this ranch and the general set-up as regards Cuesta. A map of the area and a plan of the ranch would also be useful.'

'I'll see to that.'

'Thank you, sir.' Jessica looked at the commander.

'Well,' he said, 'if there is nothing else at the moment . . .'

'When I think of anything else, I'll let you know, sir.'

Jessica stood up, and Adrian stood also. 'I will be waiting for you in La Paz. I will leave as soon as I know your dates.'

'Thank you.' She looked at Adams, and received a quick nod. 'Good afternoon.'

Jessica left the office, had a brief chat with Mrs Norton – a middle-aged lady who was her usual frosty self – and then waited for the elevator. When it arrived, Adrian Lichton came up behind her, and followed her into the car. 'I really can't express my admiration, and my gratitude, for the way you are taking this on,' he said.

'It's my profession, sir.'

'That doesn't make you any less courageous, or admirable.'

'Thank you, sir.'

'It strikes me that perhaps I should give you some more background to this whole sorry business.'

'I thought your friend in La Paz was going to do that.'

'I'm sure I can be of some help. Perhaps we could talk about it over dinner.'

Jessica considered, briefly. He was certainly a fast worker. He was also an aristocrat to his toes, and very good-looking. On the debit side she was deducing that he was after all probably younger than her, and he was definitely attracted more by her looks and the slightly sinister aura that Adams had suggested than her brains. She was a woman who would shoot her way out of trouble; she had to be exciting, and perhaps immoral.

She had no doubt that she could deal with any attempt to get his hand into her knickers, even if he was a lord and more than twice her size. But the fact was, in her present mood she wasn't certain that she would want to deal with it. It would be one in the eye for Tom.

'Or is it against the rules for you to dine with your clients?' he asked, studying her.

'I dine with my clients all the time,' she said. 'Usually to protect them. Sometimes even from themselves.'

They gazed at each other for several seconds while the lift came to a halt. Then he said, 'Touché. Shall I pick you up?'

'Ah . . . no.' Tom might be a cheating bastard, but he was also a jealous bastard; the idea of him and this man having a brawl over her was not attractive. 'It would be better if we met somewhere.'

He frowned. 'You're not married?'

People were waiting; Jessica stepped out and walked across the lobby. Adrian followed her. 'I am not married,' she said. 'At the moment. Where would you like to meet?'

'Well . . . the Savoy?'

'The Savoy.' She had in fact eaten there before, but only while on duty.

'Seven?'

'The Savoy at seven. Very good, sir.'

'Ah . . . I think if we're going to have dinner together, we could drop the "sir". My name is Adrian.'

'Very good . . . Adrian.'

'And . . .' He looked up and down her trouser suit.

'I shall wear a dress . . . Adrian.'

'Great. May I drop you somewhere?'

'I'll find my own way, thank you. See you at seven.'

She left him standing there, looking after her. She wondered if he was considering whether he might have made a mistake – dating below stairs, as it were.

Tom was out, which she supposed was predictable. She knew he was off duty, but was due to commence a new assignment in two days' time. As they never discussed their assignments – it was not departmental policy to do so – she had no idea where he was going, with whom or for how long. But with any luck she'd be away before he came back.

She sat at her desk, flicked through the e-mails on her computer – none were of any importance – and dialled.

'Hi,' said the seductive voice at the end of the line. Jessica reflected that if she herself sounded as if she'd like to go into the bedroom, Andrea always sounded as if she was already there – with company.

'JJ.'

'JJ!' Andrea's voice became animated.

'How'd you like an overseas assignment?'

'I'd love it. With you?'

'Chloe too.'

'That sounds tremendous.' But a little of the enthusiasm had gone from her voice. Someone else with emotional problems, Jessica deduced. 'Trouble is, there's this woman from Siam—'

'Thailand.'

'You got it. She's old-fashioned.'

'I'll have you replaced. Is Chloe involved?'

'No. She's got someone else.'

'I'll sort her out too. Listen, Andie, you both have to volunteer. It could be a little rough.'

'As long as you're in command, JJ, I volunteer.'

There was more than professional loyalty involved, Jessica knew, which was why she had decided to take them both. Andrea might be the most reliable back-up in the business, certainly amongst the female members of the department, but when they had last worked together, protecting Princess Karina, she had revealed a distinct desire to get closer to her boss than some would regard as proper. She was so good-looking as almost to be described as beautiful, and delightfully sexy in her totally laid-back way, but even before the looming spat with Tom, Jessica had had no desire to undertake any further emotional entanglements, even had it been an aspect of human relationships into which she had ever ventured or even properly understood. She sometimes reckoned she was square in every possible direction. On the other hand, Andrea and Chloe had been partners, both professionally and privately, ever since she had known them, so departing with both of them for a fortnight had seemed the safest thing in the world. But if their relationship was on the rocks . . .

Still, it was a job, and personalities should not be allowed to come into it. 'Then we'll have a briefing,' she said. 'When will you both be available?'

'Half a mo.' Andrea was clearly consulting her diary. 'Six o'clock.'

'No good. I have a date.'

'Can't he wait an hour?'

'It isn't Tom.'

Andrea was silent while she digested this; Jessica supposed she was finding that piece of information as interesting as what she herself had deduced about Chloe. 'Sounds great,' she ventured.

'He's a hoot. Straight out of Rudyard Kipling, or whatever, not to mention *Burke's Peerage*. He's a lord, speaks with marbles in his mouth, and refers to his father as the "pater". He's also a captain in the Horse Guards, six foot plus a whole lot of inches, and could have walked straight off a Hollywood set. He had poor old Adams virtually kowtowing.'

'And you have a date with him?'

'Dinner at the Savoy.'

'And?'

'I've been told to play this assignment by ear.'

'Some people have all the luck,' Andrea commented without conviction.

'He's also our employer for this one.'

'You mean I get to meet him?'

'You will. When I'm done with him, I'll let you have a go.'

Andrea made a strangled exclamation.

'So, our meeting will have to be tomorrow. Come here for breakfast. Both of you.'

'Will do,' Andrea said. 'Have fun.'

Jessica showered, added make-up – a rare luxury for her – and surveyed her wardrobe, wishing she had had more time to prepare. Her duties seldom required her to wear a dress, but she had a sufficient collection of both evening gowns and smart frocks for whenever her client of the moment wished to go out on the town; for obvious reasons those clients were always women, except when she was required to back up a senior male officer, and thus she was never expected to outshine her principal in any way – rather the reverse. And going out with Tom was a matter of the pub, except on very special occasions. In fact, she realized, as she had already been in the force when she and Tom had got together – he had introduced her to the Special Branch soon after her divorce, for which she remained grateful even if she had never doubted he simply wanted to get hold of her body – this was the first real date she had had in a very long time. Since, in fact, before her marriage. And with a lord!

She had to look good, but neither garish nor overwhelming. After some lip-chewing, she chose a pale blue number which clung to her rather like a second skin, thus accentuating both her slim hips and her rather full bust, which had earlier been disguised by her trouser suit. It was also short enough – just below the knee – to reveal her very good legs, also hitherto concealed. So just what am I aiming to do? she asked herself. Why, play it by ear, as she so often had to do when on duty, while being prepared for every eventuality, again as she was required to do by her job.

But she changed the shoulder bag and its pistol for a small purse; she surely did not need to be armed tonight.

Tom appeared in the doorway while she was inspecting herself in the wardrobe mirror. 'You look good enough to eat. Assignment?'

'Ah . . .' She wondered if she should go along with that; possibly it could be so considered. 'Sort of.'

'I think you should explain that.'

'And I see no reason why I should. I am going out to dinner. Don't wait up.'

'You mean I have to get my own, again?'

'Whatever turns you on.' It was a warm October evening, so she chose a light cloth coat.

'Would you mind telling me what's going on? I said I could explain about the shirt.'

'And I said I look forward to hearing your explanation. When I'm in the mood. Probably tomorrow.'

'And until then?'

'As I said, do your own thing.'

'You are a bitch!' he snapped.

'So you said this morning. Listen, if you ever call me that again, you can pack up and leave.' The apartment was in her name.

He goggled at her, never having known her in this mood before. She swept past him and down the stairs, pausing before going out to get her breathing under control.

'That was a delicious meal,' she remarked as she and Adrian sipped their coffee. She was telling the truth, and not just on account of the food and the wine and the service in the Riverside Restaurant. His manners had been impeccable, as she had supposed they would be, enhanced by the obvious fact that he was known to both the maître d' and the wine waiter. But now she supposed they were coming up to the crunch – if there was going to be a crunch.

'Liqueur?'

'Thank you. Brandy.'

He signalled the waiter. 'Do you know that you are quite the most handsome policewoman I have ever known?' he asked.

'How many policewomen have you known?' she countered.

'Touché,' he said. 'You have a very quick brain.'

'I'm alive.'

'Ah. Yes. One doesn't really take these things on board in the abstract, as it were. Have you ever been in danger?'

'Yes. Haven't you?'

'I'm a soldier.'

'And I'm a little woman. But ours is a sexless occupation, when it comes to protection.'

'So you've been under fire. Have you ever had to return fire?'

'I'm afraid so.'

'And actually hit someone?'

'I am reputed to be the department's best shot.'

'Good lord! You really are a most exciting person.'

'Thank you. I'm sure you are too.'

'I'm not sure I can compare with you. But your obvious ability, your experience, the way you are so laid back, does inspire confidence. Do you really think you can pull it off?'

'Yes. If you play your part.'

'Sadly, I'm to be a bystander.'

'Only up to a point, Adrian. I am confident that my team and I can get your sister out of Cuesta's ranch and as far as

51

La Paz. But he will undoubtedly come behind us. When we reach La Paz, it is up to you to get us out of Bolivia in a hurry and back here just as quickly as possible.'

'Oh, quite. I understand. Don't worry about that. I will have a chartered aircraft standing by, and you'll be away in no time at all.'

'Then I'll say that *your* ability, and experience, and money, gives me every confidence as well.'

'So, will you include me in your team?'

'I thought my team is yours.'

'I like that.' He raised his glass. 'To us.'

She brushed hers against his and drank.

'Now,' he said. 'Where would you like to go?'

She looked at her watch. 'I'm afraid I'm an early bird. Most days I need to keep my wits about me.'

'I've taken a room for the night. Actually, I've been staying here for several days, sorting things out, don't you know. Would you care to come up, have another brandy, use the facilities . . .' He paused to gaze at her with arched eyebrows, cheeks pink.

'Perhaps some other time, when we know each other better.'

'Is that a promise, or a put-down?'

'It is neither. It is simply that I make it a rule never to sleep with a man on our first date.'

'How about the second?'

'You never know.'

'So . . . when can we meet again?'

'I'd say probably in La Paz.'

Oh, she thought, actually to be as sophisticated as she could make herself sound. She took a taxi home; one could hardly tell the doorman at the Savoy that she was going to walk to the tube station.

Tom was in bed, and asleep; it was just past eleven. She got in beside him, and he woke up. 'Oh, it's you.'

'Who did you hope it would be?'

'I was dreaming,' he explained enigmatically. 'Had a good evening?'

'Yes.'

'Great. About that shirt . . .'

'I'm too tired to discuss it right now.'

'Ah. Well then . . .' He rolled her over and put his arm round her, reaching down to squeeze her bottom as he knew she liked.

'I'm too tired for that, too,' she said.

And then found she couldn't sleep. She kept thinking about Lord Lichton, and wondering . . . Suppose she *had* accepted his proposition? And what would happen when they met again?

The Aristocrat

'I go on assignment tomorrow,' Tom said, actually bringing her a cup of tea in bed.

'Snap.'

'You never told me.' He sat beside her.

'I didn't find out until yesterday. And it may not be quite tomorrow. But when I go, I'll be away for a few weeks.'

He frowned at her. 'Are you trying to tell me something?'

'It's a job, Tom. Same as any other.'

'So you will be coming back.'

'If not on my feet, in a box.'

'Shit! It's not one of those?'

'I'm hoping not.'

'Well . . .' He eased the sheet down from her throat, and began stroking her nipples – something else he knew she liked. 'Seeing as how we're going to be separated for a couple of weeks . . .'

Jessica looked at her watch. 'Half past seven. I have to get dressed. Andie and Chloe are coming at eight.'

'What the fuck for?'

'For breakfast, and to discuss things.'

'You're not teaming up with them again?'

'They're the best we have.' She moved his hand and nudged him with her knee. 'So give.'

'Bloody lezzies!' Instead of moving he held her shoulders and laid her across the bed, rolling between her kicking legs.

'Get off!' she gasped. 'I'm not in the mood.'

'You'd rather have it off with them, right?'

Jessica lost her temper. He was attempting to push himself into her, but was making no progress as she had every muscle tensed and her arms were free. She didn't want to hurt him seriously, but she certainly didn't intend to be raped, so she resorted to basic unarmed combat training and clapped her hands together, one over each of his ears.

He uttered a shriek, and his entire body sagged as the pressure all but punctured his eardrums. Jessica slid out from beneath him and gained her feet. 'That is it,' she said. 'Absolutely it. Get yourself dressed and get out. And take all your gear with you.'

She went into the shower. A few minutes later he followed her into the bathroom. 'You could have killed me.'

'I deliberately didn't.'

She stepped out and he handed her a towel. 'OK, OK. I was out of line. You drive a man mad. And I want you so . . .'

'Incidentally,' she said, 'you are not invited to breakfast. It's a confidential matter.'

'OK, OK. I know you're still mad about that shirt.'

'As far as I'm concerned,' Jessica said between strokes of her toothbrush, 'that shirt is history. So are you.'

'It was just a moment of madness. She's such a pretty little thing . . .'

'So go to her.' She stepped past him, returned to the bedroom, and began to dress.

Again he followed her. 'Don't you even want to know her name?'

'No.'

'Shit! Listen, JJ . . .' He reached for her.

'Touch me, Tom, and I really will hurt you.'

His hands fell to his sides. More than twice her size, he could probably kill her with a couple of well-placed blows. The trouble was, he knew he would never have the mental

55

strength to deliver those blows on her. He also knew that when she got her dander up, she could develop a furious intensity which was as frightening as it was deadly. 'We'll talk about it when you come back,' he said.

'Don't hold your breath. And if any of your things are still here when I come back, they go straight in the trash burner.'

She was still seething when she opened the door for Andrea and Chloe. As they could see at a glance. 'Bad time?' Andrea asked.

'I invited you, didn't I?'

The two policewomen – neither was in uniform – exchanged glances. Although they were both in their late twenties, they were a strongly contrasting pair. Andrea Hutchins was tall and slim, her splendid boot-encased legs exposed by her short dress; she had immaculately groomed auburn hair, which, like Jessica, she wore long and unconfined when not on duty. Chloe Allbright, on the other hand, was short and somewhat plump, with a large bust and wide thighs; her curly yellow hair was as untidy as her shirt flopping out of her very well-filled jeans. But they had always, in Jessica's experience, been very fond of each other, and, again in her experience, as a pair they could be very nearly as deadly as herself.

'Sit down,' she invited.

'Andie said something about South America,' Chloe remarked. 'I've always fancied sunning myself on Copacabana.'

'Where we are going is the other side of South America, and is a long way from any beach.'

'Next you'll be telling me it's Lake Titicaca.'

'Never was a truer word spoken in jest.' Jessica had been studying her atlas. 'I don't suppose either of you speaks Spanish?'

'I can get by,' Andrea said.

'Great. How did you manage that?'

56

'Before I joined the force, a friend and I ran a bar in a place called Javea for a couple of years.'

'I honeymooned in Javea,' Jessica said. 'Seaside place between Valencia and Alicante.'

'That's right. Honeymooned? When was that?'

'Fourteen years ago.'

'Fourteen years ago,' Andrea said reminiscently, 'I was a schoolgirl.'

'Ah, yes, of course. Still, I hope you haven't forgotten your Spanish.'

'Morning, Tom,' Chloe said as he emerged from the bedroom, fully dressed.

'He's just leaving,' Jessica said.

'Fucking lezzies,' Tom muttered, and banged the door behind him.

'It *is* a bad time,' Andrea suggested.

'What was that he called us?' Chloe inquired.

'Forget it, and listen.' Jessica poured coffee while the girls buttered their toast. She outlined the situation as succinctly as she could.

'Golly!' Andrea commented. 'Damsels in distress and all that.'

'Is she good-looking?' Chloe asked.

'I believe she was once voted the most beautiful woman in England,' Jessica said. 'But that was a couple of years back. God knows what this husband of hers may have done to her in the meantime. Now listen very carefully. This is probably the most dangerous assignment you will ever have.' She didn't include herself in that statement. Going after Korman, the mad bomber, in the Turkish mountains had been the most dangerous assignment *she* had ever had; the difference was that on that mission she had had the support, and indeed been part of, the SAS. 'It is dangerous on two counts. One, we are dealing with a killer, who appears to kill in a most unpleasant manner.'

'I hate crocodiles,' Chloe confided. 'More than ever, now. And snakes,' she added as an afterthought.

'These are alligators,' Jessica said reassuringly.

'I never could tell the difference.'

'I think it has something to do with the jaws or the teeth; one can close its mouth completely and the other can't. Don't ask me which. The important point is that alligators are a lot smaller.'

'We're not really going to run into one of these creatures, are we?' Andrea asked.

'Not if I can help it. But we do have to remember that they are there, just waiting to sink their teeth into some succulent female flesh.'

Chloe hugged herself.

Andrea was more practical. 'What do we shoot them with? Our pistols?'

'We're not carrying weapons, at least not from here. We're tourists, remember, until we actually get to Bolivia. This chap Smart in La Paz will equip us.'

'What with?'

'We'll have to wait and see. Whatever he's got is probably old-fashioned. We'll just have to make do. Which brings me to our second point. We are going to be operating outside the law – Bolivian law certainly, but also British law – at least until we get back here with the young lady. There will be no official recognition of what we are doing, and if we get caught, no one is going to come to our help, at least openly.'

'What's it like in a Bolivian gaol?' Chloe asked.

'I should think it is a bit worse than being raped. Except that you probably *would* be raped every day you're there.'

'Ugh! I need the loo.' She got up and left the table.

Jessica waited for the bathroom door to close, then she asked, 'Is everything all right?'

'Ah, well . . . is everything all right between you and Tom? I've never seen him so grouchy.'

'I asked you first.'

Andrea made a moue. 'She's got the idea that I have been seeing someone else.'

'M or F?'

Andrea gave one of her sleepy smiles. 'Oh, M.'

'You mean, you have?'

'Well . . . just a drink and that sort of thing.'

'That sort of thing means different things to different people,' Jessica pointed out.

'Well . . .'

'Look, I am not prying into your private life. I have explained that this is a tricky assignment. Which means we have all got to be totally on the ball at all times, and have total confidence in each other at all times. I just want you to tell me that Chloe is up to it. We don't want to have another Louise.'

The original fourth member of the squad had got herself killed in the line of duty only six months earlier, all because she had had domestic man trouble and had not been fully focussed. But then, Jessica realized, *she* was in the middle of man trouble now, and she was as fully focussed as ever, maybe more so. But she knew she was a far stronger character than Chloe.

'I think so,' Andrea said. But her tone lacked certainty.

'Then I'm making you responsible for her behaviour.'

Andrea gulped. 'What about Tom?'

'He isn't coming with us.'

'I meant, him and you.'

'Him and me are history.'

'Oh.' Andrea gazed at her across the table.

Chloe came back.

'Right,' Jessica said. 'What I have been leading up to all this time is that you have both got to be absolute, genuine volunteers. I am not going to hold it against you if you have second thoughts now. But once we go, we go, and there can be no second thoughts then. If we come back it's going to be because we will have acted as a team. So?'

'I volunteer,' Andrea said. 'Again.'

'Count me in,' Chloe said.

'Right. Now, Mrs Norton is organizing our trip, but it'll probably be a couple of weeks before she can get us on a tour, so you will continue with your present assignments for the time being. I will see Superintendent Manley and arrange for you to be replaced in good time and given three weeks' leave of absence.'

'Will he go along with that?' Chloe asked.

'Yes, because Adams will tell him to. However, there are things that we have to do while we're waiting. Shots. Are you up to date?'

Andrea and Chloe looked at each other. 'Well . . .'

'Get up to date,' Jessica said. 'The medical people will tell you what you need, but I would say that malaria, cholera and smallpox will be high on the list. Oh, and tetanus.'

'I hate being pricked,' Chloe said, and flushed.

'Once it's done, you're OK for about ten years,' Jessica pointed out. 'Who knows, you may like Bolivia so much you'll want to go back. I'll look after currencies and traveller's cheques and things; I don't suppose too many places in Bolivia take cards. Clothes. Not too light; we're going to be spending most of our time in some pretty high mountains. A couple of dresses for evening wear, nothing long, but in the main, long-sleeved shirts and thick pants, socks and ankle-length canvas boots.'

'And bikinis?' Chloe suggested.

'If you must, although I don't see us doing any swimming. Remember those alligators.'

'I'm going to have nightmares about them. I know I am.'

'Sunscreen might be useful, though. And insect repellent. Citronella.'

'Ugh! I hate the smell. Do they have bugs up in the mountains?'

'I doubt it. But our operation will take place down in the bush. We're supposed to be in and out in a single day, but you never can tell. And make sure your first-aid boxes are up to date.'

'Names?' Andrea asked.

'Our own. We're not likely to meet anyone we know. Save for his lordship. Just check that your passports are in order, and turn them in at the Yard. They'll obtain the visas we need. That's about it. If I think of anything else I'll let you know. And, of course, this deal is known to only the three of us. And the commander and Norton. It must stay that way.'

'It's also known to his lordship,' Andrea pointed out. 'And his family? Don't they know what he's planning?'

Jessica considered; she hadn't thought of that. 'I'll have to check that out.'

'Who are they, anyway?' Chloe asked.

'His father is the Earl of Clandine. But Adrian uses the family name, Lichton. He's Lord Lichton.'

'Adrian?' Andrea raised her eyebrows.

It was Jessica's turn to flush. 'He likes informality.'

'How do you spell that, anyway?' Chloe asked.

'A – d – r – i – a – n.'

'I meant this Lichton.'

'L – i – c – h – t – o – n.'

'That's Lickton.'

'It's pronounced Lighton. Okay, kids, get on with your lives, and wait for my next phone call.'

Andrea and Chloe finished their coffee and got up. 'When *do* we get to meet the great one?' Andrea asked.

'When you get to La Paz,' Jessica said.

She got dressed, then checked out her own wardrobe. She would have to buy things like the boots and the thick socks, as well as the thick pants. A hat! She'd forgotten to tell them about hats.

Those were details. The point Andrea had raised about the Lichton family's involvement was, or could be, a serious matter.

She went to the Yard and had a session with Superintendent Manley, who was, as always, a reluctant partner in her activities. 'The calls these special assignments make on my manpower – and womanpower. And three of you, for three weeks . . . Don't tell me,' he said as Jessica opened her mouth. 'If I have any complaints I must take them to the commander. One of these days I may well do so. Very well, Sergeant, I will make the necessary arrangements. How soon do you want Hutchins and Allbright released?'

'You'll have to check with Mrs Norton about this, sir. But I would like them available at least two days before the date she gives you.'

Manley cleared his throat. 'Very good, Sergeant. Now, I'm sure you have things to do.'

Jessica went upstairs. 'Ah, Sergeant Jones,' Mrs Norton said. 'I hoped you'd drop by. I have your bookings.'

'That was quick. When?'

'There is a tour leaving on Saturday, and you are on it – with two companions. You'll have to let me have their names.'

Jessica sat down, unbidden. 'You have got us on a tour starting Saturday? That's only four days away. That's not possible. Aren't these tours fully booked months in advance?'

Mrs Norton gave one of her cold smiles. 'Everything is possible if you have sufficient clout, Sergeant.'

'May I ask how you did it?'

'You may ask, certainly. But I don't think it is necessary for me to tell you.'

'I think it is very necessary, Mrs Norton. This is supposed to be a covert operation, and we appear to be dealing with people who will stop at nothing to protect their interests. If you leaned on people to find us places on this tour, presumably you did so in the name of the Metropolitan Police?'

'Well . . . it was necessary to make them understand that the matter was important.'

'So what did you tell them?'

'Well, really, Sergeant, I do not think you have the authority to interrogate me.'

'Mrs Norton, I do have the authority to protect the lives of myself and my team. What did you tell the tour operator?'

'Nothing that could in any way endanger your assignment, Sergeant. I simply told them that we wished to send three of our officers to South America, incognito. They quite understood.'

'Oh, my God. My *God*,' Jessica commented.

'You are being hysterical.'

'Mrs Norton, do you have any idea how many companies have tours to South America?'

'I would have thought several. But surely that is added protection for you.'

'Out of all of those tours, which go to exciting and exotic places such as Rio and Buenos Aires and Manaos, you have chosen one going to Bolivia, which does not have the best of communications with anywhere else save Peru. Now, why should you have done that, if we were going to anywhere other *than* Bolivia?'

'Well . . .' Mrs Norton actually managed to look flustered. But she recovered quickly enough. 'Even if they do deduce that you are going to Bolivia, they're hardly likely to take a full page advert in *The Times* to publicize that fact.'

'But there is always the chance that their staff may discuss it amongst themselves, and then with their friends. These are international drug dealers we are facing, Mrs Norton. They have their tentacles in every country in the world. I need to know how they found us places.'

'Well . . . I believe they told a family of three, who were recent bookings, that there had been a mistake and this tour was actually fully booked.'

'And how did this family take it?'

'I have no idea. I do know that they were given another tour as compensation, free.'

'Something else for chatting with friends about. I need to see the boss.'

'Have you an appointment?'

'This won't wait on an appointment.'

'If you mean to complain about the travel arrangements, he already knows about them.'

'Then he'll see me. Now.'

Adams looked somewhat apprehensive, as he invariably did when alone with Jessica. 'Problems?'

'Not from my point of view, sir.'

'Excellent. Your young ladies have both signed on, have they?'

'They were happy to do so, sir. On the understanding, which they shared with me, that this is to be a covert operation and that our destination and identities as policewomen were to be kept secret.'

'Ah. I don't really think you have been in any way compromised.'

'We won't know until we get there, will we? The point is that however incognito we manage to be, the tour operator's people will still know that Messrs Jones, Hutchins and Allbright, three girls apparently out for a good time, are actually members of the Special Branch. I presume our guide on the ground will be a Bolivian, or at least a Bolivian resident. Don't you think he, or she, will be informed?'

'Hm. I take your point. I'll have Mrs Norton call them back and tell them that this is strictly confidential.'

'With respect, sir, if that horse hasn't already left the stable,

64

any attempt to close the door now will merely make it a more interesting topic for gossip.'

'Are you saying you wish to drop out?'

'No, sir. But I would like to be reassured that there will be no more leaks.'

'You have my assurance.'

'Does that cover the Lichton family?'

'Eh?'

'Do we know if Lord Lichton is acting on his own in setting this up, or if his parents and his brother and sister know about it?'

'I have no idea. But even if they do, they would hardly do anything which might endanger Mrs Cuesta.'

'I am sure they would not do so deliberately, sir. But just for instance, if I have my facts right, Lady Miranda met her husband at a ball here in England. That means when he was here he was moving in the same social circles as herself, and thus must have friends in that circle. Should the business be discussed in those circles, some of those friends may be close enough to Cuesta to feel it their duty to inform him that three British policewoman are on their way to sort out his marital problems.'

Adams stroked his chin. 'It's a point. The first thing we need to do is have a word with Lord Lichton and find out how many people are in on this.'

'Leave that with me, sir,' Jessica said.

And why not? she asked herself. For the first time in a very long time, she was footloose and fancy-free. And suddenly she was enjoying it, even if she was still feeling outraged at Tom's behaviour and had no intention of forgiving him, ever. But she knew this was going to be a temporary frame of mind; she had become accustomed to sharing her bed, on a more or less permanent basis. This was not merely a matter of sexual satisfaction, or even companionship: she needed the security, both of knowing that someone was beside her and of feeling a pair of strong arms around her. She lived her life on a knife-edge, and for all her public persona of ice-cold, ruthless efficiency, when she turned that off she was as vulnerable, mentally and physically, as anyone else. Thus Tom was going to have to be replaced. The problem was, with whom?

By the nature of her peculiar profession, pillow talk could only be indulged in with fellow members of that profession. She was terribly aware that she was now on the wrong side of thirty-five, and if just about all of her male colleagues still apparently considered her worth a second look, by the time *they* passed thirty-five they were all either married or known to be gay.

So, go gay herself? She had absolutely no hang-ups about sexual mores; it was the personality, the character, the brain that mattered, not the physical attributes, or lack of them. She had no doubt at all that Andrea would move in with her tomorrow, and despite her priorities Andie was such a beautiful woman she could not help but find that an intriguing thought. But Andie, however attractive in the short term, was not the commitment she sought. She wanted children, and a family life. To reach that goal, she would have to leave the force. So which came first? Leave the force and then look for a husband? Or find a partner willing to go all the way, and *then* quit. But that last option was further complicated by the fact that any man who took her on as Detective-Sergeant Jessica Jones would do so mainly because she was the fearless protector of her assigned clients, a woman who had iced water in her veins rather than blood, so it was said, who never turned her head or blinked.

Besides, to take up with Andie would mean a bust-up between her and Chloe, and that would split the team right open.

So in the meantime, she asked herself again, why not a lord

as a fill-in? It would certainly be different. Supposing he hadn't gone off the boil.

Jessica telephoned Andrea first. She was back on duty protecting a visiting female diplomat, but was able to answer on her mobile.

She gave a little shriek. 'Saturday? We only get our shots on Friday. As for shopping . . . And what about the visas?'

'You're being relieved tomorrow night,' Jessica said. 'So you'll have a couple of days to get ready. Hats! Don't forget to buy yourself a hat each. Something broad-brimmed and sun-proof, but not frilly. I'll have your doctor's appointment brought forward. Meanwhile, get your passports to the Yard today. Will you bring Chloe up to date?'

Then she called the Savoy. 'I'd like to speak with Captain Lord Lichton, please.'

'May I ask who is calling, madam?'

'Just tell him JJ.'

'Please hold the line, madam.'

Jessica waited. She was in a corner of the ladies' restroom, using her mobile.

'JJ? How good to hear from you so soon.'

'I hope I'm not interrupting anything?'

'Nothing that cannot wait for the pleasure of seeing you again.'

So he definitely had not gone off the boil. 'There are some important matters I need to discuss with you.'

'Of course. Let's see . . . Ten past twelve. Lunch with me.'

'Thank you, sir. Where?'

'Oh, here. It's the most convenient place.'

Convenient for what, she wondered. 'At what time?'

'What's wrong with right now? As soon as you can get here.'

'I should warn you that I'm wearing pants.'

'I don't think we'll let that bother us. Shall we say, fifteen minutes?'

He was certainly a master of innuendo. But she began to feel pleasurably excited. She checked herself out to make sure she was as neat and tidy within as without, then went outside and called a taxi. Twenty minutes later she was dropped off at the hotel. She went into the lobby, expecting to see him waiting for her, but he was not. She hesitated, wondering if she should go into the bar, or try the Grill Room, when she was approached by an under-manager. 'Miss Jones?'

'Yes.'

'His lordship asked for you to go up to his suite. Seventh floor, number sixteen. I'll tell the floor waiter to expect you.'

He was also not one for clandestine arrangements. Jessica rode up in the lift, and was met on the seventh floor, as promised, by a waiter who escorted her along the wide, carpeted corridor to number sixteen. He knocked. 'Miss Jones, my lord.'

Adrian himself opened the door. Somehow Jessica had expected at least a butler. He was again wearing his blazer over slacks. 'JJ! How good to see you. Thank you, Alphonse. I'll see you later.'

Alphonse bowed and withdrew, and Jessica stepped into the room. 'Do you have to tip him every time he does you a service?'

'That depends on the service. In this case, most definitely.'

Jessica walked into the room. It was a sitting room, lavishly furnished with a settee and several chairs as well as a coffee table, while large windows overlooked the Thames. On the sideboard there was an ice bucket and a bottle of champagne with a tray of glasses; beside it there was a minibar. On the right, a half open door clearly led to the bedroom.

Adrian closed the outer door. 'I thought we'd lunch up here. It's far better for a private chat than downstairs. Don't you agree? You said you had something important to discuss.'

'I do.'

'Well, then, do sit down. And have a look at the menu. I like to get the sordid details out of the way first, don't you? Drink?'

She decided that he probably drove a Porsche, and wondered how often he was done for speeding. 'Thank you.' She sat down, picked up the menu. 'What do you recommend?'

He opened the bottle with a great deal of expertise; there was only the tiniest pop. 'I would try the turtle soup, and then the York ham and sweet corn, topped off with prunes in brandy. Plain fare, I'm afraid, but they do it awfully well.'

'Then I shall accept your recommendation.'

He held out her flute, and their fingers touched. 'Here's another toast to our joint venture. Excuse me.' He picked up the phone and ordered the food – he chose the same – and then looked at her. 'I'm afraid when it comes to wine, I'm a bit of a slummer. My favourite is Chateau Batailley. The '93 is very good.'

'On top of champagne, in the middle of the day?'

'Surely you're not working this afternoon?'

'As a matter of fact, I'm not.' She began to feel deliciously wicked. It was a very long time since she had allowed herself to feel that.

He completed the order, then sat beside her. 'Do tell me. No problems, I hope? When are you away?'

'Saturday.'

'Right. I shall have to get my skates on. I'll leave on Friday.'

'Just like that?'

'Oh, there'll be no problem getting a flight to La Paz.'

Because he would be travelling first-class, naturally. 'Don't you have military duties, or whatever?'

'I'm on extended leave of absence.'

'Just like that?'

'Well, when my CO understood the situation, he was more

than happy to help. Providing I don't bring the regiment into it.'

'Ah.'

He frowned. 'What's on your mind?'

'Your CO knows the score. The entire score?'

'Well, he had to be put fully in the picture.'

'How large is the picture you sold him?'

'Ah. I see what you mean. But there is nothing for you to worry your pretty little head about. He knows nothing about you. He has given me extended leave to see what I can do about my sister. He doesn't want to know how I do it. As I said, his only caveat is that I should not involve the regiment.'

'Well, that's something. How about your folks?'

'What about my family?'

'Do *they* know what you're about?'

'Oh, good heavens, no. It would drive Mumsy' – he flushed – 'that's my mother, into a decline. She has a very nervous disposition. Anyway, they don't suspect that there is anything wrong. They think Miranda's having the time of her life. Her letters give that impression, don't you see?'

'What about this code?'

'They don't know anything about that.'

'What about your brother and sister?'

Adrian nodded. 'They know the code. But Yolanda is married to some Scottish laird chappie. She doesn't come down very often. In fact, we haven't seen her since the wedding. She didn't approve of Ramon.'

'Sensible girl. But Tom is here all the time, right? Has he seen the letter?'

'Yes. But I made him swear secrecy and leave the whole thing to me.'

Jessica made a moue.

'I know,' Adrian agreed. 'But I think he'll go along with it. Providing we get a fairly rapid and successful solution.'

'But he knows you intend to do something about it.'

'Yes, he does.' There was a knock on the door. 'Come.'

A trolley was wheeled in, the covers were taken off the plates, the wine was opened and the cork sniffed, and the waiter withdrew.

'Looks tremendous,' Jessica said.

'Let's hope it is. Would you like to take off your jacket?' He took off his own, draped it across a chair. Jessica did the same. 'So tell me, why this sudden concern about people learning our plans?'

While they ate Jessica told him about the tour operator.

'Hm,' he commented. 'Pretty long shot.'

'If this man, your brother-in-law, *is* a drug baron, he will have agents all over the place. And we must assume, as he was moving in your social group while he was here, whether he bought his way in or not, that at least one of his agents might be in that group. People with whom your brother presumably mixes on a regular basis.'

'Hm,' Adrian said again. 'I'll have a word with him.'

'May I also assume that while he knows you are meaning to do something about your sister, like your CO he does not know who you are going to do it with?'

'Ah. Well . . .'

Jessica put down her fork. 'You didn't!'

'I think I may have mentioned that I was going to be helped, undercover, by the police. In fact, I think I mentioned you.'

'For God's sake. You told him my name?'

'Well . . . you're so damned attractive. I told him I was going on a South American safari with the most gorgeous girl I had ever known. I'm sorry. I'll sort it out.'

'Will you? Can you? And you have every reason to be sorry. You were wrong on three counts. One is that I cannot be the most gorgeous girl you have ever known. The second is that I am not a girl; I am thirty-six years old. And the third is that you have very likely buried me, and my team, up to our ears in shit.'

'Are you really thirty-six? You don't look it.'

'Compliments aren't going to help.'

'Look, I said I'm sorry. I said I'll have a word with Tom. I only told him on the phone last night. He hasn't had the time to spread it about.' He picked up her hand. 'Do forgive me, JJ, and finish your meal. I'll make sure nothing is spilt about this business. If anything were to happen to you, I'd never forgive myself.'

'Well . . .' She freed her hand and resumed eating. 'Have you written your sister, giving her the magic words?'

'Yes. It was posted this morning. Trouble is, you're moving so fast you're likely to get there before she gets it.'

'I think that's unlikely. Apparently we spend some days in Peru before going to Bolivia, and then some more days before our ranch trip.' She finished her meal. 'That was delicious, Lord Lichton. Now—'

'Am I that much out of favour? Last night you called me Adrian.' He refilled her wine glass before she could protest.

And she had sipped out of it before she caught up with herself. 'Don't you think it would be best if we kept our relationship strictly business?'

'I don't think it would be a good idea at all. Try some of these; they're stoneless.' He ladled prunes soaked in brandy on to a plate.

'If I have anything more to drink, I won't be able to stand up.'

'Were you meaning to stand up?'

They gazed at each other, then he placed a prune in his mouth and leaned forward to kiss her. She opened her mouth, and he thrust the prune between her teeth with his tongue. Then he closed his mouth on hers. She had to regain her breath and stop herself from swallowing the prune whole. When he took his mouth away, she felt she should say something like, you have done this sort of thing before, but that would have been inane. What really mattered was

72

that *she* hadn't done it before . . . and that she was enjoying every moment of it.

Now he was releasing the waistband for her pants, pulling her shirt out and unbuttoning it while she stared at him as if she were hypnotized. His movements were too gentle to be resented. She chewed vigorously and swallowed, getting her tongue into action. 'My lord . . .'

'Adrian,' he reminded her, opening the shirt wide. 'I think the prunes will keep.' He stood up. As she had supposed would be the case, she felt quite incapable of moving, so he thrust one arm under her knees, wrapped the other round her shoulders, and carried her into the bedroom, which was furnished on the same scale as the sitting room. He laid her very gently on the covers, and then took off her shoes.

'The loo,' she gasped. 'I must go to the loo.'

He pointed at an inner door. 'Can you manage?'

'Yes,' she said. 'I think.'

She staggered across the room, got into the large and elaborate bathroom – which contained a tub big enough for four people at once – and got her pants and knickers down. When she was finished she held on to the basin to peer into the mirror. To her surprise she looked exactly as she had always looked, cheeks a trifle flushed, perhaps, but still wearing her normal slightly quizzical expression. This was what he saw when he looked at her. This was the calm self-confidence he would suppose lay behind the mask – even if he obviously knew she was a trifle squiffy. This was the role she had to play if she was going to go through with it.

And how she wanted to go through with it.

She took off her pants and knickers altogether and returned to the bedroom carrying them. Adrian lay on the bed, naked. Back to the Porsche syndrome. She stood by the bed, and he watched her take off her shirt and then her bra and deposit them beside her other clothes. Then he put his arm round her thighs and brought her down on top of him. 'You,' he said, 'are utterly delicious. I would like to love you forever and a day.'

She kissed him, while allowing her body to move on his. 'I am going to reach that day before you. You do understand that.'

His hands closed on her buttocks. 'Then let's enjoy the days we do have, JJ.'

Miranda Cuesta dismounted in front of the porch and tossed her reins to the waiting groom. The two men who had accompanied her on her morning ride touched their hats and walked their horses towards the stable. Despite their presence, and the fact that she went nowhere without someone at her shoulder, she felt more relaxed after her morning ride than at any other time of the day. Or night.

But now she had to enter the house. Her prison. Her utterly delightful prison where she had everything she could wish, was given everything she could wish . . . and yet lived in abject fear. Her heels clicked on the floor. Immediately inside the door, Felicity waited, bowing at the appearance of her 'mistress' – Ramon insisted that the charade be carefully kept up. Every morning Felicity attended her to present the day's menu for her approval. She was often tempted to reject it, but she never did. For one thing, most of the time she had no idea what the various dishes meant. For another, she had decided on a course of action, and she was determined to see it through. She had written Adrian, using their code, and she knew he would not let her down. Or had he already done so? That had been six months ago, and while he had replied to two of her letters, he never used the magic word. She kept telling herself that he would have all sorts of arrangements to make, leave to be arranged, a team to be got together – he would have more sense than to try to deal with the business entirely on his own – and their escape from Bolivia to be planned: she didn't doubt that Ramon would do everything in his power to stop them from leaving, and here in Bolivia it was Ramon who had the power.

But six months! As luxurious as the ranch was, it was still six months in prison. It was evidenced every time someone came out from La Paz, or when the tourist groups came to admire the ranch; on those occasions she was always confined to her room, locked in and guarded by her maids so that she could not even go out on to the terrace: Señora Cuesta was unwell.

And every night she was even more his prisoner. She did not know what his ultimate plans for her were; she did know that for the present he still loved at least her body. She was terrified of becoming pregnant, with all the ramifications that would have. But so far she had escaped. And the truly terrifying thought was that he still turned her on, still made her yearn for his embrace, that with every day that passed her resolve to destroy him weakened until she wondered whether all the effort – and the risk – was worth it. But she had started something, and she didn't know how to finish it. Adrian's elaborate code had one fatal weakness: there was no way of saying, as you were, it was all a mistake, call off the dogs. She did not doubt that, however slowly, the wheels of her rescue were turning; the day was coming closer when this cosy little world, however criminal, however downright ghastly, was going to be blown into a thousand pieces.

Thus days like today made her more than usually excited, as well as apprehensive, because the weekly mail plane had landed from La Paz. As always, it had required all of her self-control to go for her usual morning ride, feigning complete indifference to what letters might have arrived. But now . . .

She took off her Stetson, let it trail from her fingers, and walked across the vast expanse of floor to where Ramon sat behind his desk. 'Mail,' he said jovially, indicating the pile of envelopes. 'One for you from your parents, and one from your brother.'

Miranda picked up the two envelopes, slowly and carelessly,

and slit the first open. Commonplaces from Mumsy and Daddy; they thought she was blissfully happy in her new home. She laid the sheets on the desk; Ramon always wished to read her mail. Then she slit open the second envelope, unable to stop her fingers from trembling. She scanned the single sheet. More commonplaces, until the very end. *There was a wizard game of polo yesterday. In fact, it was a wizard day.* She read the words again, feeling almost about to faint. He was coming! He was on his way!

Ramon watched her, then stretched out his hand. She placed the sheet of paper in it without hesitation; now more than ever she had to behave absolutely normally. He read it in turn, then raised his head. 'Tell me what it says.'

'Can't you read?'

'Not between the lines, unfortunately. Why don't you sit down.' Cautiously she lowered herself into the chair before the desk; the hat fell to the floor. Ramon opened a drawer and took out a mirror. 'Look at yourself.'

Miranda took the glass reluctantly. She knew her breathing had quickened when she had read what Adrian had had to say. And now, as she had feared, she could see the flush in her cheeks. 'You are excited by what is in this letter,' Ramon pointed out. 'Yes?'

'I am always excited when I hear from my family.'

'Sometimes more than ever. So tell me, what is really in this letter?'

'You mean you wish me to read it to you.'

'I wish you to stop playing games, or I will be very angry. Let me bring you up to date. My agents in London have been required, for obvious reasons, to keep an eye on your family, and their comings and goings. I have this morning received an e-mail informing me that your brother Adrian has visited Scotland Yard on more than one occasion over the past week. What, do you suppose, could a peer of the realm who is also an officer in the Blues possibly have to do with Scotland Yard?

And these visits have been made alone, unaccompanied by a solicitor, as one would have supposed if he had committed some offence. But here is another interesting point: Adrian has also been given extended leave of absence from his regiment. Why, do you suppose? Is he going to sail round the world, row single-handed across the Atlantic, climb Mount Everest by himself? Those I believe are the sorts of challenges for which army officers get extended leave. But none of them can possibly require repeated visits to Scotland Yard.'

Miranda had got her breathing under control. 'You will have to ask him.'

'Oh, I shall do that. Probably quite soon. Because having found out these interesting facts, my agent hunted a bit further, and has learned that Lord Adrian Lichton will be leaving London on Friday morning, flying first of all to the United States, but with a through ticket to La Paz. Your brother is coming to see you, Miranda. Isn't that nice of him? But he doesn't mention it in this letter. Is that not strange?'

Miranda licked her lips.

'But you know that it is not strange at all,' Ramon went on. 'Because he did mention it in this letter, didn't he? Just as you managed to call for his help in your letters without actually saying so.'

'You're dreaming,' she muttered.

'Am I? Tell me why he should be coming here, secretly, if he was not invited. After having been told, some months ago, that he would not be welcome.'

'I have no idea. If he *is* coming here.'

'I wish you to tell me this code of yours. I know there is one.'

She stared at him. 'And I say there isn't.'

He got up. 'Come upstairs.'

'I am not in the mood for sex, Ramon.'

'You are always in the mood for sex, my darling. You have got to be one of the most erotic women I have ever met. But

77

as it happens, I am not in the mood for sex, either. Not your sort of sex. Upstairs.'

Miranda got up and went to the stairs; she did not wish a scene in front of the servants. She went up, conscious of him just behind her. Her two maids were as usual fussing about the bedroom, and paused to curtsey as she came in. This was normal; she usually had a shower after her ride.

'*Abandonen!*' Ramon said.

They looked at Miranda, then curtseyed again and hurried from the room, whispering to each other as always.

'*They* think we are going to have sex,' Miranda remarked.

'Who can tell?' Ramon closed the door. 'Now give me this code.'

'I keep telling you, there is no code. You are paranoid. Your guilt has made you paranoid.'

Ramon went to the French windows, looking out at the distant airstrip. 'You intend deliberately to defy me?'

Miranda did not reply.

He turned to face her. 'Do you know what I do to my peons who deliberately defy me?'

She tossed her head. 'Feed them to your pet alligators?'

'No, no. That is reserved for my enemies. But I make them suffer. I am sure you have sometimes heard their screams, even up here. I have two methods of punishment. One is to sentence the condemned to be hung, naked, between two posts, and whipped until he, or she, bleeds. This is in public, you understand.'

She caught her breath. 'You would not dare!'

'You are my wife. You are my property, here on my ranch. I can do what I like to you.'

'My family will never let it rest.'

'Oh, I am not going to whip you. It would mark you permanently, and you are too beautiful for that. But I have a second means of punishment, which leaves no mark whatsoever, but which is never forgotten by the person who undergoes it. Take off your clothes.'

Miranda got her chin up, as defiantly as she could. 'What are you going to do?'

'I am going to make you feel. Unless, of course, you decide to be a good and loyal wife and tell me how you communicate secretly with your brother.'

Miranda stared at him. She had no idea what he intended to do, unless it was to have sex with her against her will. But that happened often enough – and she nearly always enjoyed it in the end. Besides, she knew she had to keep defying him to the very end. Or until Adrian could get here.

'There is no code,' she said in a low voice.

'As you wish. I must tell you, my darling, that nothing irritates me more than people who consider that I am a fool. And when it is my nearest and dearest . . . Strip!' Suddenly his voice cracked like a whip.

Miranda sat down and kicked off her boots, then stood up to remove the rest of her clothing. He watched her. 'Every time you do that you look more desirable,' he said. 'But then, it makes what I am going to do to you more desirable also.' Her head jerked as he picked up the phone. 'Felicity? Come up here, will you. Bring some *pimienta roja* with you.'

The Rendezvous

'Now, today,' said Señora Barrientes, 'we will take the coach to La Paz.' She smiled reassuringly at her twelve charges. She was a surprisingly young woman – or perhaps, Jessica thought, this was merely a reflection of her own age – who wore a smart suit and had long black hair; her features betrayed her strong Indian blood. She could be described as handsome rather than pretty. And she was Peruvian, which made Jessica feel more comfortable. She also spoke reasonable English, as eight of her charges were British. 'From here in Puno it is a journey of only two hundred kilometres and will take about three hours of actual driving. We go by bus instead of airplane, so that we can break the journey, eh? So that you can go for a boat ride on the lake.' She threw out her arm to indicate the broad waters of Titicaca. 'Now, if you will please take your places in the bus.'

They climbed in, Jessica choosing a seat well to the back, where there was room for both her broad-brimmed felt hat and her shoulder bag; she would have felt naked without the bag, even if it was strangely light without her pistol and magazines. But it still contained such essential items as her first-aid kit, housewife, money, mobile, compass and GPS receiver – as well as citronella spray, which, fortunately, she had not yet had to use. Andrea and Chloe, also equipped with their hats and shoulder bags, sat towards the front. After the disturbing lack of security she had discovered before leaving England, Jessica had determined to pick up what pieces she could, and thus they had travelled as two distinct entities. Andrea and Chloe were a pair of young women out for a good holiday; she was a widow who was getting over her bereavement, which was not altogether untrue. Thus, although they had been on the same plane from London to Miami, and again from Miami to Lima, they had done no more than nod to each other courteously. During the tour of Peru, they had allowed themselves to become friendlier, but they had done this with all the other members of the party as well.

Obviously, after Mrs Norton's heavy-handed negotiations with the tour company, some people there knew the group included at least one police officer. But apparently no one had considered the possibility that there might be more than one, and at least if anyone was monitoring them he or she would hopefully be confused by their arrangement.

Apart from necessary considerations of what might lie ahead, Jessica had been happy to have the week to wrap herself in her own thoughts. Her own guilt? She had never done anything like that before, could not now believe that she had actually done it at all. A complete stranger, but also the most exciting man she had ever met, quite apart from his elevated position in the world. So, did she regret it? How could she, when she remembered his fingers sliding over her breasts, and then between her legs, his gentle but persistent entry, the sudden surge of sexual energy which had left her breathless? No regrets. Her only caveat might be his utter orthodoxy, and his haste – she would have liked their mutual exploration to last for another hour. But perhaps that was a compliment to her, that she had turned him on so much he couldn't wait. As for what might happen next . . .

There could not be a next time until this assignment was completed. During the coming week she had to be a totally professional block of ice. And if they did ever decide to get together again, that decision would have to be entirely his. This was not in keeping with her character; she had always been the one to lead, whether in her profession or her private life. But here again she was terribly conscious of her age vis-à-vis his and, although she hated to admit it even to herself, of his social standing, again vis-à-vis hers.

And if his sole ambition had been to fuck a handsome woman? Well, she reflected, her sole ambition, at the time, had been to be fucked by a handsome man. But she could not stop her heartbeat from quickening as she thought that she would be seeing him again within twenty-four hours.

Despite her precautions there had still been problems. She did not think that Señora Barrientes actually knew her identity, but she had certainly been informed that the widow Jones was a VIP. On the day the party had arrived in Lima, and after their initial briefing on local manners and mores, she had taken Jessica aside. 'I am to assist you in any way you wish,' she had said in an arch whisper.

Jessica had had to make a very quick decision. To pretend that she had no idea what the woman was talking about would, she felt, be a mistake: she had obviously been told *something*. So she had smiled and said, 'That is very kind of you, señora. Be sure that I will let you know if I need anything.'

Señora Barrientes had tapped her nose. 'I understand. I know it is Bolivia you go. I will, how do you say, brief Señor Garcia.'

'Who is Señor Garcia?'

'He will join us as an additional guide, after we cross the border. He is Bolivian.'

'Ah. Actually, señora, I would prefer it if you didn't brief him. I am sure we two can cope together, eh?'

Señora Barrientes had given a complimented giggle. But she continued to treat Jessica as her most important charge, which could not help but be noticed by the rest of the party. There were other complications as well. As with all tours, the group soon settled down into cliques; in this case the division was four-way, which was a lot for twelve people. This was because Andrea and Chloe kept very much to themselves, as instructed, and Jessica kept very much to herself. Of the other nine, four were married couples, and two of these couples were Danish friends who were holidaying together, so they had naturally divided into two groups of four.

That left one man, who was travelling by himself. His name was Wesley, and he appeared to be English. He was in his early forties, wore a little moustache, and was tall and quite good-looking, a fact of which he was too obviously aware. He also very rapidly determined that as Jessica was an extraordinarily good-looking woman – and a widow, as everyone quickly found out, courtesy of Señora Barrientes – touring by herself, and he was, in his opinion, an extraordinarily good-looking man touring by himself, it was nature's law that they should get together.

Jessica had not resisted his advances in the beginning; her sole aim was to merge as far into the background as she could possibly do. But they had become more persistent as the first week had passed, so much so that Señora Barrientes had asked if she wanted anything done about it. 'Thank you, but I don't want to cause any trouble in the group,' Jessica had said.

But then, yesterday, after a hard week peering at ruins and artefacts and mountains and valleys they had been given the afternoon off in Puno before beginning the Bolivian part of the tour. After lunch she had strolled down to the waterfront to look at the rippling waters of the lake and she had found him beside her. 'Isn't that a beautiful sight?' he had asked. 'Did you know that Titicaca is the highest lake in the world?'

'I probably read it somewhere. This is certainly the highest I have ever been outside of an airplane. I feel quite breathless.'

'Twelve thousand feet,' he agreed. 'And yet, you know, the lake is nowhere deeper than fifteen feet. One feels that something so majestic should stretch down to the bowels of the earth.'

'One does, doesn't one. You are a fund of knowledge, Mr Wesley.'

'Oh, please call me Ted. And you are . . . Jessica?'

'However did you find that out?'

'I sneaked a glance at Barrientes' list. I hope you don't mind.'

'I suppose I should be flattered. But wouldn't you do better with that gorgeous girl . . . Miss Hutchins?'

'No way. I'm not into lezzies.'

'Is that what you think she is?' She would have to warn the girls not to be too demonstrative. In fact, Andrea was not the least demonstrative, but Chloe certainly was.

'Plain as the nose on your face,' Wesley said. 'But I'd rather talk about us. I mean, you. Are you feeling better?'

'Was I feeling ill?'

'Well . . . I was thinking of your husband. Your late husband.'

'I think of him all the time,' Jessica said.

'But this trip is doing you good.'

'I'll have to decide that when the trip is over. Now I really must get back to the hotel. It's going to rain.'

It certainly felt like rain, as the mountains became shrouded in cloud.

He walked beside her. 'Eerie, isn't it? What are you going to do with the rest of your afternoon?'

'I think I shall join the prevailing local custom and have a siesta. It's the weather for being in bed. And I gather that we have a pretty hectic schedule when we get to Bolivia.'

'Oh, indeed. You know, I've a bottle of Scotch in my room. Why don't you join me for a snorter? Make you sleep better.'

'I'm afraid I don't drink Scotch, Ted. It makes me aggressive. And I never have any trouble sleeping.'

'Ah,' he said. 'Well . . .'

'And after fourteen years of sharing my bed,' she went

on, lumping Brian and Tom together, 'I am discovering the delights of sleeping alone. I'll see you at dinner.'

She had hoped that would be a sufficient put-down. But here he was hurrying up the aisle to sit beside her before anyone else could do so. 'Lovely morning,' he remarked, as if yesterday afternoon hadn't happened. She supposed she would have to put him in the Robert the Bruce class, in that he clearly felt that if he persevered long enough he would have to triumph in the end. That would entail a very definite put-down, something she was reluctant to do. Not that she felt the least attracted to him, but because she had not yet found out enough about him. It might be flattering, and not at all unlikely, to believe that he *did* find her attractive. But she was so conditioned to thinking the worst of people that she felt that any man, or woman, who attempted to attach themselves to her had an ulterior motive for doing so. If he had managed to look at Señora Barrientes' list, what else had he managed to look at? At least in that direction he only had a few days left to show his hand, just as she only had a few days left to endure him. But she still intended to check him out at the first opportunity.

The bus followed the southern edge of the lake to the border, where formalities were minimal, and then continued at the same high level for a few more miles, the lake always on their left, while Señora Barrientes did her bit from her position beside the driver. 'Bolivia,' she said into her mike, 'is of course named after the Great Liberator, Simon Bolivar, but it is also known as the Republica del Altiplano, that is, the Republic of the High Plateau. This is not to say that the entire country is situated at this altitude. The Altiplano only covers a relatively small area. When we leave it, briefly, in two days' time, we plunge from the bracing coolness of where we are now to a dense tropical heat. As I say, we shall only be spending a brief time in those conditions. But the Oriente, which means the east of the country, the lowlands of the great forests and the great swamps and the rivers, comprising as it does two-thirds of the country, while it is very sparsely populated, is also a place of great cattle ranches. We shall be visiting one of these cattle ranches on our excursion.'

She paused to have a drink of water. 'More than one thousand years ago, Bolivia was the centre of a great empire, that of Tiahuanaco. When this empire collapsed in about the twelfth century, a measure of independence was achieved by the Indian tribes. Contrary to what is generally supposed, the Incas, who succeeded the Tiahuanaco as the dominant force in western South America, never had more than a toehold on the Altiplano. However, following the conquest of Peru and Chile by the conquistador Francisco Pizarro at the beginning of the sixteenth century, it passed under Spanish administration and remained a Spanish colony until 1825. During these centuries Bolivia was perhaps the most important and wealthiest part of the Spanish American Empire. This was because of Potosi, the silver mountain, perhaps the richest vein of silver in the entire world. But when the mine started to run out of ore, its importance declined. Then, during the social upheaval caused by the Napoleonic Wars in Europe, Bolivia joined with the other Latin American colonies, revolted against foreign rule, and gained its freedom in the movement headed by General Bolivar.

'Actually, there is no evidence that General Bolivar ever visited Bolivia. The country gained its independence thanks to the victories of General Antonio Jose de Sucre, and it is General Sucre who was elected the first president of Bolivia.'

Jessica removed Wesley's hand from her knee, where he had apparently inadvertently placed it in his fascination at the story he was being told.

'Since independence,' Señora Barrientes went on, 'the country has had a difficult time. This is because it is land-locked. It was not always so. In the beginning it had territory which gave it access to the sea, but this was lost in a series of wars with Chile and Peru. In recent years it has achieved a certain measure of prosperity, but it remains very poor when compared with the industrialized countries. For instance, the GNP is only just over one thousand US dollars per head. The GNP in America is more than thirty times that. Ah, we have arrived.'

The bus was stopping at what appeared to be a small port on the lake, and the tourists got down to board a launch flying the red, yellow and green ensign of Bolivia for the trip to the Island of the Sun, an Incan sanctuary.

'It's not going to be rough?' Chloe asked, finding herself next to Jessica. 'I get seasick.'

'It doesn't look rough to me,' Jessica said.

'And how are you getting on with your friend?' Andrea asked. 'Got any knickers left?'

'He is a pain in the ass,' Jessica agreed, glancing over her shoulder to see if Wesley was within earshot, but he had apparently gone to the loo.

'So, now we're here, what's the drill?'

'Here starts in La Paz. Just continue as normal while I check things out.'

'And get together with his lordship.'

'If he's here,' Jessica said sweetly. My God, she thought, supposing he isn't?

Having inspected the ruins, they returned to the bus, Wesley resuming his place walking beside Jessica. 'Moderate prosperity, she says,' he remarked. 'Do you know what funds this prosperity? Drugs. Cocaine.'

'Never!' Jessica said disbelievingly. She was distracted by the sight of Señora Barrientes speaking with a small dark man she had not seen before. The guide always did convey a sense of urgency whenever she spoke on any subject at all, with much arm waving, but it seemed she was being even more urgent than usual. Or was she just becoming paranoid?

She wasn't. 'This is Señor Garcia,' Señora Barrientes said as the other tourists boarded the bus. 'He will be our guide for Bolivia.'

'Oh,' Jessica said, as if she had forgotten. 'Aren't you staying with us?'

'Oh, yes, señora. But Señor Garcia knows more about Bolivia than I do. I shall be, how do you say, second in command.'

Garcia actually kissed Jessica's hand. 'It is my pleasure, señora. And it is not to worry. Señora Barrientes has, how do you say, put me in the portrait, eh? Anything you wish, you have but to say.'

'My needs are very small,' Jessica assured him, giving Señora Barrientes a censorious glance to remind her that she had broken her promise.

Needless to say, Wesley had kept the seat next to him vacant. 'You seem to have a lot of clout with these people,' he remarked. 'All these asides.'

'They happen to be very sympathetic to a widow,' she said. 'Especially a recent widow.'

'If you'd let me, I'd be sympathetic too.'

'Let's admire the view,' she suggested.

La Paz was only sixty-odd kilometres south-east of the lake, and they reached it in an hour, despite the fact that the roads were much more crowded as they approached the city, with vehicles of every description from new limousines through clapped-out-looking lorries to donkey-carts ambling along the centre of the highway, their owners turning with resentful glares when the bus driver blew his horn at them.

But the view was certainly breathtaking. Jessica knew they were some eleven thousand feet up, but still, in the distance, she could see even higher snow-covered peaks. To reach the city they descended into a shallow valley through which there flowed a river, while the city itself was a surprise after its somewhat primitive hinterland. Jessica had expected to see a great deal of old Spanish architecture, but instead she found herself looking at a profusion of high-rise buildings, both apartment and business.

'The city of La Paz,' Garcia told them, having taken over the mike, 'was founded in 1548 by Captain Alonzo de Mendoza, one of Francisco Pizarro's lieutenants. It was originally the site of an Incan village, a crossing place for the Rio de la Paz, which is also called Choqueyapo. Captain Mendoza named the town, as it then was, Nuestra Señora de la Paz, which means Our Lady of the Peace. However, after the decisive Battle of Ayacucho in 1825, when General Antonio Jose de Sucre finally defeated the Spanish to secure Bolivian independence, it was renamed La Paz de Ayacucho. At that time it was the capital of the country, but that is now the city of Sucre, named after our first president. La Paz, however, remains the business capital. It is, how do you say, as New York is to Washington. La Paz has airline connections with all the major cities of South America. You can see the international airport on that plateau beyond the city.'

They were now in the crowded streets, doing an obligatory circle of the huge and ornate government palace before arriving at their hotel.

'Now, señores and señoras,' Garcia said as they gathered in the lobby. 'And señoritas,' he added, giving Andrea and Chloe appreciative looks. 'The hotel staff will show you to your rooms. We will assemble for dinner at half past eight, following which we have arranged to take you all to a nightclub. You will enjoy this, eh?' he declared optimistically, surveying the unenthusiastic faces in front of him.

They trooped to the lift and rode up to their various floors and rooms. Jessica followed a young man in a bright red jacket to hers, and he placed her suitcase on the rack. She waited for him to leave – the tour price was supposed to include all tipping – but he remained standing by the door, which he now closed.

'Was there something else?' Jessica inquired.

'You are the Miss Jones?'

'Actually, Mrs.'

'Ah.' He looked disconcerted. 'I have something for the Miss Jones.'

'I know,' Jessica said, subduing her sudden surge of excitement. 'It confuses many people. What do you have for me?'

'I have a message for the Miss Jones.'

'And I am she.'

'But you are the Mrs Jones.'

It occurred to Jessica that if she was going to receive the message, she had only two options. One was to grab this youth by the neck and shake it out of him – but that would undoubtedly cause comment. The other was to descend to first principles. She opened her shoulder bag and took out an English five-pound note. 'Can you change this at the bank?'

His eyes gleamed. 'Oh, yes, señora.'

'Then you may have it, in exchange for the message.'

He felt in his breast pocket and held out an envelope.

'Thank you.' She gave him the money. 'Now, if you would mind leaving . . .'

He looked reluctant. 'If there is anything you wish, señora, anything at all . . .'

'I know. I'll call on you. I promise. Whenever I need anything.'

His eyes gleamed again, and he left the room. Jessica locked the door, then sat on the bed and slit the envelope. Inside there was a single sheet of paper. And on the paper there was a single line of writing: *71, Street of the Conception.* She gave an irritated click of her tongue. The idiot had not told her what name he was using, and whether this address was an hotel or an apartment or a house. Or, indeed, even if the note had actually come from Adrian.

However, if they were going out to the ranch the day after

tomorrow – sooner than she had expected – she had no time to waste.

She was in the shower when her phone rang. Muttering curses she left a trail of water as she crossed the carpet. 'Yes?'

'Just checking,' Andrea said.

Even Andie was not sufficiently security-conscious to realize that almost certainly every call any of them made would be monitored, at least by the hotel exchange. But there was no help for it now. 'I am very comfortable, thank you, Miss Hutchins,' she said. 'It is good of you to inquire.'

'Oh,' Andrea said.

'However, if it is of interest to you, I have been invited out to dinner tonight, and have accepted. So I will not be accompanying you to the nightclub.'

'Oh,' Andrea said again. 'It's not that Wesley creep?'

'No,' Jessica said. 'I will see you in the morning.'

She returned to the shower, then dressed, putting on a frock, after which she called the desk. 'May I have the number of Señora Barrientes' room, please?'

Apparently the clerk didn't speak English, and she had to wait until he located someone who did, but eventually she was connected. 'Señora? This is Mrs Jones. I am so sorry to trouble you, but I thought I should let you know that I have been contacted by an old friend who lives in La Paz and who has invited me out for dinner. So I will not be joining you tonight.'

'Of course, señora. It is the business matter, eh? I am here to help you with your business.'

'You're so kind,' Jessica said.

At this height the nights were extremely cold, so she wore her coat. 'Is it possible to obtain a taxi?' she asked the first English-speaking clerk she could locate at the desk.

'Oh, yes, señora. They are all outside, in a row. But they do not speak the English, eh? Manuel!'

It was her friend of the note.

'You help the señora, eh?' the clerk commanded.

'You wish to go somewhere, señora?' Manuel asked eagerly.

'Yes.' Jessica went outside, where they were less likely to be overheard by anyone in the lobby. 'I wish to go to seventy-one, Street of the Conception.'

'That is some distance away. You must take a taxi.'

'This is what I am trying to do,' Jessica pointed out.

'I will arrange it. You wish me to come with you?'

'I don't think that will be necessary. Just tell him where to take me, and ask him how much. I will pay it, here, before you.'

'Ah, yes. That is very wise. You wish him to wait for you?'

'I don't think that will be necessary, either. The people I am going to see will bring me back.' She hoped. Or at the very least they would be able to call her another cab.

'But it is not good for a young lady to be out by herself on the street in La Paz after dark.'

'Point one, Manuel, is that I shall not be on the street; I shall be in a taxi. Point two is, sadly, that I am no longer a young lady. Just do it.'

But she felt slightly apprehensive when, after a rather long drive, the taxi turned down a not very well lit residential street; by now it was utterly dark, the swirling clouds eliminating any suggestion of a moon or even any stars. If by any chance she was being set up . . .

The car stopped and the driver looked over his shoulder and asked a question. She had to assume he was inquiring whether she wished him to wait. But if Adrian was here she would not need him. And if Adrian was not here she was up shit creek in any event. 'No,' she said. '*Por favor.*'

She got out and surveyed the house, which, like all the houses in the street, looked well-to-do and was fronted by a splendid garden, reached by a white-painted iron gate set in a white-painted iron fence; beyond the garden the windows glowed with light. She crossed the road and opened the gate, and the taxi driver, who had been watching her, gunned his engine and drove away.

Jessica walked slowly up the centre path, which was made of concrete, her high heels clicking, but before she reached the steps leading up to the front door, the door opened and to her great relief Adrian appeared. 'Am I glad to see you.' He ran down the steps.

'Snap!' She accepted a hug.

'Problems?'

'I don't know yet.'

'Well, come in.' He held her arm as she went up the steps and into a wide entry hall, where a short, stout, middle-aged man with thinning grey hair was also waiting. 'Joe Smart,' Adrian said. 'Detective-Sergeant Jessica Jones.'

'The famous JJ,' Smart said, shaking her hand.

Jessica glanced at Adrian, who flushed. 'I've been telling him about you.'

Not again, Jessica thought. 'I'm sure his lordship exaggerates, Mr Smart.'

'Having met you, I don't believe he does. Come in, come in. And call me Joe.' He showed Jessica into a large lounge. 'My wife, Nicolette.'

'My dear, how nice to meet you.' The initial supposition that with such a name she was not English-born was confirmed by a very slight accent. Nicolette Smart was a willowy woman with neat grey hair, several inches taller than her husband.

'Drink?' Smart had moved to a well-stocked sideboard.

'Thank you. G and T?'

'G and T. Ice and lemon?'

'Thank you.'

'Do sit down,' Nicolette Smart invited. 'And tell me, have you dined?'

'Not as yet.'

'Oh, good. Neither have we. I'll just tell Teresa there will be another place for dinner.' She hurried from the room.

Jessica accepted her drink, and Adrian sat beside her. He was drinking Scotch. 'So, all is well, thus far.'

'I didn't say that. Actually, would you by any chance be on the Internet, Mr Smart?'

'Of course.'

'May I use your computer?'

'Certainly. Now?'

'If possible. The sooner I get a reply to my query the better.'

'Come upstairs.' He led the way up to his office, Adrian following. Smart sat at his desk and booted the machine. 'Help yourself.'

Jessica sent the e-mail to Superintendent Moran at Scotland Yard. *Would like any information obtainable on one Edward Wesley, English citizen and resident, currently on Andes Tour with Breakaway Holidays plc. Reply to this address. JJ.*

'Can he find out something like that, just like that?' Adrian asked.

'We have access to every police database in the world. Well, nearly every one. Certainly all those with whom we are on speaking terms. If my friend has ever been convicted of anything, his record will be obtainable.'

'The wonders of modern science,' Smart commented.

'So who is this character?' Adrian asked.

Jessica explained.

'And you don't think he can be genuine?'

'I hope he is genuine. But we can't risk that he may not be.'

'Dinner!' Nicolette called up the stairs.

'What exactly are your plans?' Adrian asked as they tucked

into their sirloin. 'You can speak freely before Joe and Nikky. They're with us all the way.'

'And your maid?'

Who was flitting in and out of the room.

'My dear, Teresa has been with us for yonks,' Nicolette said.

Jessica didn't want to antagonize these people, who represented her lifeline. 'Well, I'm afraid we are going to have to go on playing it by ear until we get to the ranch and suss things out. You were going to obtain a plan for me. And a map of the area.' She looked from Adrian to Smart.

'I have a map here,' Smart said, sliding it across the table.

Jessica unfolded it and glanced at it. The scale was smaller than she would have liked, but as there was only the one road leading to the Cuesta Ranch she didn't suppose that mattered. She refolded it and placed it in her bag. 'And the ranch?'

'I'll have that for you tomorrow.'

Jessica looked at Adrian. Who winked. 'You are going to come to see us again, I hope.'

'If I'm invited.'

'Oh, you are,' Nicolette said.

'Do you suppose you could put us in the picture?' Smart asked. 'Or should I say, your idea of how the picture should look?'

Jessica looked at Adrian, and received a nod. 'Well,' she said, 'we obviously won't have much time to play with. I gather we arrive there about nine, and we leave again about four, to be back here before dark. So we are going to have to make some fairly instant decisions. And whatever action we take is going to happen in broad daylight, so it may have to be fairly drastic.'

'Couldn't you just sit down with this man Cuesta?' Nicolette asked. 'Put the facts to him and tell him that if he doesn't let Lady Miranda go, he will be in trouble with the law?'

Jessica scratched her nose and again looked at Adrian.

'My dear Nikky,' Adrian said. 'You've lost the plot. From Ramon's point of view, this isn't about dealing with an outraged family. If he lets Mira return to England, then he will be in trouble with the law, because she will testify against him.'

'Whereas,' Smart put in, 'as long as she stays here as his wife he is not breaking any laws at all.'

'Oh,' Nicolette said. 'Oh, dear.'

'So,' Adrian said, 'you feel you may have to, ah, snatch her.'

'It seems likely. I am relying on the fact that she will wish to be snatched.' She gazed at him.

'Oh, she does. Absolutely. Certainly when she understands that you have come from me.'

'Suppose I am unable to convey that to her before the moment for snatching arrives?'

'Ah. Let's see . . .' He fumbled with his left sleeve and released the cuff. Although he was casually dressed, he wore a tie and his cuff links were gold. 'You'll see that has my initials on it, and as a matter of fact Mira gave them to me for my birthday a couple of years ago. She'll recognize it instantly, and will know that only I could have given it to you.'

'Then it should be enough to convince her that we're on her side.'

'So?'

'Well, as I told you in London, we are going to have to extract her, covertly if possible, but as that is unlikely, by force, and return here as rapidly as possible. Where you will have an aircraft waiting to get us out of the country.'

'I arranged that last week,' Adrian said. 'The plane will be ready and fuelled on Wednesday afternoon. I have not yet given the pilot a destination, but I am told it has a range of two thousand miles, so there should be no problem with that.'

'Ahem,' Smart said. 'Forgive me for intruding, but I would like to get my facts straight. Miss Jones, you intend to enter

Cuesta's property, seize his wife, with or without his consent, and leave again. May I ask how many men you are taking with you?'

'I have two women.'

'Good God!'

'Two very capable women, I understand,' Adrian said. 'Crack shots and all that.'

'Speaking of which,' Jessica began, but was interrupted.

'Do you have any idea how many people live on Cuesta's ranch?' Smart asked.

'I imagine quite a few.'

'Approximately three hundred men, women and children, all of whom owe their entire livelihood to the *patron*, and will therefore be inclined to support him against any outside interference. You must understand, Miss Jones, that while selling cocaine to be sniffed by unsuspecting youngsters may be an abhorrent crime to us, it is not to a Bolivian Indian. They, and their ancestors, have been chewing, drinking, smoking and sniffing cocaine since time immemorial, much as our so-called civilized world indulges in Valium and Prozac. You start trouble up there, and you will have the whole kit and caboodle on your necks. You could well wind up on the menu for the local caiman.'

'Say again?'

'It is a species of alligator common to the Oriente. It comes in several shapes and sizes, and those on Cuesta's property, known as black caiman, are the biggest and most dangerous of the species. They are the creatures that did for that man Sprightly.'

'But I assume they will be put off by a bullet in the throat?'

Smart pushed back his chair to wipe his brow.

'Speaking of which,' Jessica went on, 'you were going to have some guns for us.'

'I can get you guns. But I think you are crazy. How can three women take on three hundred men?'

'You said that number includes women and children.'

'All right, one hundred men. All of whom will be armed, at least with machetes. And incidentally, if it comes to a showdown, you can be quite certain that their women will back them.'

'And are all these people liable to be in the ranch house?'

'Well . . . of course not.'

'Give me a figure on that.'

'Ah . . . maybe a dozen. Maybe twenty. Servants. But of them, several are trained gunmen, who will not hesitate at murder. Neither will Cuesta, if all one hears of him is true.'

'Still, that does reduce the odds. I know how we can pull this off.'

'How?'

'I'm sorry, but I don't think it would be a good idea for me to divulge that, even to you.'

'But there is a plan.'

'Yes. However, I and my team will require firearms.'

'You mean sidearms.'

'That depends on what you have to offer.'

'How will you be dressed?'

'Pants. The weapons cannot be concealed in our clothes. But we each have a large shoulder bag, like this one.' She held it up.

Smart stroked his chin. 'Do you know how to put guns together?'

'It's part of my training.'

'Because it strikes me that, in pieces, you could fit an M16 in that bag, with a few magazines.'

Jessica could hardly believe her ears. 'You have an M16?'

'I can get one.'

'Army surplus, eh? Would that be an A1?'

She knew that the combination of plastic and steel used in the body of the first ArmaLite rifle had often caused problems.

Smart grinned. 'No, no. This is the A2. Standard US army issue.'

'Boy oh boy. Let's see it.'

'I said I can get it. Come back tomorrow night and you'll have it.'

'With ammo?'

'You'll have sufficient firepower to start a war.'

'Which is what I have in mind, if I have to.' She winked at Adrian. 'Despite the old man's strictures. But if it's an A2, I don't suppose . . .?'

Smart's grin widened. 'Are you thinking of a 203 attachment?'

'If I had a few grenades, I *could* take on the world. Cuesta's world, anyway.'

'You are one feisty young lady. Yes, I can get you an RPG attachment. And some ammo for that too.'

'Jesus,' Adrian commented. 'I thought you thought she was committing suicide.'

'I still do. But if she's determined to go out with a bang, I'm prepared to help her do that. The world will be a better place without people like Ramon Cuesta.'

'I have no intention of committing suicide,' Jessica said. 'But I also have my team. How many of these ArmaLites can you supply?'

'Perhaps two. But they won't both fit in that bag, even in bits.'

Jessica nodded. 'I'll bring some help. That still leaves us one short.'

'How about an SIG Sauer P226?'

Jessica gazed at him in admiration. 'You are a one-man armaments firm.'

'I have my contacts. Guns aren't exactly regarded with distaste in Bolivia. How many would you like?'

'How many have you got?'

'I could manage three.'

'Christmas Day! You're on.'

'I'm delighted you're pleased. Knives?'

'You reckon?'

'Guns are all very well. But there are times when silence is a good idea.'

Jessica nodded. 'Good thinking. How many?'

'You'll have one each. I am bound to say, though, Miss Jones, that these items are expensive.'

Jessica looked at Adrian.

'I'll foot any bill that's going,' he said.

'In that case,' Smart said, 'we have a deal.'

'In *that* case,' Jessica said, 'you can call me JJ.'

The Smarts tactfully left them alone after dinner. 'Can you stay the night?' Adrian asked.

She shook her head. 'I'm supposed to be part of a group, remember? And there are already too many people poking their noses into my affairs. I'll see you tomorrow night. Hopefully by then we'll have heard from London about Wesley. Oh, by the way, I'll have my team with me.'

'Oh.' He looked disappointed.

Jessica kissed him. 'We need them to carry the merchandise. And when you've seen my number two, you won't ever look at me again, my lord.'

He held her against him. 'You take it all so lightly. Don't you realize that you're risking your life? I'm almost inclined to call the whole thing off.'

'I have to treat it lightly, don't you see? Or I'd be in the loony bin. And you can't call it off; your sister's future is at stake.'

'Not her life? If there is shooting . . .'

'My profession is protection,' Jessica reminded him. 'I am perfectly willing to shoot people to protect my client, but protecting him, or her, comes first. As of now – as of a fortnight ago, in fact – your sister is my client. If she can be got out, I will get her out.'

100

'And if she can't be got out?'

'Can't is not a word I understand,' she told him. 'Now, are you going to drive me back to my hotel?'

'Is the group back from their evening out yet?' she asked Manuel, who was waiting in the lobby.

'Not yet, señora.' Manuel rolled his eyes.

Adrian had insisted on kissing her goodnight, and it had been a long, slow, deep kiss, while his hands had roamed over her dress. It had happened in the car, but had certainly been observable by anyone looking out from the lobby.

'Then I'll just go to bed,' she said. 'Thank you for your help, Manuel.'

'You are sure there is nothing I can do for you, señora?'

'Not tonight, Manuel.'

She went up to her room, sat at the desk, and wrote a note – *Come after midnight: three knocks* – on a sheet torn from her Filofax, then went along the deserted corridor and slipped the sheet beneath the girls' door. Then she went to bed; it was just after ten. She was asleep in seconds, and was later awoken by three soft taps. She got out of bed, put on a dressing gown, and opened the door. Both Andrea and Chloe were wearing nightdresses and although she assumed they had come home some time before, they were both still on a high.

She allowed them into the room and closed the door. 'Had a good time?'

'Great,' Andrea said.

'All those guys wanting to dance,' Chloe said. 'All those hands.' She giggled.

'And you loved every minute of it,' Jessica suggested hopefully.

'Yes, she did,' Andrea said. 'And so did I. How did you get on with his lordship?'

'Very well. Sit down and I'll put you in the picture.'

They sat or lounged on her bed while she recalled the events of the evening. Andrea gave a low whistle. 'An ArmaLite? Stone the shitting crows.'

'Hopefully two ArmaLites,' Jessica said.

'I'll stay with the Siggy,' Chloe said; she had a taste for small, light weapons, although the Sauer was hardly that when compared with the Walther she carried on duty at home.

'Again, hopefully we'll have one each,' Jessica said.

'So what's the plan?' Andrea asked. 'We go in like lambs and come out like lions, hopefully with her nibs between us?'

'In a manner of speaking. Concentrate, and I'll tell you how we're going to play this.'

When she was finished, Chloe scratched her head. 'Isn't that going to make us wanted criminals?'

'Only here in Bolivia. Our objective is to be out of the country, with Lady Miranda, within six hours of the snatch.'

Ramon Cuesta opened his wife's bedroom door; he only spent the night in here when he wanted sex. She was still asleep, but her eyes opened when he sat beside her. 'God,' she muttered. 'What time is it?'

'Just after six.'

'For God's sake . . .' But she licked her lips as she looked at him. As he had promised, she would never forget that day a fortnight ago when he had applied pepper to her nipples and between her legs and left her a seething, abject mass of pain, unable to resist him a moment longer.

'Tell me what you know about a woman named Jones. Jessica Jones.'

'Who?'

'You have never heard the name?'

'Should I have?'

'I thought you might have. I believe she may be some kind of private detective employed by your family.'

'Whatever makes you think that? A private detective?'

102

'I agree. It does seem bizarre. But then, you belong to a bizarre family, don't you? There are two reasons for my suspicions. One is that your brother is in La Paz, and has been there for the past week.'

Miranda sat up. 'Adrian? Here?'

'Well, a few hundred miles away. And I told you he was coming. He is staying with an English resident named Smart. A shady character. However, we may confidently assume that, as he is in the country and has not informed you of this, he has come here for you. He hasn't informed you of his presence, has he?'

She pulled the sheet to her neck. 'You know he hasn't. I have not had a letter from him since . . .' She bit her lip.

'Of course. When he used the code word "wizard". But that was to tell you he was coming. Now he is here. My second reason for supposing this Jones woman is connected with him is that my agents, who I instructed to inform me of any suspicious entries into the country, have radioed this morning. Jones is apparently travelling by herself with a tour, one of those whose itinerary includes a visit here. She is apparently posing as a widow . . .'

'Why should she be posing?'

'Well, she may actually be a widow. The point is that a message was left at her hotel to be handed to her on arrival in La Paz. This was done, following which last night, while the rest of the tour party went to a nightclub, Jones went off on her own. The address to which she went is the home of this man Smart, which as I said happens to be where Adrian is staying. This was obviously contained in the message she received. And the message was clearly sent by Adrian, who equally clearly knew she was coming and where she would be staying, which he could only have discovered by knowing which group she was touring with, which can only have been done before she, or he, left England, which means he probably arranged the whole thing. Why do you think he should do that, if she is not in his employ?'

Miranda tried to think of something, anything . . . 'She could be a girlfriend. He has dozens of girlfriends. Is she pretty?'

'My agent says she is very pretty. But I find it strange that Adrian should travel several thousand miles to have an assignation with a woman who is surely at the end of a telephone in England. No, no. She is clearly working for him, and he has arranged for her to be a member of the tourist group which is visiting us tomorrow. This has got to be so that she can see you, and discover what is going on.'

Miranda licked her lips. 'What are you going to do? If you harm Adrian . . .'

'What would you do, my dear? But I think it would be a mistake to harm him, unless I have to. He is after all, an English aristocrat. No, I think the person for us to deal with is this Jones. And after all, she is coming to visit us, is she not? It will be interesting to learn what she has to say. But first I think we need to find out a little more about her.' He grinned. 'If she is as pretty as my agent says, asking her questions, in suitably private circumstances, should be very enjoyable.'

The Trap

'Well, señoras and señores,' Garcia said, facing the group in the hotel lobby. 'I hope you have had an enjoyable day, and are not too tired. At least now you know all about the great city of La Paz de Ayacucho. Now, tonight is free for you to do what you wish. This is because tomorrow is the early start, eh? It is necessary for us to go to the airport at half past seven of the clock. This is so we can be at the Cuesta ranch by nine. It is a slow aircraft, eh? No jet. So I have arranged for you all to have a call at six thirty. It is the wakey-wakey, eh?'

There were several groans. But he continued to smile. Jessica caught Andrea's eye as the group split up, but was immediately rejoined by Wesley; he had stayed at her shoulder through the day, which had been spent visiting museums and seeing historical sites. 'I missed you last night,' he said. 'How did your dinner go?'

'It was most enjoyable. In fact—'

'Well, how about having dinner with me tonight? À deux?'

'Oh, Ted. I'd love to. But I'm going back to see my friend again.'

He frowned at her. 'You're sure he's just a friend?'

'Actually, it's a she.' Which was only half a lie, as she had to consider Nicolette as a friend now. 'I'll see you tomorrow.' She went to the elevator, leaving him to make what he liked of that.

Andrea and Chloe had already gone up, and were waiting

in the corridor. Jessica unlocked her door, and they followed her in.

'I am going to shower and change, and then I am going out, exactly as I did last night. You'll want to change as well. Look presentable; these people live in some style. Now, when you are dressed, go down to the bar and have a drink. Give me an hour, just in case. Then leave the hotel and walk away from it, as if out for a stroll, in a westerly direction. Move slowly, but make sure you are out of sight of the hotel, at least two blocks down. You'll be picked up.'

'More than once, I should think,' Chloe objected. 'Can't we just take a taxi as well?'

'No, because you can't reveal that you're going to the same address that I am.'

'Who's going to pick us up?' Andrea asked.

'I imagine it'll be Adrian.'

'Adrian being?'

'Lord Lichton, Booboo.'

'Whoopee!'

'Then I'll see you later. Oh, by the way, when we leave here tomorrow morning, we won't be coming back. I mean, back to the hotel. Which means our luggage is going to go AWOL, probably permanently. Therefore, if you have any favourite pieces of underwear, wear them, even if they may seem inappropriate for a day in the bush. Same goes for jewellery. Just remember that we can only carry our shoulder bags, and there has to be room for our weapons.'

'Bang goes those sexy thongs you bought in Lima,' Chloe said.

'No way,' Andrea said. 'I'm going to wear them.'

'Imagination boggles,' Jessica said. 'See you later. Oh, just one more thing. No one, but no one, must be told how we intend to pull this thing off. That includes his lordship, no matter how much he may turn you on.'

*　　*　　*

106

Needless to say, Manuel was waiting in the lobby; he seemed to have adopted her as his very own, or was hoping to do so. 'You wish the taxi, señora?'

'Thank you.'

'To go where?'

'The same as last night. Seventy-one, Street of the Conception.'

'I remember. I will fix it. But you no wish to come back?'

'My friend will bring me back, as he did last night.'

'I will fix it,' he repeated, and asked casually over his shoulder as he went to the door, 'You come back late, eh?'

'I should think very late,' she replied.

Bumptious little bastard, she thought as she got into the taxi. But now that they were actually on their way, she felt totally relaxed and fully focussed. She was utterly confident that her plan would work, at least as far as getting off the ranch with Miranda Cuesta went, simply because, however hackneyed, it would almost certainly take the opposition by surprise. The only mistake she could make would be to underestimate that opposition, and she had no intention of doing that.

But when they left the ranch, they would be in the hands of Adrian. She didn't like being in the hands of anyone when it came to life-or-death situations, but she didn't see how his plan could be improved upon, and anyway, it was too late to make any alternatives now. All she could do was make sure that he was also fully focussed.

Only Smart bothered her. But perhaps Adrian would be able to explain his place in the business.

As always, Adrian appeared delighted to see her; his hug and kiss were quite proprietorial. But that was something to be worried about after the job was completed.

She went with him in Smart's Mercedes to pick up the girls, and found them just in time, she supposed, as they were surrounded by a gaggle of young men with whom Andrea

107

was trying to cope in her limited Spanish while Chloe giggled girlishly. Jessica knew that with their training in unarmed combat they could take care of themselves if push came to shove, but she had some doubts as to whether they would *want* to, and was happy to have them in the car.

'Hi,' Adrian said. 'I'm Adrian.'

'I thought you were a lord,' Chloe said.

'To you, Adrian.'

Chloe gave one of her giggles. Andrea appeared to be struck dumb, and stayed so throughout the evening, even when, after dinner, Smart took them into his office and showed them his goodies – which, as he had promised, consisted of two ArmaLite rifles, one of which had a grenade-launching attachment, and three Sauer pistols. There were spare clips of ammunition for the pistols, spare boxes for the rifles, and six grenades.

'Wowee!' Chloe said. 'With this lot we *could* start a war.'

'Quite a weight, I'm afraid,' Smart said apologetically.

'We'll manage.'

'Let's see you strip the rifles down.'

Jessica gave one to Andrea, who was so nervous she took a while to get going, but that she knew what she was doing was obvious to both men.

'Now,' Smart said, 'obviously that is how you are going to take them out of here. But your lives may depend on how quickly you can put them back together.' He took a stopwatch from his desk. 'Go!'

This time Andrea had her fingers under control, but Jessica still beat her to it.

'Forty-three seconds,' Smart said admiringly. 'Pretty good. And . . . fifty-two. Good enough. I think we could have a drink.'

'You have some things for me, I hope,' Jessica said over the meal.

'Ah, yes.' Smart left the table to fetch the plan. 'I've never been there myself, so I can't guarantee its accuracy.'

Jessica scanned the rather rough drawing. 'It doesn't have a scale.'

'No, it doesn't. I'm sorry about that.'

'This garage that's marked looks somewhat large. Or is that artistic licence?'

'I believe it is large. Cuesta keeps several vehicles in there.'

'That's what I wanted to hear. Now, this river which runs round the southern edge of the property, is *it* large?'

'No really. About a hundred feet across. But—'

'And deep?'

'I believe so, several feet. But—'

'And this bridge over it, that leads to the road, right?'

'Yes. But—'

'Is it open? I mean, can one just drive across it, or are there any barriers?'

'I do not believe there are any. But I am trying to tell you, be careful of the river. It's full of black caiman.'

'What's a black caiman?' Chloe asked.

'A species of alligator. They come in several shapes and sizes, and have several names, but the black are the largest and most dangerous.'

'Are they what did for this fellow Sprightly?'

'So I believe.'

'Ugh! So if one tries to hold my hand I shoot first and ask questions afterwards?' She looked at Jessica.

'I think that would probably be a good idea. But our object is not to get close to these creatures in the first place. Okay, Joe, I'll take this and study it. Now, what about Wesley?'

'Ah, yes. Nothing important, I'm afraid, at least from your point of view. The only Edward Wesley your people could come up with is a character who was charged with harassment of a TV newsreader a few years back.'

'That sounds like my man. Age?'

'Early forties.'

'That's him.'

'Wasn't he sent down?' Chloe asked.

'Suspended sentence.'

'Don't tell me: it was a male magistrate. So now he's harassing women in South America.'

'Forget it,' Jessica said. 'Well, thanks a million for all your help, Joe. And yours, Nicolette.'

'Where on earth did you get those two?' Adrian asked, getting Jessica alone after dinner.

'What do you mean?' she asked suspiciously.

'Well, they're so . . . well, that girl Andrea should be in movies.'

'I told you she was out of my class. But kindly do not mention movies to her. We can't spare her.'

'Has she been with you long?'

'About six years. Four in the Special Branch.'

'She must be good at her job.'

'She is, very.'

'And is she . . . ah, married?'

'Not at the moment. Is that a pertinent inquiry?'

He flushed. 'Good lord, no. I mean . . . well, it's the thought of someone that good-looking firing an ArmaLite in anger. Imagination boggles.' He squeezed her hand. 'God, I am scared stiff. Aren't you?'

'I can't afford to be. I'll get the heebie-jeebies when it's all over. Can we talk timings?'

'Shoot.'

'I'm having to work on certain assumptions. One is that we will be given lunch in the house, and equally, that we will not be allowed into the house until lunch. Two is that your sister, as the hostess, will join us for the meal. I don't suppose she'll come on our tour of the plantation. That would be just too good to be true. So it would appear, in the light of our present knowledge, that we cannot make our play before lunch, but it needs to be made immediately after the meal. I can't give you any timing on that, but as these people keep Spanish hours it is likely to be quite late. On the other hand, as we are supposed to leave the ranch by four, it can't be after that.'

'You mean you're going to bring Mira out on the tourist plane?'

'No. That won't be possible unless all the gods in the pantheon turn out on our side. We're going to drive out.'

'Two hundred miles?'

'Give or take.'

'But, that'll take . . .'

She nodded. 'Bad roads. We should still do it in five hours, but allow six.'

He whistled. 'Ramon has planes up there. He'll come after you.'

'It's my intention to arrange things so that they may have second thoughts about that. Even if I can delay them for a couple of hours, that'll bring us close to dusk. They'll have a hard time locating us in the dark. What we shall need, when we come close, is guidance to the airport.'

He nodded. 'Let's see that map.'

They were sitting beside each other. Jessica spread the map on her lap.

'You'll see that this road, which for most of the way is just a track,' Adrian said, 'becomes a highway as it approaches La Paz. By then you'll be back in the Altiplano. Eventually it runs into the city itself. But here' – he made a mark with his ballpoint – 'it bifurcates; the left-hand branch, as you will look at it, leads to the airport. I'll be waiting at that turn-off.'

'In?'

'Joe's Merc. He'll be with me.'

'Right. We should be there about ten o'clock tomorrow night. But I hope to confirm that by my mobile, as soon as we're clear of the plantation. However, don't panic or change any arrangements if you *don't* hear from me. Things may be fraught. Can your man take off in the dark? Will he get clearance?'

'I'll see that he does. It's just a matter of greasing a few palms.'

'Does he have any idea what it's all about?'

'No. But he's being paid well enough to ask no questions. He's a pretty shady character, but he'll do anything for money.'

'Where did you find him?'

'Joe found him.'

'Hmmm. As Joe also found us a small modern armoury. How shady is *he*?'

'He was at Cambridge with the pater.'

'I know. But with respect, that would have to be something like thirty years ago. Time enough for people to change. What exactly is his line of business?'

'I have no idea. I thought it best not to ask.'

'But you trust him.'

'I'm trusting him with my life. All of our lives. Including that of my baby sister.'

Jessica studied him. There could be no doubt that he *did* trust the older man. 'Then it's all systems go.'

'JJ . . .' He held her hands. 'I don't know what to say, other than I adore you.'

'Keep it until we're airborne. You're sure there won't be trouble for you?'

'Nothing I can't handle.'

'Even if we have to shoot one or two people to get Mira out?'

He grinned. 'As you say, we'll worry about that when we're airborne. You know that when this breaks I am of course going to have to deny that I knew anything about it, or that I have ever known you.'

'Will you be able to do that?'

'Of course. No one even knows I'm in Bolivia. Joe has been handling all the arrangements. When I turn up at the airport, with company, we are just some of his people.'

'I hope you're right.'

'But as soon as the dust settles, we'll be getting together. You have my word.'

'Like I said, let's worry about promises when we're both in a position to keep them. Now, will you take me back to the hotel?'

'This early? I thought . . .'

'We all need to concentrate. You can drop me at the door, as you did last night. The hotel staff are expecting that. Then come back for the girls. But remember to drop them a couple of blocks away so that they'll appear to be returning from their stroll.'

'Won't it have been rather a long stroll?'

'They'll have stopped in a bar for a couple of drinks.'

She gave Andrea and Chloe their instructions – to return to the hotel after being dropped off by Adrian and go straight to bed – then said goodbye to Joe and Nicolette.

'Will we see you again?' Nicolette asked.

'I don't wish to sound ungrateful, but not if I can help it.'

'I meant, perhaps, in England, next time we're over.'

'I'd like that,' Jessica said, and meant it.

Joe kissed her on both cheeks. 'Here's wishing you all the luck in the world.'

'You've been tremendous.' She kissed him back. 'I'll see you tomorrow,' she told the girls. 'Be good.'

'Aren't they always?' Adrian asked as they drove through busy streets; it was only ten, and La Paz was just waking up.

'They can be.'

The car stopped in the hotel forecourt. 'Well . . .' he said.

'I'll see you tomorrow as well.' She allowed him to kiss her,

113

got out, hefted her now very heavy shoulder bag, and went into the lobby. The reception clerk had seen her coming, and had her key ready. She took the elevator, walked along the softly carpeted corridor to her room, and checked when she saw the line of light beneath her door.

Instinctively her hand dropped to her bag. But whatever was going to happen was liable to be public, and thus it would be highly risky to reveal herself to be armed. She mentally sized up the possible opposition. Garcia? Or Señora Barrientes? She hoped it was Garcia; she hadn't liked him from the start.

She inserted her key in the lock, and the light went out. But there was no way out of the room except through the door – unless the intruder tried jumping from the window, and her room was four floors up.

She pushed the door in, and smelt a faint tang of garlic. He, or she, was very close, probably intending to slam the door on her wrist if she put her hand inside to find the light switch. She called up a mental picture of the room. To attack her as she entered, the intruder would have to be standing on her right; the door opened to the left. She stepped out of her shoes, drew a deep breath, and pushed the door again, as hard as she could, entering behind it at speed and then slamming the door behind her. She heard a stifled exclamation, followed by a thud and a gasp of pain. Her assailant had been caught in his own trap, having missed her and having his own hand struck by the door.

Now he was pulling the door open again, but she had no intention of letting him get away. She had turned and already identified the shadow, now illuminated as he got into the hallway light. Jessica seized him by the collar of his jacket and pulled backwards with all of her highly tuned strength, at the same time kicking the door shut again. He crashed to the floor, and before he could recover Jessica had rolled him on his side, hitched her skirt to her waist, dragged his head between her thighs, and clamped them on his neck in a classical scissors hold, crossing her ankles to be able to exert maximum pressure. Then she seized his right arm and bent it back as far as she could.

Only then did she discover that it was Manuel. 'Aaagh!' he squealed. 'You are breaking my arm.'

'I haven't done it yet,' she pointed out, and closed her thighs.

'Aaagh!' he shrieked again. 'You are killing me!'

'I haven't done that yet, either,' she said. 'And aren't you where you always wanted to be?'

He gasped, his face suffused with colour, and she slightly relaxed the pressure, still retaining her grasp on his arm. 'Tell me what you were doing here?'

He did some more gasping. 'I wanted a memento, of the beautiful lady.'

'I don't suppose you have ever been strangled by a pair of beautiful thighs,' she remarked. 'They tell me it's a lovely way to go.'

'Señora . . .'

'But I think I'll just break your arm first.'

'Señora, please! I beg you.'

'Then tell me the truth. Who employs you?'

He licked his lips. 'Señor Cuesta pays me.'

'Shit,' she muttered. But who else could it have been? 'Why did Señor Cuesta wish you to search my room?'

'I do not know, señora. He just said to find out about you. Everything about you. I did not expect you back so early,' he added ingenuously.

'That was bad luck, wasn't it?' But for her more than him. So, Cuesta had some inside information . . . 'Who told the señor that I was here?'

'I do not know. I think maybe Señor Garcia.'

Which was what she had anticipated. But she had to cover every eventuality. 'Not Señora Barrientes?'

'No, no.' His voice was faintly contemptuous. 'She is Peruvian.'

'True. So, Garcia informed Señor Cuesta that a widow lady named Jones is a member of this tour group. That hardly seems a reason for him to wish to have my room searched.'

'I do not know, señora. I do not know. Señora, my arm . . .'

'If we stay like this long enough, it'll go to sleep. Then it'll stop hurting.' But what the hell was she to do? Once he left here, if he wasn't under arrest, he'd be in touch with Garcia, who would be in touch with Cuesta. And how the hell had Cuesta found out about her? He couldn't have picked her out as possibly hostile simply because she was travelling alone – Ted Wesley was also travelling alone. Possibly his information could be a spin-off from Mrs Norton's ham-handed handling of their bookings. Or perhaps it had been carelessness in the Lichton family. But whose carelessness? Because if it was Adrian's, then she, and the girls, were up a very long creek without a paddle.

The more important question now, however, was *what* had he found out about her? And did he know that Andrea and Chloe were her partners?

She should call the whole thing off, inform Señora Barrientes that she had received bad news from home and was having to return immediately, and depart with the girls. The tour people could make of it what they wished. But she knew she wasn't going to do that. She had been given a job to do, and she would do it. Think positively, she told herself. Be real. Point one: Cuesta had been informed that she was a suspicious character simply because she was being given special treatment by the tour guides, but he *couldn't* know anything more than that – or there would have been no necessity to search her room to find out just what or who she was. Point two: that he had overreacted so strongly had to mean he was at least nervous, if not scared stiff. Point three: he obviously didn't have any suspicions about Andrea and Chloe, or their rooms would have been searched as well. That needed checking out, but she felt, and hoped, that they remained her aces in the hole. Point four:

if, in the absence of any information to the contrary, she still turned up at his ranch as bright as a button and as a member of a tour group, any move he made would have to be very subtle or he would have to wait for her to move first. That suited her. The fact that she now knew he might be *expecting* her to move did not greatly increase the risks – he could not possibly suppose that, on her own, she was intending to extract Miranda. The most he would suppose was that she was an agent of the family sent to discover the truth of the girl's situation.

That left her only the immediate problem of handling this lout. And there was only one thing she could do. To call the desk would involve the police and perhaps even make her miss the trip to the ranch, while she had no idea how many of the police might be in Cuesta's pay. She could only rely on the fact that nothing Manuel did or said now could make matters any worse, and that her treatment of him might both confuse Cuesta and make him wonder if he was after the right woman. 'So, tell me what you have found out about me.'

'Nothing. Nothing. I swear it. I have found nothing. Oh, señora, the pain . . .'

'Then what would you tell Señor Cuesta, if you could?' She applied some pressure on both his neck and his arm.

'Aaagh! What can I tell him? Nothing. Only . . .'

'Yes?'

'That you know how to hurt a man, so badly. Señora, if you let me go, I will be your slave for life.'

'That makes me very happy,' she said. 'So I am going to be very generous. Although I should think that having held you in such a position for so long, I have been generous enough. Please remember that what I have done to you, and am doing to you, is nothing to what I can, and will, do to you if you encourage me.'

She released his arm, and then uncrossed her ankles and pushed herself backwards, allowing him to slide out from between her legs. He rolled on to his face, hands clasped to his neck, panting.

Jessica got up and switched on the light, then opened the door to retrieve her shoes. The corridor remained empty; she didn't know if the girls had got back yet, but she suspected not.

Manuel had got to his knees, still holding his neck. 'Off you go,' she said. 'Sleep well.'

He reached his feet, and looked at her, his eyes rolling. She blew him a kiss, and he stepped past her and into the corridor.

Jessica locked the door and then placed a chair against it so that anyone equipped with a duplicate key – as Manuel had been, obviously – would not be able to get in without disturbing her. Then she went to bed and slept soundly, to be awakened by the call at six thirty. She had briefly considered calling Adrian and alerting the girls, but decided against it. There was nothing she wished them to do about it, and it would only alarm them. Until she started something, Andrea and Chloe were safe. Once something started, whether it was by her or Cuesta, she expected their back-up, but it would be better if they came in as previously decided than to have them expecting catastrophe at every corner, so to speak.

She showered and dressed in the thick shirt and pants, socks and ankle-length boots she had purchased in London, added the broad-brimmed hat, and thought she looked rather good as she surveyed herself in the mirror, her expression as calm as always. She repacked her shoulder bag, squeezing a spare pair of knickers, a bra, a clean shirt and a pair of socks in amongst her usual gear as well as the Sauer and the pieces of the ArmaLite, the spare magazines and the six grenades; the clothes made very little difference to the already heavy load but they certainly crammed the bag to bulging capacity. She then made sure both guns were readily accessible, and went downstairs to join the rest of the party for breakfast.

'Well, hey, which are you, Butch Cassidy or the Sundance Kid?' Wesley inquired, sitting beside her. 'And what have you got in that bag? The kitchen sink?'

'I never travel without one. You never can tell when you'll need to wash your hands.'

He snorted, and looked across the table. 'You know, those two could have been shopping at the same store.'

Jessica also looked across the table at Andrea and Chloe, and gave a mental gulp. That had been careless of her. Even their shoulder bags were too similar for comfort, although he hadn't apparently noticed that. 'These things happen,' she said. 'At least we're not wearing the same evening gown at a posh bash.'

But she was more concerned to note that both girls seemed in a highly nervous state, Andrea spilling her coffee and Chloe dropping butter on the tablecloth. Had their room been searched after all? But surely if it had they would have let her know.

She watched Garcia come in and sit down next to Señora Barrientes. They chatted, but as far as she could tell from their expressions it was a light-hearted exchange, and it was several minutes before Garcia looked at her. Then she smiled at him and waggled her eyebrows. Again there was no response. She wondered if Manuel had reported to him, or just made himself scarce; he was certainly nowhere to be seen now.

A few minutes later the guide stood up. 'It is time to go, eh? How do you say? To the woods!'

Ramon Cuesta spoke into his mobile phone. 'You gave him orders to do that?'

'I thought it might be good to find out something about her.'

'And she beat him up? How big is this woman?'

119

'Oh, she is not big at all. She is very small. Maybe one metre sixty.'

'Manuel is one eighty.'

'Yes.'

'And he is a man. And she beat him up. And used the scissors on him?'

'He said she was very quick. Very efficient. He says he thinks she must be a black belt or something.'

'Yes,' Ramon said drily. 'Describe her to me.'

'As I say, she is small, but clearly very strong. She is also very handsome. She has yellow hair.'

'I see. And what did Manuel find out for his pains?'

'Nothing. He says there was nothing.'

'Surely she had a passport?'

'He could not find it. He thinks she must have taken it with her when she went out. He says she carries a big bag. But you know what is strange, señor? After having caught him in the act, and apprehended him, and beaten him up, she did nothing. She did not even report the incident to the desk. She just told him to get out. Do you not think that is very strange?'

'Perhaps,' Ramon said. 'But perhaps what she did, or did not do, may have told us all we wish to know. What about her companions?'

'Señor?'

'Unlike you, Garcia, who sends someone to go blundering around people's bedrooms in the dark, I simply asked my agent in London to track down this Jones. She is a sergeant in the Special Branch of the Metropolitan Police.'

'Oh, señor!'

'There is no need to be alarmed. She is a long way from home, and flashing her badge will not accomplish anything here. But my man also informs me that she is travelling with one, perhaps two companions. Have you identified these?'

'I was not told of this, señor.'

'I only found out myself yesterday. Is there no one else in the group who has behaved suspiciously?'

'Ah . . . there is a man. An Englishman, named Wesley. He and Jones apparently pretended to be strangers at the start of the tour, but they spend much time together, whenever possible, alone.'

'An Englishman named Wesley. Thank you, Garcia. That may be very useful. Now, have you seen Alonso?'

'I saw him yesterday.'

'And?'

'He knows nothing, other than that he has been hired by the English aristocrat to fly him to an unknown destination sometime tomorrow.'

'You mean today?'

'Ah . . . yes, that is it.'

'And he does not know the time he is to leave?'

'No, señor. He is on stand-by for the whole day.'

'I see. Thank you, Garcia.'

'Do you wish me to do anything more? I could leave this woman behind, by accident. And the man, Wesley.'

'No, no. It is better to deal with the situation now. And it is best done here on the ranch. You need do nothing more, Garcia. Just your job.'

Ramon replaced the phone and sat for a few minutes, thinking. It was very early in the morning, and the ranch was just stirring. And he was about to be visited by a police task force, it appeared. His idea that the woman was being employed privately by the Lichton family to make contact with Miranda had to be wrong. So, the information that he had received from London had to be correct, which indicated a far more serious situation than he had suspected. He personally had committed no crime in England. Thus if the Metropolitan Police were after him it could only be to do with drugs, and such an operation might well also involve the DEA. But she was also obviously connected with Adrian Lichton and therefore with this chartered plane that Lichton had standing by. That could only mean she had some scheme for spiriting Miranda off the plantation. He simply could not determine how she could hope to do this, but equally he could not take the risk that she might attempt it. Thus she needed to be dealt with. And her partner? He couldn't afford to go overboard.

He picked up a house phone. 'I wish Duarte. Send him to me.'

The overseer appeared a few minutes later; not only was he fully dressed but clearly had already been out – he carried his riding crop. 'Trouble?'

'A nuisance. Which must be dealt with. In the party coming in this morning there is a woman named Jones. She is small, blonde, and according to Garcia she is very good-looking. I have known about her for some time, but I was assuming she was only an investigator. Now I have discovered that she is actually an English police sergeant, and that she is accompanied by a man, presumably also a policeman. I do not know what these people intend, but I believe they must be considered dangerous.'

'Will they be armed?'

'There is no indication of it, but we should assume so.'

'What do you wish done with them?'

'I do not feel we should take any risks. We do not know what plans she may have laid, and what other back-up she may have arranged. I know she has support in La Paz.'

'Two hundred miles away?'

'We cannot risk that there may be some closer than that. You will arrange an accident during the tour of the ranch.'

'For both of them? That will be very difficult. Would it not be better to arrange for them to miss the return plane?' Duarte licked his lips. 'Then we could question her at our leisure. If she is handsome . . .'

'I know. You would enjoy that.' Ramon grinned. 'I would too. But we cannot take the risk. I think the accident need only apply to the woman, who is clearly the leader. If it happens in front of the rest of the group, and clearly *is* an accident, her assistant will have to accept that and will have to return, at least to La Paz, but probably to England, for further instructions. And I would estimate that the English police would be very reluctant to risk any more of their people. You will take today's group to the North Pond, as usual?'

'Oh, yes. The trip would not be complete without a glimpse of the caiman.'

'Arrange for her to fall in.'

Duarte scratched his chin. 'In front of eleven other people, who will remember what happened and probably sell their story to a newspaper? Several newspapers?'

'Arrange it. Have someone make a terrible mistake. We shall see to his punishment, if it is necessary. But I am sure, if you choose the right man, it will not be necessary. As for the publicity, the more the better. We will have ten innocent bystanders swearing to what happened.'

Duarte considered. 'I suppose we could—'

Ramon held up a forefinger. 'I do not wish to know how it is to happen. I must be as shocked and horrified as anyone when I learn the news. I know you will do a good job, because you will enjoy it. If you cannot torture this handsome woman, at least you can watch her being eaten alive.'

'Hard to believe there are still places like this left in the world, eh?' Wesley shouted into Jessica's ear as the twin-engined aircraft droned over the Oriente at a height of two thousand feet, allowing its passengers to study the terrain beneath them; below them were unending areas of either forest or swamp, and a total lack of any sign of human cultivation except in small patches around the occasional village that studded a single white ribbon of road winding through the wilderness.

The road was at least reassuring, from Jessica's point of

view, and made up for the discomfort of the journey. The scenery might be dramatic – if somewhat monotonous – but the plane did indeed fly rather slowly, there was no air-conditioning, the noise was frightful, and she had Wesley virtually in her lap as he leaned across her to look out of the window. 'Terrifying,' she suggested. 'Suppose we were to come down in that?'

'Oh, they'd have search parties out for us in no time at all. I gather from Señor Garcia that this fellow Cuesta is a bit of a bigwig.'

'And he should know,' Jessica said without thinking.

'Eh?'

Hastily she corrected her error. 'I mean, if he regularly brings tour parties up here, he must know all about this fellow. What did you say his name was?'

'Cuesta.'

'Ah, I must remember.'

'Ladies and gentlemen,' said the loudspeaker. 'If you care to look ahead, you will see the ranch. We will be landing in a few minutes, so will you kindly fasten your seatbelts.'

'Silly oaf,' Wesley growled. 'How does he expect us to see in front of the aircraft?'

A moment later they were circling over the ranch and the house and the river – to a chorus of 'oohs' from the group – and then settling on the airstrip. As soon as they were on the ground, Garcia left his seat and came down the aisle, leaning across to open several of the windows. This was very necessary, because almost immediately the plane seemed enveloped in a considerable heat, while the difference between the atmosphere down here and that of the Altiplano took their breaths away.

'You will quickly adjust,' Garcia assured them. 'It is easier to do this coming down than going up, eh?'

The aircraft rolled to a stop before a small terminal building, and the door was opened. The tourists went down the steps, eyes watering although all wore sunglasses. 'Does it get any hotter than this?' someone asked.

'Oh, yes. Now, it is just past nine of the morning. By noon, it is very hot. And you see . . .' Garcia pointed to the east, and they saw the great clouds banking. 'Soon after noon it rains, every day at this time of the year. Very heavy. But by then we will have completed our tour, and you will be at the house. This is Señor Duarte Tejada.'

'Señoras, señores.' Duarte came to them and shook each hand. '*Bienvenida a Cuesta.*'

Jessica was studying her surroundings, relating them to the plan she had been given and which was in her bag. To her relief it appeared to have been fairly accurate. The house was perhaps half a mile in the distance, beyond the stables and a large swimming pool. It was impossible to determine anything of what the inside of the building might be like, but she noted with satisfaction that the garage was where it had been indicated – beside the stables, only a hundred yards from the house – and she could see that it contained several vehicles. Then she realized that the man Tejada was standing in front of her, smiling at her. '*Bienvenida, señora.*'

'Ah . . . *gracias, señor.*'

He continued staring at her for several seconds while still holding her hand, then released her and moved along the group.

'You've made another conquest,' Andrea muttered at her shoulder.

Jessica doubted that. The man had undoubtedly liked what he was looking at, but there had been no warmth in his eyes.

'Now then, ladies and gentlemen,' Garcia was saying. 'The tour will now begin. First, there is the comfort stop, eh? That is in the building. Then, as soon as you are finished, we go. You see there are four jeeps waiting, eh? You go three in each jeep, with the driver and a guide. Five minutes, please.'

'I thought he said as soon as we were ready,' one of the women remarked as they trooped off to the toilets.

Andrea stayed close to Jessica. 'How do we handle this?' she asked.

'By ear. Nothing can happen till after we get to the house. Just be cool. And tell me what's troubling you. Quickly.'

'Well . . .' Andrea looked at Chloe.

'Was your room searched last night?'

'Eh?'

Obviously it hadn't. 'So give.'

Chloe snorted. 'She got kissed.'

It was Jessica's turn to say, 'Eh?'

'His lordship gave her a whammy when he said goodnight.'

Jessica looked at Andrea, who blushed.

'Now she's like a bitch on heat,' Chloe complained.

'So snap out of it,' Jessica said. 'You can't have another go at him until this job is completed, and you won't ever have another go at him if it isn't. I want one hundred per cent concentration, as of now.'

Andrea swallowed. 'You got it.'

Jessica only hoped she did have it.

When they came outside, Wesley was waiting for her, as she had expected. 'I've bagged a jeep,' he said.

She allowed herself to be escorted to one of the vehicles and sat in the back; thankfully they all had their awnings in place. The others were arguing over who was going in which jeep, while Andrea and Chloe quietly took two seats for themselves. Jessica used the opportunity to take in as much more of her surroundings as possible, and finalize as many plans as possible. So far it was looking promising. There was no sign of Cuesta. If he was really interested in her, she would have expected him to be about.

She was not so happy when Tejada took his seat beside their driver, having persuaded the four married couples to

126

split up; one of the Danish women, whose name was Helga, had reluctantly accepted being separated from her husband and friends, and sat beside Wesley and Jessica.

'Didn't you say you spoke Spanish?' Jessica asked Wesley.

'Oh, yes. Why?'

'There are so many things I want to know. I mean, maintaining a ranch this far from civilization must be an enormous job. You saw all those trucks and cars in the garage. Is there a petrol station around?'

'I'll ask him.' Wesley did so, and Tejada turned round to smile at them and explain. 'No filling station,' Wesley said. 'They bring their petrol up in barrels, and store them in the garage. Wouldn't get past British regulations, but I imagine these chaps make their own laws.'

'Ah,' Jessica said. That could be a problem, but only a slight one.

They left the road, and bumped, uncomfortably, over the nearest pasture, where there was a considerable herd of cattle that lowed and moved restlessly towards each other as the vehicles surrounded them. Garcia got down from his jeep – he was driving with Andrea and Chloe and one of the English men – and used his loudspeaker to tell them all about the breed and the various markets. His voice seemed to upset the cows even more.

He had just finished his lecture when there was a great deal of hallooing and several horsemen arrived, galloping up to the jeeps and bringing their mounts to a halt with admirable precision. Now it was time for those of the tourists who had got out of the jeeps to move nervously back towards their transport. Señora Barrientes looked positively alarmed, and Garcia lowered his megaphone and came towards Tejada, asking a question.

'What's the problem?' Jessica asked Wesley.

'It seems that these cowboys weren't around on the last visit.'

'Then why are they here now?'

'Tejada says it's the boss's idea, to make our tour more colourful, more exciting.'

'It's a thought,' Jessica conceded, noting that each of the cowboys carried a machete stuck through his belt.

Garcia was back to his megaphone. 'These men, these *vaqueros*, are the men who herd the cattle, eh? They are the best horsemen in the world. They will accompany us on our tour to show you their skill.'

Someone applauded, and the rest did so too, hesitantly.

'Bullsh— . . . I beg your pardon, ladies,' Wesley said.

'Be kind to our hosts, Ted,' Jessica recommended.

They drove off, and went through seemingly endless rows of drooping plants. When they stopped, Garcia addressed them again. 'Here you have the coca plant,' he said. 'It is for the making of chocolate, eh? Very good.'

'He actually means cocaine,' Wesley explained as they resumed their journey.

'Oh, really, Mr Wesley,' Helga protested.

Wesley grinned. 'You know how when you visit the Carlsberg Brewery in Copenhagen they let you drink all the beer you can? Maybe when our tour is finished Señor Cuesta will let you sniff all the coke you can, too.'

The woman shuddered.

Now they left the cultivation behind and, following a rough path, bumped across an open pasture. The six *vaqueros* galloped round and round them, hallooing and cheering, revealing their skill as promised by leaving the stirrups to stand in their saddles while they waved their machetes in the air, regularly coming close enough to each other to clash the blades together in mock combat.

'I wish they wouldn't do that,' Helga complained. 'I am sure they'll cut each other, or one of them is going to fall off and hurt himself.'

'I wonder how they'll get on in the bush,' Wesley remarked.

In front of them, at no very great distance, they could see trees, very close together, reaching high towards the sky.

'That is dramatic,' Helga said.

But the little caravan turned off well before the trees, to reach a sudden shallow cliff, at the foot of which there was a large pond of water. Now for the first time they realized that the river had curved round to keep them company, and that this pool was a backwater of the larger flow. The jeeps pulled to a halt, while the horses continued to mill around.

Garcia stepped down. 'Now we give you a glimpse of what life is like in the forest,' he announced. 'Come and look. But be careful. Do not fall over the edge.'

The tourists advanced, cautiously, and stood around him, Señora Barrientes remaining at the rear.

'You see?' Garcia pointed, and they looked down at half a dozen large reptiles sunning themselves on the bank surrounding the pool.

'Crocodiles!' someone gasped.

'No, no, señora. Those are caiman, that is, a species of alligator. You see that their hide is nearly black, unlike the usual alligator, and also that their jaws are very long. They are called black caiman.'

'Gosh,' said someone else. 'Are they dangerous?'

'Oh, very dangerous, señor. They are man-eaters.'

'Then why are we standing here?' Wesley inquired. 'Won't they attack us?'

The caiman were actually paying no attention to them at all.

'They would, if they could get at us,' Garcia acknowledged. 'But they cannot climb the slope. If any of you were to go down there, well . . .'

'That's horrible,' Helga said. 'The very thought of it. Let's leave.' She turned to go back to the jeeps, and uttered a scream.

Everyone looked round, while the halloos of the horsemen turned to shouts of alarm. One of the horses appeared to be having a fit, neighing and rearing, while its rider clung on for dear life, obviously unable to control it. Then it suddenly charged at the group on the edge of the escarpment.

'Quick!' Garcia shouted. 'Get out of the way.'

The tourists scattered left and right. Jessica ran to her right, for the moment unable to accept what was happening. But the horse now turned to its left, and came straight at her. She turned back; again it followed, and was now rearing above her. She stepped backwards, tripped, and went rolling down the slope towards the pool.

Destruction

Desperately Jessica tried to stop herself by clutching at the embankment, but she had been thrown virtually upside down and her fingers slipped on the soft earth, still damp from the previous night's rain, so that she landed at the bottom of the slope before she knew it, flat on her back and utterly winded.

Then she heard movement, and sat up, reaching for her bag – which had remained on her shoulder – but knowing that she wasn't going to make it as she watched the huge jaws opening, and saw two more of the creatures behind the first. They were each at least ten feet long. She tried to remember bits of alligator-handling advice she had gleaned from various television documentaries, which had seemed to suggest that one's best bet was to get on the back of the beast – without vouchsafing any information as to the procedure to follow when one is sitting down and the alligator's jaws are between one and the required back, while a couple of its cronies are waiting to drag one off even supposing one achieved one's objective.

From above her there was a chorus of screams and shrieks and yells, but then, when the creature seemed to be breathing on her face – at a distance of some three feet, so long were the jaws – three shots rang out. The bullets went straight down the caiman's throat. Blood gushed, and the mighty jaws snapped shut, just missing Jessica's foot. Then it lay inert, except for its tail, which still thrashed once or twice as it died.

The two other caiman appeared to be confused by what had happened, and for a moment their advance stopped. Jessica scrambled to her feet, opening her bag as she did so.

'Are you all right?' Andrea shouted.

'Yes.' Her hands were trembling, but she kept telling herself, *forty-three seconds*. She was also powered by anger: those bastards had tried to kill her. 'Hold the fort,' she called. 'Don't let anyone leave or use a phone.'

'We got it,' Chloe said. 'Just nobody move,' she shouted. 'And don't touch that mobile, Garcia. You guys, get down. All of you! Drop those machetes!'

There was a brief drumming of hooves, then the sound of another shot, followed by a scream.

Jessica screwed the barrel tight, then slapped the magazine in place. Just in time, for the caiman were advancing again, moving much more quickly than she would have supposed possible. She levelled the rifle, aiming at the eyes, and loosed four shots. The first animal made an odd sort of roaring sound, and rolled over, tail thrashing. Again this halted its companion, but there was no time to waste; three more of the reptiles were emerging from the pond. She slung the rifle beside her bag and clawed her way up the slope.

At the top, Andrea and Chloe, both with drawn and levelled pistols, faced the group of tourists, who had been joined by Garcia and Señora Barrientes. Tejada stood to one side, looking thunderstruck. Behind him five of the cowboys were grouped with their horses. The sixth horse was galloping round and round, blood streaming down its flanks. 'You shot the horse?' Jessica was aghast.

'No, no,' Chloe said. 'I shot the rider. That blood is from his spurs. He's the one who charged you. The bastard wouldn't stop.'

'Then where is he?'

'Somewhere over there.'

'Shit!'

'He tried to kill you,' Andrea pointed out. 'Pretending he had lost control of his horse was rubbish. Once they do that . . .'

'We are entitled to kill them,' Jessica said. She was in fact feeling a killing fury herself. Cuesta's people had tried to kill her, in the most unpleasant manner possible. Her plan, as outlined to the girls, had always been to kidnap him as well as his wife, to give them safe conduct to the airport, and indeed to get him out of the country to stand trial, even if she had not been ordered to do so. Now she intended to do a lot more than that. 'Assemble your gun.'

She studied the people, who were starting to recover somewhat. Everyone was talking at once, save for Helga, who seemed to have fainted; she was being supported by her husband.

'What the shit?' Wesley demanded.

'Señoras! Señoras!' Señora Barrientes wailed.

'Are you mad?' Garcia shouted.

Tejada was gabbling in Spanish, and the remaining tourists were just gabbling.

'Shut up!' Jessica shouted, and when no one paid her any attention, she fired a shot into the ground at their feet. That got a response; they seemed to press closer together.

'Jessica!' Wesley ventured.

'You too,' Jessica said. 'Just listen. I and my associates came here to do a job of work.'

'Those two?' Wesley was aghast.

'My closest friends,' Jessica told him, and heard the reassuring clicks of Andrea completing the assembly of her ArmaLite. 'We had hoped to complete our mission peaceably, but as you just saw, these people tried to feed me to the alligators.'

'It was an accident,' Garcia protested.

'Just remember that you are as guilty as any of them,' Jessica pointed out. 'Now, we are going to get on and complete our job. I'm sorry, but you are going to have to walk back to the ranch house. It can't be more than a few miles. These people will guide you. With any luck you'll make it before the rain. But first, all of you throw your mobiles on to the ground.'

'You will go to gaol,' Garcia said.

'Just do it.'

He unhooked his phone from his belt, and let it drop.

'Kick it over here.'

He obeyed.

'Now you, Tejada.'

The overseer looked at Garcia, who spoke in rapid Spanish. Tejada dropped his phone and kicked it away.

'You too, señora,' Jessica said. 'I am sorry.'

Señora Barrientes discarded her phone.

Jessica surveyed the tourists. 'Come along, now. I know some of you have them.'

They all looked at each other uncertainly.

'Now!' Jessica allowed steel to enter her tone. 'You too, Ted.'

'You realize you are in serious trouble?'

'The story of my life,' she agreed. 'Just do it.'

He threw his mobile at her feet, and the other male members of the group followed his example.

'And you, ladies.'

The women obeyed, and Jessica proceeded to stamp on each of the phones until they were reduced to scattered pieces of plastic and metal. 'Now you, come out here.' She beckoned the cowboys.

They came forward hesitantly, obviously fearing they were about to be executed. But none of them had a phone.

'Right. Keep them covered,' she told the girls, and walked past the group to the jeeps, completing the assembly of her weapon as she did so by screwing the grenade-launching attachment into place. Some more babbling broke out, although in a lower key, but she intended to save her heavy armament for more important duties.

'Take it easy, and no one else will get hurt,' Andrea told them.

Jessica selected one of the jeeps – all the keys were still in the ignitions – got behind the wheel, and drove it some fifty feet away from the other vehicles. There she stopped, got out, and walked back towards the others. 'Stand clear!'

They gaped at her.

'Go, go, go!' Chloe shouted.

'You are going to be locked up,' Wesley said again.

'But you won't be there to see it, if you don't move,' Chloe told him.

He backed away with the others, and Jessica levelled the rifle and fired a shot into the petrol tank of the first of the three jeeps she had left behind. It went up with a whoosh and she fired twice more, into the next jeep. This also exploded, igniting the remaining vehicle into a huge bonfire.

'Now turn those horses loose,' Jessica shouted.

The animals were released, and she fired three shots just above their heads. Neighing and prancing, they galloped off.

The cowboys stared after them in dismay, then one of them ran at Jessica, waving a machete he had grabbed from the pile on the ground. She shot him in the leg, bringing him down with a screech of pain; he then rolled to and fro, still screaming.

'You!' Jessica pointed at Garcia. 'Tell Tejada that as soon as we have left he can patch that fellow up, and go find the other. I'm sorry about this,' she told the tourists. 'I'm sure you'll be well looked after. Let's go.'

Still keeping their guns levelled at the group, Andrea and Chloe backed up to the remaining jeep. Jessica got behind the wheel, Chloe beside her; Andrea sat in the back, continuing to cover the waiting people. Jessica gunned the motor, and the jeep bounced over the meadow.

'I don't think we made any friends back there,' Chloe remarked.

'It's all rather fallen into our lap,' Jessica said with more confidence than she actually felt. 'We already have that head start we wanted.'

There was no way they could afford any delays now. This meant that they might arrive at the rendezvous before Adrian, but that problem could be sorted out after they had left the ranch.

'We can use one of the planes,' Andrea suggested.

'Can you fly?'

'Ah . . . no. But surely we can bully Cuesta . . .'

'Our lives would be in his hands, and we'd have to let him use his radio to obtain clearance for us to land at La Paz, where we might just find half the Bolivian police force waiting for us. We'll stick to our plan.'

'But they'll follow us in the planes,' Chloe said. 'And that helicopter.'

'They won't, you know,' Jessica promised. Her adrenaline was flowing; she was on a high of outrage. Various people had, in the past, tried to shoot her, or knife her, or strangle her, but this was the first time anyone had tried, in the coldest of blood, to feed her to an alligator. Cuesta, she was determined, was going to get his chips.

They left the meadow and were now at the pasture. There were several more cowboys here, gathered together on horse-back, staring and pointing, firstly at the distant smoke and then at the jeep hurtling towards them

'Do we . . .?' Chloe asked.

'No,' Jessica said firmly. 'Any shooting must be strictly in self-defence.'

She knew she must look a sight – her hat had floated off

her head and was held only by the strap round her neck, and her clothes were covered in mud and slime – but she gave the bemused *vaqueros* a cheerful wave as she shot past them.

'If they go to find out what happened, that's going to shorten the odds,' Andrea said. 'They'll have horses again.'

'We've still time,' Jessica told her.

They left the pasture behind and could now see the buildings. Jessica drew to a halt outside the garage. 'This first.'

They leapt down and ran at the entrance. There were two men inside the building, engaged in servicing one of the cars. They both turned in consternation as the three women pointed guns at them.

'Andie, ask them where they keep their petrol,' Jessica said. 'Chloe, find somewhere secure.'

Chloe hurried off.

'*Buenos días, señores,*' Andrea said. '*Dónde está la gasolina?*'

The men goggled at her, and she levelled her rifle. '*Pronto, pronto!*'

'*Ahí está!*' One pointed at an inner doorway.

'*Gracias.*'

'And the ignition keys?' Jessica asked.

'*Llaves por los coches?*' Andrea asked.

'*En los coches,*' the man said.

Jessica checked, and nodded. As with the jeeps, all the vehicles had their keys in the ignitions. It was simply a matter of choosing one.

Chloe was back. 'The boys' room looks pretty secure. It's not very big, but . . .'

'It'll do. Put them in.'

The two men protested vehemently, but Andrea and Chloe drove them into the small toilet and closed and locked the door. Jessica then got into a Mercedes and backed it up against the door.

'They'll still get out,' Andrea said.

137

'Not for a little while. I intend to be back by then. Now, the petrol.'

As she had hoped and expected, there was both a flexible fuel line and a pump. Of all the several vehicles available she chose a Dodge truck as being the most heavy-duty. 'We may need some protection,' she said as she pumped fuel into the tank.

The girls hunted around and found various items such as spare tyres as well as some toolboxes. These they emptied of their contents and loaded into the back of the truck, binding them together with lengths of rope, then they all got into the cab. From the adjoining stables the horses neighed and stamped.

'How're we doing?' Chloe asked.

'We're doing just fine,' Jessica told her.

They drew to a halt in front of the house. There were several gardeners to be seen, and these stopped work to stare at the unexpected arrivals, and even more so when they saw the guns. Behind them the helicopter waited on its pad; it occurred to Jessica that the department had been very remiss in not teaching her how to fly.

They disembarked and the wolfhounds bounded towards them. Jessica unslung her rifle and fired a single shot into the ground in front of the dogs. They backed off, snarling but not risking a further approach.

'Señoras?' asked one of the gardeners, an elderly man who walked with a limp.

'Just visiting,' Jessica said. 'Andie, hold the fort.'

Andrea nodded, and levelled her rifle. The men hastily retreated, muttering to each other. The front doors were open, and Jessica and Chloe ran inside. 'Holy shitting cows!' Chloe remarked, looking right and left.

Jessica did the same, but less in awe than to identify her surroundings – and the opposition. To her right, although it was only just after twelve, several servants were already laying places for lunch; the women amongst them began to scream as they saw the guns, save for one of them – a tall, handsome mestiza – who hurried towards them.

'Out!' Jessica said. 'Take your people. Out.'

Felicity checked, and looked away from her across the house. Jessica followed the direction of her gaze, and saw a man get up from a desk against the far wall and start to approach them. 'What the shit . . .?' Then he saw the guns and turned to run back to the desk.

Jessica aimed and fired, just above his head. The bullet smashed into a television set in the office, and it burst into flames. Felicity screamed and ran at her, and she swung the rifle barrel, sending the housekeeper tumbling to the floor, blood streaming from her cut cheek.

Chloe had run forward to stand over Ramon as he got back to his knees, the Sauer held in both hands and pointing at his neck. 'Cool it,' she said.

Jessica left the moaning Felicity, and the rest of the servants, who had backed against the dining-room wall, and joined her. 'Mr Cuesta?'

Ramon raised his head, and looked from Sauer to ArmaLite. 'Jones,' he said. 'Jessica Jones. But you are dead.'

'Close. You may get up,' Jessica invited. 'Chloe, cut those communications.'

Chloe went into the office and began destroying the radios and television sets.

Ramon reached his feet. 'You're covered in mud.'

'That was your idea, not mine.'

'That's an RPG!' He pointed at the ArmaLite, having identified the lower barrel.

'It doubles.'

'How the fuck did you get hold of that?'

'I always carry one,' Jessica assured him, 'whenever there's a possibility of having to wrestle with alligators.'

'Are you out of your minds?' Ramon asked, and turned to watch Chloe continuing to hurl television sets, computers and radios to the floor with crackling crashes. 'Do you know how much those things cost?'

'Put in an insurance claim,' Jessica suggested, 'when next you have the time to spare.'

'You *are* mad,' Ramon declared. 'Do you suppose you can get away with this? Where is Duarte?'

'If you mean the guy who had me pushed into the alligator pit,' Jessica said, 'he's on his way. But it'll take a little time. He's walking. With the rest of our party. We thought we'd come on ahead.'

Ramon watched in consternation as Chloe started firing into the various sets that were too heavy or robust to be destroyed by simply being hurled to the ground. 'Mad,' he said. 'You are going to go to prison for a very long time. The rest of your life.'

'Then you want to make sure you're still alive when I come out,' Jessica said. 'I want your wife.'

'She's not receiving visitors.'

'Chloe, shoot him,' Jessica said. 'In the leg will do for the time being.'

Chloe came round the desk, pistol levelled. Behind her the office was a shambles; several of the shattered sets, like the one first hit by Jessica, were burning.

'You . . .' Ramon gasped.

'Three seconds,' Jessica told him. 'One, two . . .'

'All right, all right,' he panted. 'She's upstairs.'

'Take us.'

Ramon moved towards the stairs, and checked at the sight of Felicity, who had risen to her knees, weeping and pawing at her bleeding face.

'She'll live,' Jessica told him, and listened to a shot from outside, followed by another. 'Go back Andie up,' she told Chloe. 'I can manage in here.' She noted that the servants had fled the dining room, and she didn't suppose they had stopped in the kitchen. Which no doubt accounted for Andrea's problem. But now she heard the sound of the Sauer again. There was no time to lose. 'Hurry,' she said.

Ramon went up the stairs. Jessica could imagine the thoughts that were tumbling through his brain, the ideas and possibilities that were presenting themselves. But she still held the initiative . . . and the ArmaLite!

Ramon reached the bedroom door. 'It is locked.'

'So open it.'

'It's locked in the inside.'

'Well then, tell whoever is inside to open it.'

Ramon hesitated, then called, '*Es el patron. Abran la puerta.*'

They heard the key turning immediately; clearly the people inside had been alarmed by the shooting. The door swung in and Jessica pushed Ramon ahead of her, following immediately behind him. The two maids goggled at her, and from the bed there came a startled exclamation.

'Back up,' Jessica snapped. 'On the floor, on your faces.'

She didn't suppose they understood her, but they got her drift when she pointed at the floor; they sank to their knees, and, when she pointed again, lay on their stomachs, hands on their heads.

'What's happening?' Miranda had the sheet to her throat. 'Who are you? Ramon . . .?'

'This is the Miss Jones I mentioned to you, my dear,' Ramon said. 'She seems to have some crazy idea of taking you out of here. She seems to believe she can do that.'

'Jones?' Miranda released the sheet and scrambled out of the bed. She was naked. 'Adrian . . .?'

'Is waiting for us.'

'How do I know that?'

Jessica felt in her pocket and tossed the cuff link on to the bed.

Miranda picked it up, examined it, and then almost kissed it. 'I knew he'd send someone. But you . . .' She stared at the little blonde, the mud-stained clothes, and the rifle.

'I'm the best he could find,' Jessica explained. 'Now, if you'd care to get dressed, we can get out of here.'

'But . . .' Miranda gazed at her husband. 'Are you going to let me go?'

'No,' Ramon said.

'He's my problem,' Jessica said. 'Put something on, please. Hurry.'

'Oh, I . . .'

Jessica moved to the window and looked out at the back of the house. There were several people standing by the pool, talking to each other and pointing. She moved to the front windows and looked down. The truck still waited at the porch; Chloe was in the back, and Andrea was standing beside the cab. Both had their weapons levelled, and seemed to have the situation under control, but that there had been a crisis was evidenced by the two bodies lying on the lawn, although neither appeared to be dead. However, the dozen gardeners had been reinforced by the fleeing servants, and now people were starting to arrive from the village.

She had kept her rifle pointing at Ramon while she had been at the window. Now she turned back to the room to see Miranda standing in front of the open wardrobe, pinching her lip.

'For God's sake,' she said.

'I need to know where we're going,' Miranda explained. 'Who we're going to see.'

'Just get dressed,' Jessica snapped. 'Put something on. Anything. Or come as you are. I don't mind. But we have to go.'

Just for a moment she had taken her eyes off Ramon, and now there was a click. She swung the rifle back to where he was standing, just inside the door. He had moved a few feet back against the wall, and had pressed a switch she had assumed controlled the lights. Now she listened to a whirring sound, turned again, and watched a steel shutter come down across the balcony window, and then others over the two front windows as well. The room was immediately gloomy, but the sunlight was so bright outside that it was by no means dark.

'Just hold it,' Jessica snapped. 'What the shit . . .?'

'We're in now,' Ramon explained. 'That switch controls every exterior window and door in the house. We're sealed.'

'Oh, my God!' Miranda cried.

'Get *dressed*,' Jessica snapped. 'And you, you've had your fun. Open the shutters.'

'Can't be done,' Ramon said, now again fully confident. 'Once that switch is thrown, it cannot be reversed for an hour. And in an hour . . .'

'You reckon you'll have a screaming mob out there. Well, I have news for you.'

'Shooting me isn't going to help,' he said. 'You'll be hanged for murder.'

'Life does have its problems,' she agreed, and turned back to Miranda, who had at last put on a pair of panties and a bra. 'I suppose,' Miranda said, 'that I could wear jeans. Do you think it would be all right to wear jeans? Or are we going to be seen socially?'

'No parties, so jeans will be fine,' Jessica said, having to stop herself from grinding her teeth as she listened to some more shots from outside. 'And a shirt and a pair of boots. That's all you need.'

'But what about all my good things?'

'We'll send for them later,' Jessica assured her.

Miranda considered. 'But we're leaving the ranch. I couldn't possibly go anywhere proper wearing jeans. I'll wear a dress.'

Jessica fought back the temptation to swear at her.

'Listen,' Ramon said. 'You are, how do you say, on a hiding to nothing. You cannot leave this house for an hour. By that time it will be surrounded by my people. What do you intend to do, shoot them all?'

'If I have to,' Jessica said equably.

He stared at her. 'You can't be serious.'

'We'll have to wait and see. All right, milady? Oh, my God!''

Miranda was at last fully dressed – in a skimpy summer number which finished well above her knees, and high heels. 'Don't you like it? I bought it at Fortnums.'

'You look stupendous,' Jessica agreed. 'Can we go now?'

'Well . . . I don't really like leaving my things. Couldn't I just pack a small bag?'

'No. Where is your passport?'

'In that drawer. Will we need it?'

'Yes.' Jessica opened the drawer, took out the passport, and dropped it into her shoulder bag. 'Let's go. You first, Mr Cuesta.'

She opened the door and pointed with her gun. One of the maids asked a question.

'They want to know if they can get up now,' Ramon said.

'Tell them no. Move it.'

Ramon shrugged, spoke rapidly in Spanish – to a chorus of discontent – and led the way on to the darkened gallery and then down the stairs into the well of the house.

'What's that smell?' Miranda asked, and then uttered a shriek when she saw the office. 'My God! We're on fire!'

'Only in places,' Jessica assured her.

Ramon gestured at the front doors, outside of which there was a great deal of noise. 'They know you're trapped.'

'We'll have to disillusion them, won't we.'

'Help me! Help me!'

She had forgotten about the housekeeper, who had fallen down again. She stood above her. Felicity's face was even more drenched in blood, and distorted with pain. 'I am bleeding to death.'

'I think you'll manage,' Jessica said. 'Although you may have a scar. My apologies. Just remember that you attacked me. She's your housekeeper,' she told Ramon. 'Clean her up.'

'What with?'

Jessica went to the table, seized the cloth, and jerked it off, scattering glasses and cutlery left and right. 'Try this.'

Ramon took the cloth and knelt beside Felicity, stroking her face. She gave a wail of pain, and threw both arms round him.

Jessica went to the doors to examine them.

'Those doors are made of greenheart,' Ramon said over his shoulder. 'That is the strongest wood in the world. It is so heavy it is the only wood which will not float. You'd need a bomb to get through there.'

'By golly, you're right.' Jessica unslung her shoulder bag and took out a grenade.

'You mean you have cartridges for that thing?'

'I was a girl scout. Be prepared.' She levelled the rifle and squeezed the trigger. Miranda and Felicity both screamed. Even with the butt firmly wedged in her shoulder Jessica was nearly knocked off her feet. The grenade smashed into the join of the two doors and punched a hole right through, blackening the timber to either side. But the doors were still closed.

Jessica reached into her bag for a second round, and Ramon hurled himself at her. Miranda screamed again, but a second too late for it to act as a warning. Jessica saw Ramon coming out of the corner of her eye, but did not turn quickly enough, and he slammed into her shoulder, knocking her from her feet. She struck the floor heavily, and lost her grip on the rifle, which skidded away from her. She reached for it, but it was kicked from her grasp by Ramon, who then reached for it himself, but she caught his ankle and brought him down in turn with a thump.

She got up, and he threw both arms round her knees. Miranda and Felicity both screamed again; it was impossible to tell whose side they were on. Ramon reared above Jessica and swung his fist; she moved her head but the blow still caught her on the side of the skull and made her brain spin. She understood that for all her skill at unarmed combat she was at too great a disadvantage in size and strength to risk a serious wrestling match, and again went back to first principles.

Ramon was drawing back his arm for another punch. 'I am going to feed you to my pets, slowly,' he snarled.

Jessica brought her hand up to his crotch, and squeezed with all her strength. He uttered a shriek and rolled off her, hands reaching for the afflicted part of his body. Jessica got to her knees and reached the rifle, swinging it to catch him on the side of *his* head. He went down without a sound.

'You've killed him!' Miranda cried.

'You mean you still care?' Jessica staggered to her feet – her brain was still spinning – and pointed the rifle at Felicity, who was back on her feet, and was also swaying. 'I would sit down again if I were you,' she recommended. 'You don't look well. Help will be along in about five minutes,' she promised.

Miranda was now kneeling beside Ramon, who was just stirring, and groaning. 'He *is* my husband,' she said defensively.

'I thought you wanted a divorce.' Jessica regained her bag, fitted another grenade, and fired. This time the doors sagged, and when she put her shoulder to them they fell apart. She stepped outside, and looked at what appeared to be the entire village – well over two hundred people, men, women and children, plus barking dogs, a few goats, and several horses – milling about, shouting and cursing, but being kept at bay by Andrea and Chloe, both of whom were looking extremely agitated.

'Where have you *been*?' Chloe asked.

'Coping.'

'How do we cope with this lot?' Andrea asked.

'Half a mo.' She went back inside. Ramon was sitting up, holding his head; blood seeped through his fingers.

'I think he has concussion,' Miranda said. 'You must have hit him awfully hard.'

'It's the only way to hit people,' Jessica pointed out. 'Come on, Cuesta, on your feet.'

He blinked at her. 'Bitch!' he snarled. 'Bitch!'

'You're begging for another one.' She levelled her rifle, and he staggered to his feet, holding on to Miranda. 'Get him outside.'

They stumbled on to the porch, and the noise from the crowd grew as they recognized their employer.

'Shut up!' Jessica shouted.

No one paid any attention to her, so she fitted another grenade, aimed at the helicopter, and fired. The results were spectacular as the machine burst into a thousand burning pieces, showering those standing near it with glowing fragments. They screamed and retreated, but the rest had fallen silent.

'Chloe,' Jessica snapped. 'Help her ladyship get him into the truck.'

Chloe tucked her pistol into her waistband and hurried over. Jessica went round to stand beside Andrea. 'You'll have to do the shouting,' she said. 'Tell them that we are driving out of here with the *patron*. Tell them that if any attempt is made to stop us, or to follow us, he will be killed. Make them understand that.'

Andrea swallowed as she tried to get her Spanish together, then began shouting. Jessica watched Chloe and Miranda push Ramon up and into the back of the truck. 'Do you think he's going to die?' Miranda asked. 'I really would not like him to die.' She seemed to notice the burning helicopter for the first time. 'Oh, my God! He's going to be *furious*!'

'Not if he dies,' Jessica told her. 'Unfortunately, I don't think he's going to do that – unless I shoot him.'

'You can't!' Miranda screamed.

'I'll try to restrain myself. OK?'

Andrea and Chloe nodded.

147

'Right. You two in the back. Milady, you'll sit in the cab with me.'

'Shouldn't I be with my husband?'

'Milady, try to understand. My associates and I are risking our lives and creating mayhem in order to free you from your husband, and hopefully, with your testimony, send him to prison for the rest of his life.'

'Ramon? Prison? He couldn't go to prison. I mean, he'd die if he was shut up.'

'That's a problem most criminals have to face when they're sent down. You'd be surprised how many of them decide to grin and bear it. Now, ma'am, with respect, can we continue this discussion when we're out of here?' She looked out of the cab window. 'All set? Hold him up so they can see him.'

Andrea and Chloe pushed Ramon into a sitting position, and Chloe rested the muzzle of her pistol on his neck. Jessica started the engine and turned the truck. The mob backed off, muttering and shouting, the sunlight glinting off their machetes. Not, Jessica realized, that there was going to be too much more sunshine; the black clouds which had been threatening all morning were now definitely gathering overhead.

She swung to her left and drove round the house, the crowd continuing to part in front of her, but now puzzled by her movements; the bridge was behind her. She drove away from them and to the garage. 'Just don't move,' she told Miranda, but as she could no longer be sure of her loyalty, she pocketed the keys. Then she jumped down. 'Chloe, free the horses. Andie, let the men out of the loo and tell them to run for it.'

Chloe ran for the stables, opening the stalls and chasing the amazed horses out. Andrea got into the Mercedes and drove it away from the toilet door, then got down and unlocked the door. The two men staggered out and she shouted at them in Spanish. They stumbled away from the building.

The horses were now all free. Chloe fired several shots into the air to scatter them. 'Okay!' she shouted.

'Run!' Jessica shouted back. She was still standing in the garage entrance, but she could see, through the open inner door, the barrels of petrol stacked one on top of the other. Andrea dashed past her, and Jessica drew a deep breath, levelled the rifle, and fired a single shot.

The explosion knocked her off her feet, but Andrea was there to help her up, and they staggered back to the truck; behind them another series of explosions thundered across the ranch, and pieces of shattered cars and trucks showered about them. Miranda was screaming, and even Ramon was sitting up, looking dazed. Chloe and Andrea scrambled in beside him. 'Down, boy,' Chloe said.

'If he's coming round,' Jessica said, 'you'd better tie his hands.'

She got into the cab and started the engine. 'My God!' Miranda said. 'You blew the whole place up. All of Ramon's cars!'

'They didn't have anywhere to go,' Jessica pointed out. She swung the truck again, now driving towards the airstrip. As she did so, several horsemen appeared, waving and shouting. She recognized Duarte, but ignored him and continued driving towards the terminal building and the five parked aircraft, braking a hundred yards away.

Men ran out of the building, and at least two were armed and shooting – fortunately not very accurately. 'Return fire,' Jessica commanded, getting down from the cab.

Instantly there were several barks from Andrea's rifle, and the men hastily dashed back inside. Jessica fitted a grenade, aimed, and sent the shell into the executive jet. It went up, as had everything else that day. She fired twice more, the first into the turbo-prop, and the second into the waiting twin-engined tourist plane.

The two small training aircraft had got caught in the explosions and were also burning, as was some of the terminal building. There were still shots coming from inside, but all went wide, so terrified were the men inside. Jessica checked her bag. There was only one grenade left, and she felt she might still need it.

She got back behind the wheel. 'My God, my God, my *God!*' Miranda shouted. 'Is there anything left?'

'I can't think of it, at the moment,' Jessica conceded, and drove back towards the village.

The crowd was still gathered, now on the street, and was being harangued by Tejada, waving his arms and shouting; he had armed himself with a pistol, as had several other people, but Jessica did not suppose they would do much shooting with Ramon in the firing line. She blew the horn, loudly, while Andrea and Chloe held Ramon up so that his people could see him; he was now suitably pinioned by a length of rope. 'They will follow,' he said. 'They will never let you get away.'

'I'm sure the boss has that in mind,' Andrea said.

As Jessica did. The truck bounced across the bridge, beneath which the turgid dark water flowed slowly; the eyes of several caiman could be seen just breaking the surface. On the far side Jessica braked and got out of the cab, fitting the last grenade to her rifle while studying the joists of the bridge. 'Tell those people to clear off,' she instructed Andrea.

Several of the men were beginning to cross behind them. Andrea waved her arms and shouted at them to go back.

'Tell them they have five seconds, or they'll be swimming with caiman,' Jessica said.

Andrea shouted some more while Jessica levelled the ArmaLite. The men began to back away. Jessica counted to five, as promised, then fired, aiming at the centre joist. The grenade exploded and the bridge sagged, and then began collapsing into the water.

Ramon looked from the bridge to the smoke billowing from the garage and, further on, from the wrecked aircraft; closer at hand the helicopter still smouldered, and wisps of smoke were issuing from the ranch-house windows. 'Bitches!' he said. 'You have destroyed my ranch.'

'Think of all the fun you'll have rebuilding it,' Andrea said, 'when you get out of gaol.'

'That's going to be about the year 3000,' Chloe pointed out. 'You'll have time to make plans.'

The truck roared south. The road was every bit as bad as Jessica had expected, but she maintained forty miles an hour, and within minutes the ranch was out of sight behind them as they drove through a little wood.

'Where are we going?' Miranda asked.

'To join your brother.'

'Adrian? Oh, super. What about Ramon?'

'He's coming with us.'

'He's going to be frightfully angry.'

'I already am,' Jessica pointed out. 'That husband of yours tried to have me served up for alligator lunch.'

'Oh! That must have been *awful*! How did you get away?'

'I shot it.'

'Oh. You're good at that.'

'Yes, I am,' Jessica said modestly.

'He told me he only fed his enemies to the caiman.'

'Well, I don't suppose he'd describe me as a friend. But you say he told you that?'

'Oh, yes. The night Sprightly died.'

'Just let me get this absolutely straight. Your husband told you he had fed Sprightly to the caiman?'

'Yes. Well, I knew something awful had happened.'

'You'll testify to that in court?'

'Court?' Her voice had become a squawk.

'Milady, that is the object of this exercise. To place your husband in court.'

'On a charge of murder? Oh!'

'I think that may be the minor charge. He is also, with your help, going to be charged with drug smuggling on a large scale. You are prepared to testify to that?'

'Oh. I hadn't thought of that.'

Jessica became aware of lead balls gathering in her stomach. 'Listen! You sent a coded message to your brother asking for help. Didn't you?'

'Well, yes, I did.'

'And you knew what would be involved?'

'Well, I couldn't stay with him, not after Sprightly. And then . . .'

'Yes?'

'Well, he tortured me.'

'Eh?'

Miranda shuddered. 'He had that woman hold me down, and he put pepper, well . . . It was awful. I couldn't *go* for hours, I was so swollen.'

'Shit,' Jessica muttered. 'You're making me feel I didn't hit him hard enough. Still, that's another charge against him.'

'Oh, I couldn't possibly tell anyone about it. I mean, it would be so embarrassing. Anyway, a wife can't testify against her husband, can she?'

'A wife cannot be *forced* to testify against her husband. There is no law to prevent her from doing so if she wishes to.'

'Oh. I hadn't thought of that.'

'What *were* you thinking of, when you sent to Adrian for help?'

'I thought he'd come and get me out. I thought that's what you came for. Didn't you?'

'Sure I did. But I also came to rescue a witness who has the power to put Ramon Cuesta away for the rest of his life.'

'The rest of his life? But that would be *awful*!'

'Mrs Cuesta, that man is a murderer – probably several times over – and a drug smuggler, and God alone knows what else.

152

He is also, as you said, a torturer. Don't you want to see him punished?'

'Well . . . think of the scandal. Mumsy will have a fit.'

Jessica gave up. 'You'll have to discuss it with your brother.'

They had been driving for an hour, and her arms and legs were feeling like lead, not to mention her stomach. She simply was not in the mood to argue any more with this absurd creature. Now they came to a village, but she didn't slow down, and people scattered out of her way. The houses, and the people, looked terribly poor, and she did not suppose they had much in the way of communications equipment even if Tejada was somehow able to get a message down the road.

She drove for another half an hour, then slowed and put her head out of the window. 'You guys all right?'

'It's starting to rain,' Chloe said.

Jessica watched the huge drops splattering on the windscreen; the sky was now entirely black. She stopped the truck and got down, and was immediately wet. 'You'd better come inside,' she said.

'What about him?'

'We'll have to do a good job on him.' She climbed into the back, while the rain now started to fall heavily, great drops pounding through her hat and even slashing through her thick shirt.

'You can't leave me out in this,' Ramon protested.

'We'll make sure you don't drown,' Jessica promised. She used some more of the rope to bind his ankles, then propped him up against the toolboxes. Then the three of them climbed down again.

'Bitches!' he shouted. 'When I get my hands free . . .'

'Shall I gag you as well?' Jessica asked.

He glared at her, but closed his mouth.

'Now,' she said. 'One of you can spell me.'

'I'll drive,' Andrea said.

The downpour was so heavy they were soaked by the time

they were all in the cab, huddling against Miranda. 'Oooh!' she complained. 'Now I'm all wet!'

'It's warm rain,' Jessica assured her.

There was a searing flash of forked lightning, seeming to strike the road only yards in front of them, while the instantaneous crack of thunder had them all quite dizzy. 'Jesus,' Andrea muttered, sawing the wheel back and forth to keep the truck on the road, which had suddenly turned into a water slalom.

'Try not to oversteer,' Jessica recommended.

Miranda was weeping. 'I hate these thunderstorms. They're so frightening. I mean, suppose we get hit?'

'We won't; we've got rubber tyres,' Jessica said, hoping that her very elementary knowledge of physics was accurate.

'Listen!' Miranda said. 'Isn't that Ramon?'

Jessica listened to the distant shouting. 'I would say that you are right.'

'He can't stay out there in this! He'll catch pneumonia.'

'Even if I was prepared to consider it,' Jessica said, 'there's no room in here. Look out!'

Visibility was now down to a matter of yards, except during the lightning flashes, and in front of them there was suddenly a fallen tree lying right across the road. 'Shit!' Andrea shouted, and wrenched the wheel round. The truck skidded violently, and went sideways into the obstruction, then, as Andrea tried to turn the wheel again, it slid off the road into the ditch, which by now was filled with water.

Escape

Jessica found herself half sitting on Miranda's lap, while they were both lying on top of Chloe against the nearside door. 'God!' Miranda screamed. 'Oh, God!'

Andrea was hovering above them, still hanging on to the wheel. 'Sorry about that. It got away from me.'

The shouting from the back had gained in intensity.

'He's hurt,' Miranda moaned. 'I know he's hurt.'

'So am I,' Chloe complained from beneath them.

'Will this thing still work?' Jessica asked.

The engine had died, and now Andrea turned the key several times, but was rewarded only with a whirring sound.

'Don't kill the battery,' Jessica said. 'Who did mechanic's training?'

'Me,' Chloe groaned.

'Then you'd better take a look under the hood.'

'How do I get out? This door is jammed against the earth. Ugh! There's water coming in.'

'We'll have to get out your side, Andie. Move it.'

Grunting and breathing heavily, Andrea forced her door open, letting in the pouring rain. 'Shit, shit, shit!' she commented, but held on to the surround and dragged herself up and then out.

'You next, milady,' Jessica said.

'I couldn't possibly get up there,' Miranda complained.

'Well, you can't possibly stay here,' Jessica pointed out. 'Lend a hand, Andie. I'll give her a push.'

Andrea reappeared, looking like a drowned rat but reaching through the doorway. Miranda got herself up, giving a little squeal as Jessica grasped the bare flesh of her thighs to push, and a moment later she was out, legs and high heels waving.

Jessica passed up the shoulder bags and the rifles before scrambling out, then Chloe followed. The rain continued to teem down and the thunder to crackle and the lightning to flash, and Miranda continued to moan. 'OK,' Jessica said. 'Is anybody really hurt?'

'Yes,' Miranda said.

'Chloe?'

Chloe felt herself. 'I'll live. Nothing broken.'

'Great. See what you can find.'

Chloe looked into the ditch, which was now about three feet deep in water. 'Fuck it,' she commented, and slid down. 'Someone has to release the catch.'

Andrea lay on her stomach to reach into the cab and release the hood.

'What about me?' Miranda inquired.

'Anything broken?'

'Well, I don't think so. But I'm awfully bruised. I know I am.'

'You'll feel better tomorrow.' Jessica went to look at the back.

'What are you trying to do, kill me?' Ramon demanded.

'When I try to kill someone, I usually succeed,' Jessica told him. 'Right, Andie, give me a hand to shift this tree.'

'You'll never move that,' Miranda said, staring at the fallen trunk.

'Doesn't look too promising,' Jessica agreed.

'Wouldn't do us any good anyway.' Andrea had been inspecting the truck. 'This wheel's all bent. The axle is gone.'

Chloe joined them. 'I think I can get her going.'

Andrea pointed to the wheel, and Chloe grunted. 'What are we going to do?'

'Walk,' Jessica said.

'Walk?' Miranda shouted. 'You must be out of your mind. Do you know how far it is to . . . Where are we going, anyway?'

'La Paz.'

'Oh, my *God*! That's two hundred miles away, and ten thousand feet above where we are.'

'It can't still be two hundred miles,' Jessica pointed out. 'Hang on and I'll see just where we are.' She used her GPS to obtain a reading, then crawled beneath the truck to check it on her map.

'I am drowning,' Ramon complained from above her.

'It could happen,' Jessica agreed. She dialled a number on her mobile, but there was no reply from the number Adrian had given her. 'Shit,' she muttered, and re-emerged. 'We are one hundred and forty-three miles from La Paz, give or take a hundred yards.'

Andrea and Chloe gulped.

'And you expect me to walk a hundred and forty miles?' Miranda demanded. 'In this rain? And with . . . Oh, shit. My dress is torn.'

'I told you that jeans would have been more sensible.'

'But what about my shoes?'

'Your best bet is to take them off.'

'Take them off? You want me to go barefoot, in the mud and the bugs?'

'I've never tried it myself,' Jessica agreed. 'But I've been told that walking barefoot through mud is a great sensation. I can't speak about the bugs.'

'Listen,' Miranda said, 'the sensible thing to do, the only thing we *can* do, is to get into the cab and wait for someone to come along.'

'How often does that happen?' Chloe asked.

'Well, I'm sure there'll be something along tomorrow. Or the day after.'

'Shit!' Andrea commented.

To sit tight, at least until the rain stopped, was a temptation, if only because they were all exhausted. But Jessica knew that she could only risk that if she could contact Adrian and get him to come for them. Otherwise . . . 'I'm afraid we cannot wait for something to come along,' she said. 'Because the first thing that does is likely to be a busload of policemen, looking for us. However, things aren't as bad as you might think. According to the map, there is another village just three miles along the road. There is sure to be a vehicle there that we can, well, requisition. So, let's move it.'

They pulled Ramon out of the back. 'What are you going to do?' he asked nervously.

'Take a little walk.'

'You expect me to walk in this?'

'Don't you start. What have you guys got against water?'

Ramon was looking at his wife. 'My God!' he said. 'You look like a drowned rat.'

'I feel like a drowned rat,' she snapped. 'These people are absolutely mad.'

'The only way to cope with mad people is to humour them,' Jessica recommended. 'Let's go.'

'You must untie my hands,' Ramon said.

'I don't think I want to do that.'

'I cannot walk with my hands tied behind my back.'

'Don't worry about it. If you fall down, I promise we'll pick you up.'

'I am going to feed you—'

'You are starting to sound like a broken record,' Jessica said. 'I really do think you'd do best by saving your breath.' She poked the muzzle of her rifle into his back. 'Move it.'

They walked through the still heavy rain, Miranda and Ramon in front – Miranda uttering little shrieks from time to time as her bare toes encountered obstacles in the mud – the three policewomen behind. At least the thunderstorm seemed to have passed.

'What has this done to our schedule?' Andrea asked.

Jessica looked at her watch. 'Just on two. Adrian isn't expecting us until ten tonight. We've got time, thanks to our early start.'

'Two,' Chloe said. 'That's why I'm so hungry. When do we lunch?'

'We'll get something at this village,' Jessica said with more confidence than she actually felt. Because . . .

Andrea had had the same thought. 'We couldn't possibly have destroyed all the mobiles on the ranch.'

'I'm sure we did not.'

'Well, then . . .'

'So they'll be calling. All depends on who. But they can't possibly know where we are. The people in that last village didn't react.'

'That was nearly an hour ago. But the people in this village . . .'

'Look on the bright side. We have three bright sides. The first is that there aren't likely to be too many mobiles in a remote Bolivian village. The second is that even if Tejada or Garcia or someone else does manage to raise them, they'll be expecting us to be charging by in a pick-up truck, not walking in the rain. And the third is that if push does come to shove, we have the sort of firepower which is again unlikely to be found in said remote village.'

'But we're only three, with at least one hostile in our midst.'

'Trust me,' Jessica said, which she knew from past experience Andrea would be perfectly happy to do. They had been under fire together on three previous occasions before today, and had come out on top each time – entirely because Andrea had been prepared to obey orders without hesitation.

But for all her confidence that they could handle any

immediate situations, the overall prospect looked very grim unless she could raise Adrian, and if something had happened to him they were once again right up the creek. She tried him again after they had walked for half an hour, but again there was no reply.

'What's he at?' Chloe asked.

'He must have switched off,' Jessica said. 'We'll get him.' Again she was expressing a confidence she was a long way from feeling.

They walked for another fifteen minutes, splashing through the increasing water on the road; Miranda was complaining bitterly both about her feet and about how exhausted and hungry she was when suddenly Andrea said, 'Houses.'

Like most of them Jessica had been walking with her head bowed to keep the rain out of her eyes; her hat had collapsed into a sodden mess. Now she looked up to see roofs appearing through the trees and round a bend in the road.

'Right,' she said. 'Volunteer.'

'Me,' both the women said.

'Chloe. You'll stay here with these two.'

'Oh!' Chloe had assumed she was volunteering for action.

'I need Andie's Spanish,' Jessica explained.

'You want us to stay here?' Miranda demanded. 'In the rain?'

'It'll be just as wet in the village. You can sit down, if you like,' Jessica suggested. 'In the mud. We won't be long. Chloe, I'm giving you carte blanche to shoot Mr Cuesta if he starts making a racket or tries anything you don't like. But try not to kill him.'

'She can't do that,' Miranda protested.

'Try me,' Chloe suggested. 'What about her?'

'We're supposed to be rescuing her. Do try to be good, milady. We really are on your side, and we expect you to be on ours. However, if you can't be good . . . You

160

may hit her, Chloe. But only just hard enough to shut her up.'

'You lay a finger on me . . .'

'I never could resist temptation,' Chloe warned her.

'Ramon . . .'

'Shut up,' her husband said. 'We do not wish to go into that village.'

'Why not?'

'Just shut up.'

Miranda subsided, looking ready to burst into tears to join the water already dribbling out of her hair and down her cheeks. Jessica reflected that one's sins will always find one out: Cuesta had clearly had dealings with this village at some time in the past, and was not popular here. Which might come in handy.

She left them to it.

'What about these?' Andrea asked, raising her rifle.

'We can't conceal them, and I'm certainly not leaving them behind,' Jessica said. 'They'll just have to put up with them.'

Andrea blew through her teeth.

They rounded the bend, and saw a slip road which led off the 'highway' to the village. They went down this and came into full view of the houses. Predictably, both on account of the rain and the hour – it was a quarter past three, the middle of the siesta – there was no one to be seen, but as they approached a dog barked, and then another, and one of the animals left the shelter of the overhang beneath which he had been lying and came towards them, teeth bared. 'Don't bug me, dog,' Jessica warned.

He got the message from her tone, both that she wasn't afraid of him and that she might be more dangerous than him, and retreated, growling.

'Do you see what I see?' Jessica asked.

At the far end of the street there was a lean-to garage which contained a pick-up truck.

'The answer to a maiden's prayer,' Andrea said. 'Do you think they'll let us rent it?'

'Whether they will or not, we are going to have it,' Jessica said.

The door of the nearest house opened – there were only a dozen in all – and a man stepped out on to the shallow porch. He was heavily built, not very tall, had a broad flat face and lank black hair. 'He's Indian,' Andrea whispered.

'He's bound to speak Spanish,' Jessica said. 'Try him.'

The man stared at the two bedraggled figures for some seconds, and Andrea said politely, *'Buenas tardes, señor.'*

He studied them some more, taking in the guns, which they both held upright against their shoulders. But clearly he did not identify the weapons as assault rifles; he probably assumed they had been hunting. *'Qué desean ustedes, señoritas?'*

Andrea broke into a torrent of Spanish, speaking too quickly for Jessica to understand more than the odd word. But she did gather that she was explaining that their car had broken down and that they would like to hire a vehicle. While she was speaking a woman and three small children came out to stare at them. They all looked desperately poor, ill-dressed and undernourished. Jessica fervently hoped they would not have to take them on.

Andrea turned to her. 'He says there is only one truck, and they cannot allow us to have it.'

'I see. Well, ask him if we can have some food.'

Andrea resumed her conversation, then made a face. 'He says no.'

'All right,' Jessica said. 'Tell him to come here.'

Andrea spoke, and he replied. 'He says, why should he do that?'

Jessica levelled the rifle. 'Tell him because if he doesn't I am going to blow him apart.'

Andrea gulped, and then relayed the message. The man stared at them in disbelief, while his wife started to shout. Now more doors opened, and more people emerged. None seemed very eager to come out into the rain, but Jessica could not believe they did not possess at least one weapon among them. If they were going to get out of this mess it had to be done now. She levelled the rifle, aiming at the floor of the porch between the man's feet, and fired. He gave a scream of pain and fear, and began hopping about as wood splinters cut through his pants into his legs.

Andrea shouted at him, and he staggered down the steps into the rain and splashed towards them. A ripple seemed to spread through the village.

'Pistol, and arrest,' Jessica said.

Andrea hooked the strap of her ArmaLite over her shoulder and drew the Sauer from her bag. As the man limped up to them, face working in a mixture of outrage and apprehension, she levelled the gun.

'Tell him we want that truck, now,' Jessica said.

Andrea did so. The man spluttered in Spanish.

'Now,' Jessica repeated.

'He says that if we take the truck they will have no means of taking their produce to market.'

'Tell him we are renting the truck and will pay him for it. And he will get the truck back. And tell him also to warn his people not to attempt to stop us, or someone is going to get hurt, beginning with him.'

The man looked as if he would have argued some more, but Andrea snapped at him, using the word *pronto* several times, and at last he shrugged and shouted at his people. They retreated into the houses and he indicated the street. Andrea turned him round and stepped against him, her pistol jammed into his back. Jessica followed immediately behind, her rifle moving from left to right, but for the moment at least the villagers did not appear to wish to risk any action that could involve the death of their compatriot.

The truck was a Ford; it looked at least ten years old and was clearly held together by rust. 'Check it out,' Jessica said, and now levelled her rifle at their captive. Andrea put away her pistol and climbed into the cab. The engine started easily enough, and she inspected the dashboard. 'Not quite half full. Will that take us a hundred and forty miles?'

'Probably, but we can't risk it. '*Gasolina, señor.*'

The man pointed to the corner, where there was a stack of jerry cans.

'Tell him to fill her up.'

Andrea did so.

'Then ask him to name a price.'

Andrea chatted while their captive poured petrol into the truck's tank. 'He says a thousand Bolivian pesos.'

'Tell him we want to rent it, not buy it. What is a Bolivian peso worth, anyway?'

'Haven't a clue.'

'Ask him.'

Andrea did so. 'He says it is on a par with the US dollar.'

'Tell him we weren't born yesterday.' Jessica opened her bag – which was waterproof, so its contents had remained dry throughout the downpour – and took out the pouch in which she carried her passport and their money and cards and traveller's cheques, as well as her ballpoint. Using the bonnet as a table she filled in a traveller's cheque for one hundred pounds. She held it out and the man peered at it. 'Tell him to take this. Tell him that it is worth more than the truck, in my opinion.'

Andrea interpreted, and the man slowly took the piece of paper; Jessica wondered if he had ever seen a traveller's cheque before.

'Now, food . . .' Her head jerked as she heard the sound of a shot, followed by another.

*   *   *

'Chloe!' Andrea shouted.

'Let's go. Stand aside, señor.'

The man might not have understood her, but he got the message as she scrambled into the cab and Andrea started it up, and hastily jumped to one side. Andrea drove out of the shed and along the street. People had re-emerged in front of their houses, no doubt equally alerted by the gunshots, and were shouting and waving their arms. Some of the men ran on to the street, but Andrea blew her horn and managed to avoid hitting any of them. The truck skidded round the corner on to the main road, where they saw Chloe just getting to her feet. Miranda was sprawled on the road, and of Ramon Cuesta there was no sign.

'Shit!' Jessica snapped.

'Chloe!' Andrea said, braking in a flurry of flying water and leaping from the cab to run to her friend.

Jessica followed more slowly, pausing to make sure that Miranda was alive. She was trying to get up, but blood was dribbling down her cheek. 'She hit me,' she moaned. 'The bitch hit me!'

'What happened?' Jessica asked. 'Where is Cuesta?'

'They jumped me,' Chloe said.

'For God's sake, Chloe. You have a pistol.'

'Somehow he got free. I don't know how. I suppose because his hands were tied I wasn't watching him all that closely. Then her ladyship said she wasn't feeling well, and went down to her knees. I went to see what was wrong, turned my back on that bastard for a moment, and he clobbered me. Well, that bitch was holding on to my legs, so I had to hit her to get free. Hubby was trying to strangle me, so I hit him as well. He moved away from me and I managed to get rid of her and turn round, and there he was, running into the trees. I fired at him, twice, but you had said not to kill him, so I was trying to hit his legs and . . . I missed. Then he was gone.' She looked

165

from face to face. 'I couldn't go after him, could I, without leaving her. And I reckoned she was more important.'

'I'm bleeding!' Miranda wailed.

'What do we do?' Andrea asked.

Jessica gazed at the trees. They knew nothing of the South American jungle, and Ramon obviously did. Meanwhile there was a lot of noise from behind them as the villagers were summoning sufficient courage to investigate.

'We get out of here,' she decided. 'Into the cab.'

'What about Ramon?' Miranda cried. 'You can't leave him.'

'Milady, he obviously didn't want to stay.'

'But out there in the jungle, unarmed . . . There are spiders and things! Ants! Jaguars! Alligators! And snakes! Something called a bushmaster. If it bites you, you're dead in ten seconds.'

'I'm sure he'll get on very well with all of them. Hurry.'

They piled into the cab.

'You drive, Andie,' Jessica said.

Andrea gunned the motor. 'I thought we were taking him back for trial?'

'We were. But it can't be helped. As Chloe said, her ladyship is our first priority, and his capture wasn't in the original script.'

'Have I messed it up?' Chloe asked.

'You took the only reasonable course of action,' Jessica said. 'In the circumstances. The mistake you made was underestimating the opposition.'

'Oh,' Chloe said contritely.

They swung round the bend and saw what appeared to be the entire village gathered at the slip road. Several of the men were carrying long bamboo poles.

'Windows up!' Jessica snapped.

Chloe, again seated at the nearside door, hastily obeyed, and just in time: as they drew level with the crowd several small darts splattered on the glass.

'What the shit . . .?' Chloe inquired.

'Those are blowpipes,' Jessica told her. 'The darts are probably dipped in something unpleasant.'

'*Wourali*,' Andrea suggested.

'Absolutely.'

'I am in such pain,' Miranda complained. 'My entire head hurts. And my feet. And I am bleeding to death.'

'Patch her up, Chloe,' Jessica said.

'If that woman touches me again . . .'

'All right, let me.' Jessica opened her bag, found her first-aid kit, wet a tissue with her saliva, and stroked the blood away from Miranda's forehead. 'Hm. You may have a scar for a while.'

'A scar? On my face? I'll sue.'

'Your brother? He's our employer.' She smoothed a small strip of plaster over the wound. 'What you'll have to do is a Veronica Lake. You know, have your hair set so it droops over this eye.'

'My head hurts.'

'So you said.' Jessica found a couple of aspirin. 'You'll have to swallow them dry, I'm afraid.'

'I can't do that.'

'Try.'

Miranda put the pills into her mouth and gave a convulsive swallow, appearing to gag before getting them down.

'What I would give for an ice-cold beer,' Andrea said.

'And I'm all muddy,' Miranda said. 'There is mud everywhere. I can feel it between my legs. Ugh!'

'It was your idea to dress for a summer stroll in Green Park,' Jessica reminded her.

'I don't suppose you did get anything to eat,' Chloe remarked disconsolately. 'I'm so hungry I could eat a live horse.'

'Just be quiet,' Jessica suggested, 'and I'll see what I

can do.' She punched numbers on the mobile. Come on, she thought. *Come on.* She desperately needed to get hold of Adrian; while kidnapping Cuesta had not been in their original remit, possession of him had been their one guarantee of getting out of Bolivia alive. Of course, she told herself, alone and unarmed in the jungle he'd be concentrating more on his own survival than on making contact with any of his people, but as he seemed to have people everywhere she couldn't even be sure of that.

The phone was actually buzzing. 'Thank God,' she said.

'Captain Lord Lichton.'

'Adrian!' Miranda shrieked, and snatched the phone from Jessica's hand. 'Oh, Adrian, it's been terrible.'

'Mira! Are you all right?'

'No, I am not all right. I have a headache, and a bruise on my head, and I'm soaked through and covered in mud, and I have no shoes and Ramon has gone missing in the bush, and there's been shooting and all sorts of things, and my house is on fire.'

'Good lord! Where are you now?'

'I don't know. In a crummy old truck on a crummy road with, well . . .'

'Don't say it,' Jessica recommended.

'JJ! Is that you?'

Jessica took back the phone. 'Present and correct, sir. Do you always answer the phone with your full name?'

'Well, of course I do. Don't you?'

'Not when I am in what might be considered hostile territory, sir.'

'But you have managed to get hold of Miranda. That's tremendous. My best congratulations. Ah . . . was anything she was saying true?'

'Of course it's true, you great oaf,' Miranda shouted. 'I'm bleeding!'

'JJ?'

168

'Yes, sir. I think Lady Miranda outlined the situation fairly succinctly. However, we have stopped the bleeding.'

'But . . . is she hurt?'

'Of course I'm hurt, you idiot,' Miranda shouted.

'Only slightly,' Jessica said.

'Good lord! And is her house really on fire? Did you set fire to it?'

'We were responsible, yes. But I don't think it should any longer be considered your sister's house. And I'm quite sure the fire has been put out by now.'

'Good lord! But where are you?'

'About a hundred and twenty miles out of La Paz.'

'But . . . it's just four o'clock. You weren't going to leave the ranch until now.'

'The situation became fluid. May I ask where you have been the past couple of hours?'

'Well, I was lunching with the Smarts. Why?'

'I tried to get you, but you never replied.'

'Well, I had the phone switched off, don't you know.'

'Why?'

'Well, it really isn't very good form to have the old phone buzzing while one is lunching with friends, don't you know. Was it important?'

'Ah . . . yes, I think you could say that it was important. However . . .'

'Has there really been shooting?'

'I'm afraid so.'

'Around my sister?'

'Seeing that she was the reason for us being there in the first place, the answer has to be yes. Don't worry, she wasn't hit.'

'What about this wound in the head?'

'I meant she wasn't hit by a bullet. With the greatest respect, my lord, will you kindly shut up and listen.'

'Ah . . .' He was clearly taken aback. 'Well?'

'Unless we have another accident—'

'Accident? You have had an accident? With Miranda?'

'Just listen!' Jessica shouted. 'We should be roughly with you at about seven tonight.'

'Seven? You said ten.'

'As I have tried to explain, sir, things moved faster than I had expected. I would like to take off as soon as possible after we get there.'

'Ah. Tricky. I told Alonso – that's our pilot – that he needn't report before eight.'

'Can't you tell him there's been a change of plan?'

'Well, I suppose so. It's a matter of getting hold of him, don't you know.'

'Surely you have his address and phone number?'

'I think Joe has it. Yes. I'll see what we can do.'

'Please.'

'But what's the rush? I mean, you say you're out of the ranch and on the road. Isn't that it?'

'Sadly, sir, that is not it. I don't know how close behind us Mr Cuesta and his people are. And I estimate he is in a fairly aggressive mood.'

'Because you burned his house down, eh? Well, you know, you can't really blame the chap. But I thought Mira said that he was lost in the bush?'

'He went into the bush, certainly.'

'What an extraordinary thing to do.'

'He thought it was a good idea at the time. And I suspect he knows his way around when in it. So if you could change the arrangements . . .'

'Yes, yes. I said I'd see what I can do.'

Jessica had to make a great effort to restrain herself from being very rude, reminding herself that he was her temporary employer, that he was really a very nice 'chap', and that when he was making love in surroundings with which he was familiar he was a great deal more than that. 'Thank you, sir. Now, as I

170

say, we should be with you by seven. That means we should be met and guided to the airport about six. Or at least you should be in position by then. Can we count on that?'

'Six? I say, that's a bit short notice.'

'Is the road junction very far from La Paz?'

'Not really. But I have to have a bath, and pack. I didn't bring my man with me, you see. Thought it might be a bit obtrusive.'

'Absolutely. But you are packed already, aren't you?'

'Well, no, I was going to do it after dinner. Nicolette is laying on an early dinner, you see.'

'Dinner,' Chloe moaned, clutching her stomach.

'But you won't be having dinner at all, will you, sir, in view of the change in plan.'

'Ah, no. I suppose you're right. Oh dear, it'll upset her arrangements.'

'I'm sure she'll understand, sir. So perhaps you could pack. *Now.* And be at the junction by six o'clock. We really won't mind if you have to skip the bath.'

'Ah . . . well . . . Yes, I suppose I could do that.'

'Food,' Chloe said.

'And beer,' Andrea put in.

'Also, sir,' Jessica said, 'do you think you could bring some food with you?'

'Ah. Yes. I see what you mean. Something for my dinner, you mean.'

'Something for *our* dinner, sir. We haven't had any lunch.'

'I am starving,' Miranda said loud enough to be overheard at the other end of the phone. 'And my head hurts.' Just in case he had forgotten.

'I'll see what I can do.'

'And something to drink, sir. Cold beer would be best.'

'Ah. Yes. Does Miranda drink beer?'

'Right now I'd drink a bucket of warm piss,' Miranda shouted.

'Cold piss,' Andrea insisted.

'Quite. Well, then . . .'

'There's one thing more,' Jessica said.

'Yes?' He was starting to sound a little tired.

'Ponchos.'

'Say again?'

'You know those cape things all the locals wear? We need four of those.'

'Whatever for?'

'Because Lady Miranda isn't the only one of us who is covered in mud and sopping wet; we all are. And if we have to walk through a terminal building we will arouse comment. So we'd like to cover ourselves up.'

'Ah. Good thinking.'

'And shoes,' Miranda said.

'Shoes. What sort of shoes?'

'Any sort of shoes. Size six.'

'Hm. I'll see what I can do. Well, as they say, *adios*. I'll see you in a couple of hours.'

'He really is awfully nice,' Andrea said.

Chloe snorted.

The rain stopped as they climbed out of the Oriente, but now they went in and out of cloud, which in patches brought visibility down to virtually nothing. There was also more traffic; vehicles loomed out of the mist behind glowing headlights and blaring horns.

'Please be careful,' Jessica suggested. 'Another accident now and we've had it.'

'What happens when we blow up?'

'Eh?'

'Can't you smell it? I think the radiator is running dry. It's all this climbing in low gear.'

Jessica looked at her watch; it was past five. 'Just keep it going for another forty-five minutes.'

'I don't think that's going to be possible.'

'Well, as long as you can. If we have to walk the last bit, that's life.'

Thanks to the aspirin, Miranda had dozed off. Now she woke up. 'I am so cold,' she complained. 'I think I have caught pneumonia.'

'You could have company,' Jessica said, and sneezed.

'If we don't die of starvation first,' Chloe remarked.

'Houses,' Andrea said.

They had actually passed through several villages, which were closer together as they approached civilization, but this was a sizeable town.

'Oh, boy,' Andrea said. 'A petrol station. Do we have any local money?'

Jessica pointed. 'They take cards, so they say. Rifles on the floor.'

They pulled into the forecourt, and Andrea got out. She engaged the attendant in animated conversation while he studied her bedraggled but still most attractive form with interest: her shirt was so plastered to her chest she might have been taking part in a wet T-shirt contest. Jessica leaned out of the window. 'Is there a problem?'

'He is saying I am all wet.' Andrea giggled. 'He says, the beautiful señorita is all wet.'

Chloe gave another snort.

'Andrea, you're on duty,' Jessica reminded her. 'Look at the steam coming out of the radiator.'

'Right. Let's see.' Andrea released the catch for the hood, and it flew up with a force that threatened to tear it from its hinges.

Miranda gave a shriek.

Jessica got out to join Andrea and her new admirer at the front of the truck, from which clouds of steam were issuing. The mechanic made a remark.

'He says, another beautiful lady, all wet.'

173

And she had considerably the larger bust. 'Tell him it's his lucky day. Here's number three. Shit.'

Chloe had joined them; her shirt had been torn, either in getting out of the original truck or during her tussle with Ramon and Miranda, and she was revealing a good deal of very ample white flesh: her bust was as big as Andrea's and Jessica's put together. The mechanic made another remark, and rolled his eyes.

'Don't bother to translate that,' Jessica said, but she was more concerned about what might be happening inside the cab. She returned to it and looked through the window, and just in time: Miranda was leaning down to reach the rifles. Now she jerked upright again. 'Have you ever used one of those?' Jessica asked.

'Well . . . no. But I'm sure it's not difficult.'

'It is very difficult,' Jessica assured her. 'And very dangerous, at least for you. Because if you lay a finger on them I am going to break every bone in your body. Savvy?'

Miranda's eyes filled with tears. 'You are a horrible bully. I hate you.'

'That is perfectly permissible. But do try to make up your mind whose side you are on. We are not kidnapping you; we are rescuing you, at the request of your brother. Who, like us, is risking his life to get you out of the mess you so happily made of your life. Try to cooperate.' She returned to the front of the car where Andrea and the mechanic were still engaged in animated conversation. 'What's the hold-up? All we want is some water in the radiator.'

'And food,' Chloe said. 'Do they sell food?'

Andrea translated. 'He says there is food in the office.'

'Great. Do they take English money?'

'Tell them I'll be in in a moment and pay by card,' Jessica said. 'And try not to get raped. Now, señor . . .'

Chloe hurried off, and the mechanic donned a pair of heavy-duty gloves and after a struggle managed to loosen

174

the radiator cap. He promptly jumped back, and just in time, as the cap burst off and went sailing through the air. Andrea retrieved it, kicking it along the ground, as it was too hot to pick up. The man was again becoming voluble. 'He says we cannot put water in now. We must wait for it to cool down.'

'We don't have the time. What happens if we put water in now?'

Andrea listened. 'It will go *phut*. Holes.'

'Tell him we'll chance it.'

More chat. 'He doesn't want to do it,' Andrea explained. 'He says he knows this truck. It belongs to Miguel Santos of Araguey Village. He asks, what are we doing with it, anyway?'

'Tell him we rented it.'

More chat. 'He says he should see the rental agreement.'

'Tell him we lost it.' Jessica herself picked up the watering can that stood beside the pump and began filling the radiator. Steam rose. The mechanic protested. Chloe returned with four long pieces of bread and four beers.

'Is that all you could find?' Andrea asked.

'They've got some kind of sausage inside,' Chloe promised her.

'So get in,' Jessica told her. She took the radiator cap from Andrea and screwed it down, then closed the hood. There were huge gurgling sounds from beneath it.

The mechanic was still expostulating. 'He says he thinks he will have to call the police,' Andrea explained.

'Well, in that case . . .' Jessica opened her bag and found some English notes. 'Here's ten pounds. I'm sure that will cover the water and the *bocadillos*. Thanks for your help, señor. Let's go, Andie.'

The mechanic took the money but continued to protest. Jessica got into the cab and Andrea sat beside her and switched on. The mechanic hastily got out of the way, while a man and a woman appeared in the office doorway, both talking.

'Think he will call the cops?' Andrea asked.

'Probably. But we should be away in another half an hour. Just keep her going.'

Steam was starting to rise again.

'So, feed me,' Andrea said.

Chloe and Miranda were already chewing between swigs of beer. 'I don't usually drink beer,' Miranda confided. 'But this is rather pleasant.'

'That's because you're thirsty,' Chloe pointed out.

They seemed to be almost friends now.

Jessica held the fourth *bocadillo* to Andrea's mouth, and she bit into it. 'Jesus! That has to be the toughest piece of bread in the world.'

'You haven't got to the meat yet,' Jessica reminded her.

She was feeling slightly hysterical, as she always did when a mission was successfully accomplished. Had this mission been successfully accomplished? Providing Adrian was capable of keeping up his end – and she felt, and hoped, that despite the silly-ass image he kept projecting he was far tougher than he looked – she did not see what was going to stop them now. So far as she knew Ramon Cuesta was still cut off from all support, and even if the garage had called the police they would not catch up with them in time. The radiator continued to steam, but it was ten to six, and according to the last position she had taken they were only a couple of miles from the rendezvous. And then? Presumably Ramon had some kind of clout with the Bolivian government, if only because he was able to donate large sums of money to its support, but she did not suppose that, even though he knew her name and identity, an official complaint about the behaviour of her and her team was going to cut any ice in London once Miranda started giving evidence – presuming she was not going to backslide, that is.

Jessica glanced at her. Miranda's eyes were closed as she chewed slowly and thoughtfully – obviously she had never eaten a *bocadillo* before, either.

'A parked car,' Andrea said.

Jessica sat up, and peered through the cloud mist; the car was a Mercedes. 'Oh, boy,' she said. 'Pull in.' But she reached to the floor and picked up her rifle, just in case.

Andrea braked behind the waiting car, in which there were two men. But now Adrian got out. The women tumbled from the cab. 'Adrian!' Miranda shrieked, throwing herself into his arms. Since he was, as always, immaculately dressed in blazer and tie, he fielded her with some reluctance. 'My dear,' he said. 'You look like—'

'A drowned rat. I know. Everybody says that. What I want is a hot bath.'

'Yes. Well . . .' He looked past her at Jessica.

'Drowned rat number two, sir. I'm afraid the hot bath will have to wait. I hope it's all systems go?'

'Oh, indeed. I had a bit of trouble getting Alonso to change his schedule, but Joe worked it out.' He looked at Chloe and Andrea. 'I say, you *have* been in the wars.'

'In the line of duty, sir,' Andrea said, cheeks pink.

Chloe snorted.

Joe Smart also got out of the car. 'Those things any help?' He was looking at the guns.

'Without them, we wouldn't be here,' Jessica said. 'I'm afraid I used up all of your grenades.'

'My God! You must tell me about it sometime. Do you mean to take them with you on the aircraft?'

'I'm sure that won't be necessary,' Adrian said.

'Well . . .'

'You'll never get them through security.'

'Do we have to go through security on a private charter?'

'Actually, you don't,' Smart said. 'But you'll never get through the terminal with two ArmaLites.'

177

'We'll take them to pieces in your car.'

'Well . . .' He pulled his nose.

'I don't see why you still need them,' Adrian said. 'Your part of the operation is over now.'

'Nothing is ever over until the fat lady sings,' Jessica reminded him. 'My part of the operation is over when I escort your sister from an aircraft into the terminal building at Heathrow. Or Gatwick. I'm not fussy. Besides, these guns are old friends. I'd hate to lose them. Now, sir, did you bring the ponchos?''

He didn't argue further, and Jessica, Chloe and Andrea got into the back of the Mercedes. Miranda sat in the front with her brother; Smart was driving. Jessica reckoned they had definitely been relegated to the position of servants. Which suited her well enough.

'Shoes,' Miranda said. 'Where are the shoes? Don't tell me you forgot the shoes.'

'They're in the paper bag.'

Miranda peered into the bag. 'Sandals? You brought sandals?'

'They were the only things we were sure would fit.'

'But sandals don't go with this dress!'

'Darling, right now nothing would go with that dress – or what's left of it.'

'Oh, you beast! Everyone is being so beastly to me.' She started to cry.

'What about that truck?' Smart asked.

'Is it possible to let the owner know where it is?' Jessica suggested. 'After we've left the country?'

'If you think he'll want it back.'

'Oh, he will. It's his pride and joy. His name is Miguel Santos, and he lives in a little village about a hundred and fifty miles down the road. I think it's called Araguey.'

'I'll see what I can do.'

'I'm sure he'll be grateful. There is also the matter of our tour group. They're stranded out at Cuesta's ranch with no transport.'

'Don't they have a plane?'

'I blew it up.'

'You . . .' Smart half turned his head.

'It was necessary, believe me.'

'I'm sure. Well, I don't think I should get involved in that. The company will presumably send another plane when they don't turn up. They'll have an extra adventure.'

'I suppose.' She accepted his point; she didn't suppose her fellow tourists would actually come to any harm. 'Now, ladies, let's try to repair some of this damage.'

'You mean we can get out of these clothes?' Chloe asked.

'I don't think that's practical until we're airborne. And the ponchos will hide most of them. But we can do something about our hair.'

'I don't have a comb,' Miranda sniffed. As no one had paid any attention to her distress, she had stopped crying.

Jessica opened her bag. 'Use mine.'

Miranda hesitated, then took it. 'I don't suppose you have any make-up?'

'I'm afraid not.'

They made themselves as presentable as possible, dropped the ponchos over their heads – the waterproof material came to below their thighs – then Jessica and Andrea stripped down the rifles, drying the parts as best they could on their still damp clothing. 'Do you really think we'll need these again?' Andrea asked.

'Let's say that I feel happier with them around,' Jessica said. Why? she wondered. They were now in Adrian's hands, and he seemed to have everything under control. If only she could get rid of the feeling that, after the traumatic events of the day, everything had started running her way just a little too easily.

But they reached the airport without mishap. 'You stay in

the car until I've located Alonso and made sure everything is going according to plan,' Smart said. 'If you'll pardon me, ladies, your appearances are going to attract attention, even with the ponchos to hide the worst, so the less time anyone has to consider you the better. I won't be long.'

'Makes sense,' Adrian agreed.

Smart bustled off.

'I don't know what we would do without him,' Adrian said.

Jessica chose not to comment. She could see his point, but she was again experiencing the uncomfortable feeling in the pit of her stomach that she always did when she could not bring herself to trust someone entirely. For an ordinary businessman, Adrian's father's friend had just too many strings he was capable of pulling, from securing modern weapons at very short notice to controlling aircraft movements. 'Where are we going?' she asked.

'Rio.'

'I beg your pardon.'

'We are going to be taken to Rio de Janeiro. You'll like it there. And once we're there, I'll fit you out with some decent clothing.'

'You mean I get to go to Copacabana after all?' Chloe asked. 'Wowee!'

'Well,' he said, 'I'm sure you can, briefly. We want to be on a plane for England just as quickly as it can be done.'

'You are saying that we are going to fly right across South America?' Jessica asked.

'It's not a problem. Only a matter of about one thousand seven hundred miles. The plane we're using will do it comfortably.'

'You said it had a range of two thousand miles.'

'That's right.'

'You wouldn't say that's cutting it a bit fine?'

'No, no. Piece of cake.'

'Does your pilot know this?'

'Alonso? He says he'll fly us anywhere within two thousand miles of La Paz. There is nothing to worry about, really.'

'How long will it take?' Andrea asked.

'About seven hours. We'll be there by dawn tomorrow.'

'Will there be food on board?' Chloe asked.

'And beer?' Andrea added.

'I believe it's all laid on. Now ladies, you have done a magnificent job. Just sit back and relax. You're in my hands now.'

'I'm not really going to have to testify against Ramon, am I?' Miranda asked.

'Darling, that is the whole object of the exercise.'

'I thought the object of the exercise was to get me out of there.'

'Well, that too, of course. But the only way I could obtain the help of the police, and thus these lovely ladies, and the only way we can make whatever happened up there at the ranch stick, is to present you to the world as a vital witness in the war against drugs. Think of it: you'll be going to the States to give evidence.'

'Oh, lord! I mean, I know Ramon is a thug, but I really don't want him to go to prison.'

'We'll talk about it later, shall we? Let's get home first.'

She subsided into a brood, while Jessica and Andrea looked at each other and waggled their eyebrows.

Smart returned in fifteen minutes as promised, and they hurried into the building. It was still only just after seven, and the various concourses were crowded. But this was to their advantage; although they received several curious glances, Jessica felt this was more on account of their looks than the fact they were there.

A man wearing uniform was waiting for them and escorted them through the throng to a gate. 'Passports.'

'I'll say goodbye now,' Smart said, and kissed Jessica on the mouth.

'We couldn't have done it without you,' she acknowledged.

'It was a pleasure. Meeting you has been one of the great experiences of my life.'

He kissed Chloe and Andrea as well, and then Miranda. 'I hope it works out for you,' he told her, and shook hands with Adrian. 'Keep in touch.'

Their passports were returned and they waved goodbye. Next they came to security. 'What now?' Jessica asked.

'No problem,' the man said.

She led the way under the arch, her bag on her shoulder. As expected, a shrill sound blared from the metal detector. The woman manning it raised her eyebrows, and their escort spoke to her rapidly in Spanish. This seemed to satisfy her, and she waved Jessica through and appeared to take no notice at all as Andrea's and Chloe's passage produced the same noise.

'What do you think he told her?' Andrea whispered.

'I shudder to think,' Jessica said.

Then they were walking across the tarmac to the waiting aircraft, still accompanied by their tame official. There were so many things Jessica wanted to ask him, particularly regarding his relationship with Joe Smart, but she didn't think she could without risking offending Adrian.

'That's not a seven-oh-seven?' she asked.

'Exactly, señorita.'

'But . . . how old is it?'

'A few years.'

'You mean less than thirty?'

'Well . . . a little.'

'And it is going to carry us right across the continent?'

'No problem, señorita. It is, how do you say, in good nick.'

'It has only two engines,' Miranda said.

'But it will fly on one.'

'I hope it can.'

'I will wish you goodbye,' the official said, shaking hands with each of them in turn. 'You will have a good flight.' He saluted, and disappeared into the gloom.

They climbed the steps, and were greeted by a smiling, very brunette young woman who, like Ramon's housekeeper, was clearly of Indian ancestry; she wore a pale blue uniform and a sidecap. 'Welcome aboard,' she said. 'You please to be seated?' Her English was remarkably good.

There wasn't much choice, as the interior of the aircraft had been stripped down to bare metal except for two rows of seats immediately behind the flight deck. Adrian sat beside Miranda, Chloe and Andrea sat together, and Jessica sat by herself.

'I will serve drinks as soon as we are airborne,' the hostess said. 'And then dinner. Then you sleep, eh? If you wish anything, ring the bell. My name is Encarna. Your pilot is Captain Alonso, and your co-pilot is Captain Garcia.'

Jessica's head jerked, as did Chloe's and Andrea's. 'Did you say Garcia?'

'Yes. Do you know him?'

'I know someone named Garcia.'

Encarna chuckled. 'Everyone knows someone named Garcia. It is the commonest Spanish surname. Like your English Smith, eh?' She hurried off to seat herself in the jump seat at the rear of the plane. The engines were already running, and a few minutes later they were airborne.

For all the discomfort of her wet clothes – she was intending to do something about that just as soon as possible – Jessica was determined to relax. They were really on their way. In not more than a few hours they would be out of Bolivian air space. She wondered what Ramon was doing now. Presumably he would have found some shelter and probably some support. But as no attempt had been made to stop them from taking off, he either hadn't got to a phone or he had less clout than she had feared.

183

Encarna brought them champagne to drink. 'How many toilets do you have?' Jessica asked.

'We have two, señorita. One forward, here, and one aft.'

'Right, gang. Let's complete those repairs.' She took the aft compartment, stripped to her skin, washed herself all over, dried herself completely with paper towels, added some perfume, then put on her change of clean underwear, shirt and socks. She was stuck with the still damp pants, but she reckoned that if she got a chill in the bum that would be the least of her troubles. Then she tackled her hair and managed to restore some order.

When she returned, Andrea and Chloe had also changed and were looking much happier, which left only Miranda in a state of discomfort – she had nothing to change into – but even she cheered up when Encarna served a surprisingly good meal. 'Do you make this flight often?' Adrian asked chattily.

'Sometimes, señor. We go where we are sent, eh?'

'But not usually with passengers,' Jessica suggested.

'No, no. It is mostly freight. This is, how do you say, special.'

'But you always fly with Captain Alonso?'

'Oh, yes. We are very good friends, Captain Alonso and I.' She bustled off.

'I wonder what she meant by that,' Chloe remarked.

'I suspect what she said,' Jessica suggested, and leaned back, her eyes drooping shut. It had been one of the most dramatic and exhausting days of her life. And when she woke up, she would be in Brazil! She wondered if Chloe would get to Copacabana, and if she would go with her. It seemed a shame to be in Rio and not do the beach.

She fell fast asleep, and awoke with a start as the engines faded.

The Breakout

Jessica sat up. The lights in the cabin had been dimmed while they slept, but now they came on again brightly, and Encarna hurried up from the rear. 'Please to fasten your seatbelts,' she said.

'What the hell is going on?' Adrian inquired. Everyone was now awake, sitting up and rubbing their eyes. The sound of the wind rushing by outside was tremendous; there was a brilliant moon, but below them it was as dark as pitch.

'There is a problem, señor.'

'A problem? There's no power.'

'That is true. I will see what it is.'

'We're going down!' Miranda shouted. 'My God, we're going down!'

The aircraft was certainly descending, and quite fast. Jessica's ears popped.

Andrea turned round to look at her. 'JJ . . .'

For the first time that Jessica could recall, Andrea's voice had a quaver in it. 'Fasten your belts,' she said. And pray? But Encarna had not appeared to be frightened; on the other hand, Encarna was probably trained to cope with emergencies of this nature. She stared out of the window, looking down into the blackness. Am I going to die? she wondered. Somehow, for all the narrow squeaks she had experienced, and the large amount of travelling she had done – usually by air – she had never once considered the possibility that she might be killed in a plane crash.

Encarna emerged from the flight deck, carefully closing the door behind her. 'There has been engine failure,' she announced unnecessarily. 'Captain Alonso hopes to be able to regain power, but it may be necessary to land until repairs are made.'

'Land where?' Chloe asked.

'Down there. It will be all right.'

'Are you trying to say that the captain intends to glide this plane down, into a forest, in the middle of the night?' Adrian demanded.

'Aaagh!' Miranda screamed.

'It will be all right,' Encarna repeated. 'But keep strapped in.' She went aft to take a seat and strap herself in as well.

Now they were dropping very fast. 'We're going to crash!' Miranda shrieked. 'We *are* crashing! We're going to be killed!'

Adrian turned round to look at Jessica, his face a picture of confused alarm.

'It's your plane,' she reminded him. But now she was again feeling the white fury she had known when sliding down the slope into the alligator pit. This was deliberate. Which meant that the pilot had to be working for . . . Ramon? Or was Smart up to something?

She looked out of the window again, wondering what they would hit first, trees or the ground – or water! The thought of again coming face to face with an angry caiman . . . She had the strongest urge to put her rifle together. But that was a waste of time until they were on the ground.

She looked out of the window again, and saw a gleam of light below them. She blinked, and looked again. Nothing. But there had been a pinpoint of light. She was sure of it. Then, without warning, the engines roared back into life.

'Holy hallelujah!' Andrea exclaimed.

Miranda burst into tears.

'This is the captain,' the tannoy said. 'I have regained power, but this may be temporary. I am going to have to set down to investigate. Please remain in your seats and keep your seatbelts fastened.'

'Set down where?' Chloe asked.

'He must know what he's doing,' Adrian said reassuringly.

Jessica had no doubt at all he knew what he was doing. The aircraft was now under full control, but was still descending quite rapidly, and now she again saw lights. They were coming down on a landing strip. The question was, where were they and who controlled the strip – it would have to be a sizeable strip to accommodate even an out-of-date jet.

There was no time to use her GPS, as a moment later they were on the ground, bouncing several times to accompanying shrieks from Miranda. Then they rolled to a stop. Encarna hurried forward. 'Please to remain seated until the doors are opened. Señora!' In her concern she had elevated Jessica – who had opened her bag and taken out the pieces of the ArmaLite – from a 'Miss' to a 'Mrs'.

'I'm a nervous traveller,' Jessica explained. 'Andie, load up.'

Encarna turned to Adrian. 'Señor . . .' She obviously held him responsible for the antics of his people.

'Do you really think that's necessary?' he asked.

'If I didn't, I wouldn't be doing it, sir. My business, and that of my colleagues, is to get you and your sister back to England in one piece. When we board a reputable airline bound for Heathrow, we will surrender our weapons.'

He scratched his head.

'I will open the doors now,' Encarna announced, attempting to regain control of the situation.

'Don't do that.' The gun assembled, Jessica released her belt and stood up, covering the bemused hostess. 'Andie, keep your eye on her.'

Andrea got up and took over, pointing her rifle at Encarna, who gave a little shriek.

Jessica knelt on a seat and peered through the window. Although the thickly packed trees made a black backdrop, in the considerable clearing created by the airstrip the moonlight was almost as bright as day. She saw a couple of shed-like buildings, in one of which there was a gleam of metal, suggesting that there was a vehicle parked under the overhang. Nearer the aircraft was a group of perhaps a dozen people, two of whom were wheeling forward a flight of steps.

Adrian had also been peering out of the window. 'Looks quite civilized. I wonder where we are?'

'That I propose to find out. I think you and Mrs Cuesta should remain seated for the time being, sir,' Jessica said. 'Chloe, you're in charge of the front.'

Chloe took out her pistol, and just in time, for the door to the flight deck was opening. Alonso was first out. 'Now, ladies and gentleman,' he said jovially. 'We are safely down, as you . . .' He gazed down the barrel of Chloe's pistol. 'What is this? What is happening?'

'That is what we would like you to tell us,' Jessica said. 'Just don't touch that door, Encarna.' Encarna was still hovering by the door, not having actually released the catch as yet. From outside there was the sound of several voices. 'But first, Captain, tell your co-pilot to come out. Tell him that if he attempts to send a radio message he is going to wind up in hospital.'

Alonso gazed at the little yellow-haired woman. Then he looked at Adrian. Who attempted a smile. 'She's very positive, isn't she? I really would do as she wishes, old man.'

'The co-pilot,' Jessica said. 'Señor Garcia.'

Alonso spoke over his shoulder, and Garcia came into the cabin looking as thunderstruck as his captain. Jessica reckoned he was no relation to the tour guide, as he was a big, tall man with quite handsome features.

'We have already sent out a mayday call,' Alonso said. 'I expect assistance to be here within the hour.'

'Here being where?'

'It is an emergency strip.'

'Conveniently placed,' Jessica remarked. 'You still haven't told us where. You took off just at seven, and it is now eleven. We have been flying for four hours, and we were told that the flight to Rio would take about seven hours. Would I therefore be right to assume that we are somewhere in Brazil?'

'Ah . . . yes. That is it. We are in Brazil. Help will soon be here.'

'Señor, you are lying. That bugs me. Chloe, shoot him in the leg.'

'Here, I say . . .' Adrian protested.

Chloe aimed.

'All right, all right,' Alonso said. 'We are in Colombia.'

'Say again?'

'We have flown north instead of east. It is very simple. There is nothing for you to worry about.'

'I see. But we did not wish to come to Colombia. Why did you alter the route without telling us?'

'Well . . .'

Someone was banging on the door and shouting.

'We must let them in.'

'What will they do if we do not?'

'They may start shooting.'

'In which case we will shoot back. You have not answered my question. Did Mr Smart instruct you to fly to Colombia instead of Brazil?'

'Here, I say . . .' Adrian protested again.

'No, no, señorita,' Garcia said.

'Then who? Was it Señor Cuesta?'

'Ramon?' Miranda cried. 'But he's in the bush.'

'He *was* in the bush, several hours ago. Señores?'

The pilots exchanged glances, then Alonso said, 'Señor Cuesta pays more than Señor Smart.'

'I see.'

189

'I don't understand any of this,' Adrian confessed.

'It is puzzling, isn't it? I'm afraid that our friend Cuesta is a lot smarter than I thought he was, and has a lot more tentacles than I supposed. He obviously managed to get to a phone long before I thought it could be possible.'

'But why Colombia? If he wanted to stop us, why didn't he just telephone the La Paz airport?'

'Because that would have made the whole thing very public, including his humiliation; he means to deal with us in private. As for bringing us down in Colombia, that's simple enough. He's a drug dealer. That means he has links with other drug dealers all over the world. I imagine he has quite a lot of friends in Colombia. Friends who are now on their way to take care of us. Am I right, Captain?'

'Well . . .' Alonso licked his lips.

'Ramon will never really hurt me,' Miranda declared.

'You may well be right,' Jessica agreed. 'Although after today he may use up a lot of pepper.'

'Oh, my God!'

'But I'm quite sure he will have no compunction whatsoever about hurting *us*. That includes you, my lord.'

'Shoot! What are we to do?'

'That, certainly, if we have to. But we are also going to leave. You got us down, Captain Alonso. Now get us up again.'

'I cannot do this.'

'I should warn you that I am operating on a very short fuse at the moment.'

'I cannot take off. There is no fuel.'

'Just what do you mean by that?'

'I was told to take on only sufficient fuel to reach this airstrip. Well, there is perhaps fifteen minutes left in the tanks. I would burn that warming the engines up for take-off.'

'So what did you intend to do with this heap of junk? Leave it here to rust? There must be a fuel store right here.'

'No, no, señorita. When the men come, they will bring a bowser with them.'

Jessica had an uneasy feeling that he was telling the truth. She looked at Adrian. Who was looking utterly crushed. 'I never inquired about the fuel load. I was told this aircraft had a range of two thousand miles. That bastard Joe . . .'

'It looks as if it might not have been his fault, apart from his having trusted the wrong people.'

'But what are we going to do? I mean, what about those fellows outside?'

As if the 'fellows' outside had heard him, there was a shot, and a great increase in noise; the bullet crunched into the fuselage.

'They are shooting at me!' Alonso shouted.

'I think they are shooting at *us*,' Jessica corrected.

'They are saying they will break open the door,' Encarna said.

'Right,' Jessica said. 'Encarna, pack up all the available food and drink you have on board. It must be in easily transportable bags, or better yet, one bag. *Pronto*. Girls – and you, milady – put on your ponchos. Now, gentlemen, I assume you have a map of this area. Show me where we are.'

Alonso muttered at Garcia, who went to the flight deck and returned with a map. 'Here. You see?'

'I do indeed. That's Brazil just over there.'

'Well, señorita . . .'

She checked the scale. 'Fifteen miles.'

'That is true, señorita, but it is not like walking a road. This is Amazonia. That is the thickest jungle in the world out there. And the border . . . *pouf*! You see it on the map, but it is not a line on the ground, eh?'

'You mean the people who are on their way to do us will follow us across the border.'

'Of course.'

'Well, they'll have fun.' She bent over the map. 'Isn't that a town?'

'Yes. It is called Uaruma.'

'And it is not more than forty miles inside Brazil.'

'But that is still more than fifty miles from here. And you see, it is situated on the river Uaupés, which is a tributary of the Amazon. All the rivers in this area are tributaries of the Amazon. And you see how many there are? So much water, impossible to cross.'

'We'll think of something.'

'And if you get there, there is nothing. Nothing!' His voice rose.

'Again, I'm sure we'll find something.'

'You will die!'

'If that is the rock, then this is the hard place, it seems.' She folded the map and stowed it in her bag. 'Now, Captain, how highly do you value your life?'

'I will do anything you say, señorita.'

'Thank you. You will precede us out of this aircraft, telling your friends to behave themselves to save you – and you, Mr Garcia – from being shot.'

'But, señorita, those men out there are not my friends. They will shoot me.'

Jessica considered.

'Just what are you planning to do?' Adrian asked. 'How do we get to this place, U-whatever? We've no transport.'

'Those people out there must have transport. In fact, I think I've seen it.'

'But what happens when we run into thick bush? Or these rivers?'

'In my book, my lord, one only crosses one bridge at a time – and then only as one comes to it. The situation is that if we stay here, Ramon Cuesta, or some of his chums, are going to turn up at any moment. I don't know what they will do to you, as you are his brother-in-law, but I have a pretty good idea what he is going to do to me and my assistants, as he has already tried to feed me to one of his pet alligators, or caiman, or whatever they are.'

'Good lord! Did he really do that?'

'I should also repeat that I have been given a job to do by my commanding officer, and that is to conduct Mrs Cuesta to England as a material witness, and this I intend to do. So, are you coming with me, or staying here?'

'Well, if you put it that way . . . But how do we get out?'

'How many people do you reckon are there, Captain?'

'I do not know, señorita.'

'Captain, you are bugging me. You have been here before. You must have, or you would not have known where to look for the landing lights and how to come down. How many people were here the last time?'

'I think . . . maybe a dozen.'

That tied in with her first estimate. 'And how long do we have before the rest of them arrive?'

'I do not know. Perhaps half an hour.'

'And what vehicle do they have over there in that shed?'

'Maybe a jeep.'

'A dozen men come in and out by jeep?'

'No, no, señorita. They mostly come in and out by chopper.'

'Right. And that's how the reinforcements are coming now.'

'I think so, señorita.'

'What about this fuel bowser you're expecting?'

'That will come later. After . . . well . . .'

'After we have been removed. Well, I would like you to switch off the cabin lights. But before you do, I wish you to understand that if any one of you attempts to lay a finger on any one of us, I am going to shoot him dead.'

Alonso looked at Jessica, and then at the rifle, clearly doubting either her ability or her mental strength.

'Shall I demonstrate?' She looked past the two pilots into the flight deck. 'What's that hanging above the window?'

'It is my good luck charm, señorita. A toy elephant.'

'Then I apologize for bringing you bad luck.' She levelled the rifle and squeezed the trigger. The plastic elephant disintegrated, and so did the windshield behind it, which would have the effect of grounding the plane for some time, Jessica reflected.

Miranda screamed, as did Encarna. The chatter from outside grew louder.

'You have wrecked my aircraft,' Alonso complained.

'I told you she was a difficult woman to get on with,' Adrian reminded them.

'So if you wouldn't mind,' Jessica said, pointing her gun at Alonso.

Alonso nodded to Garcia, and the cabin was plunged into darkness.

Jessica listened intently while she waited for her eyes to become accustomed to the gloom. Thanks to the moonlight outside this was a matter of seconds, and in fact inside the cabin it remained quite bright. She decided against further involving the crew, or attempting to use them to facilitate their escape: she suspected they would only be a liability. 'Right. Now, my advice to you is to get down on the floor and stay there until it's safe to come out. Encarna, is that food ready?'

'It is here.' Encarna's voice shook.

'Chloe, will you take charge of it. Use your flashlight.'

Chloe followed the beam down the aisle to where Encarna waited with two large plastic bags.

'Will you move down the cabin, please, my lord. And you, milady.'

Adrian helped Miranda up and they shuffled to the rear.

Jessica put on her poncho and followed. 'Now, Encarna, open the door and stand clear. Andie, you'll monitor everything that is said, but stand by to open fire.'

Andrea nodded.

'Come along. Encarna.'

'They will shoot me.'

'Not if you stand to one side. Open the door. Close up behind me, my lord. And you, milady. Ready, Chloe?'

'Ready.'

'We're going to die,' Miranda said. 'I know we're going to die. I want to stay here. Ramon will never harm me.'

'Milady, you are coming with us if your brother has to carry you.'

Adrian shuffled his feet nervously.

'Now, Encarna. *Pronto!*'

Encarna drew a deep breath, gazed at Andrea – who was standing opposite her on the other side of the doorway, rifle at the ready – then she grasped the heavy lever and forced it up before pulling the door out of its socket and back towards her. The flight of steps had been pushed against the plane, and as the door opened, a man standing on the top attempted to enter. Andrea swung her rifle and the barrel caught him across the face. He tumbled backwards with a shriek and from the continuing noise apparently fell down the steps, taking one of his companions with him.

'Good girl,' Jessica said, advancing to the door but keeping out of any line of fire. 'All right, Encarna. Tell them to assemble at the foot of the steps, without weapons, or we are going to come out shooting.'

Encarna shouted, and someone shouted back. 'They do not believe you, señorita. They do not believe you have more than a single weapon. They say you must come out with your hands up or they will shoot *you*.'

'If that's the way they want to play. Stand by, and when I say go, follow me.' Jessica stepped into the doorway and loosed off the entire remainder of her magazine. The first two shots she fired at the men who were still lying on the ground at the foot of the steps, but deliberately aimed just to miss them. The rest of the magazine she fired at the group of figures some distance away. They separated with screams and shouts, and at least two went down. 'Cover, Andie,' Jessica said. 'Go, go, go!'

She led the way down the steps, discarding her spent magazine and slapping a fresh box into place as she did so, jumping over the two men still lying there, unhurt but apparently paralysed with fright, then running across the flattened earth to the sheds and the jeep. Behind her she heard the sounds of the footfalls of the others, and Andrea, bringing up the rear, sprayed the area to left and right. Several shots were fired in return, but there were no shouts to indicate that anyone had been hit.

Jessica reached the shed and a man loomed in front of her. He did not appear to be armed, so she swung her rifle and hit him on the side of the head; he went down without a sound. The rest arrived beside her, panting. Miranda was moaning. 'You're hurting me.' Adrian had hold of her arm.

'Anyone hit?' Jessica asked.

'I'm in agony,' Miranda complained. 'I'll never forgive you for this, Adrian. Never!'

'Listen, get into the front of the jeep,' Jessica said. 'Will you drive, my lord? Mount up, kids.'

Chloe and Andrea scrambled into the back, and Jessica discovered there were three of them. 'What the hell are you doing here?'

Encarna panted. 'I must come with you.'

'Why?'

'If I stay, they will shoot me. I know this. They will say I have helped you.'

She had virtually admitted to being Alonso's mistress, but she could just be telling the truth. Anyway, there was no time for argument: her allegiance could be sorted out later. 'Well, get in, then.' The hostess scrambled in beside Andrea, and Jessica joined them. 'Let's go.'

*　　*　　*

Adrian started the engine. 'Where do I go?'

Jessica pointed. 'Follow that track out of here to begin with. We wish to place ourselves as far away as possible from that aircraft before anyone else arrives.'

'I would say that track leads north.'

'Doesn't matter. There'll be other tracks.' She hoped. But there could be no doubt that their first priority had to be to make themselves scarce.

Adrian gunned the engine and they bounced out of the shed. Several shots were fired after them, but none were in the least accurate, although they had Miranda screaming. Jessica had to restrain Andrea from returning fire.

Then she turned to Encarna. 'If you intend to come with us, you will have to make yourself useful.'

'Oh, yes, señorita. You tell me what to do.'

'All I want at the moment is information. You said you fly regularly with Captain Alonso?'

'Oh, yes. We are old friends.'

'Then you have been here before.'

'I have been here,' Encarna said cautiously.

'Have you been on this road before?'

'I have been one time on this road.'

'Great. Where does it go?'

'It leads up to join the main road at Morihal.'

'Which is?'

'A town.'

'In which direction?'

'It is north.'

'How far?'

'Fifty, maybe sixty, kilometres. But they will know to look for you there.'

'I figured that. Is there a turn-off to the east? To the border?'

'There is a turn-off to the east. I do not know if it goes to the border.'

'Lights,' Andrea said.

'Switch off yours and stop,' Jessica told Adrian. He obeyed without question, pulling in to the side of the road while Jessica and Andrea readied their rifles. But the lights, although low, were in the sky.

'Choppers,' Chloe said. She had also drawn her pistol.

'Nobody move,' Jessica said.

She suspected that the approaching helicopters – there were three – had been warned that there had been trouble at the airstrip, hence their low altitude, but they whirred overhead apparently without seeing the stationary jeep. She waited until the noise of the engines had faded before letting Adrian go on. 'How far to the turn-off?'

'Not far,' Encarna said. 'Maybe ten kilometres.'

'As fast as you can, my lord,' Jessica suggested.

They bounced over the pitted surface, often splashing through water, which indicated that there had been recent rain. 'I am going to be sick,' Miranda announced.

'Lean well out,' Jessica advised.

'Don't you think I should stop for a moment?' Adrian asked.

'No, sir. I do not think you should stop, not even for a second.'

'Turn-off,' Andrea said. As always, her eyesight was sharper than any of theirs.

But now Jessica saw the slight parting of the trees to the right. 'Hard right, sir,' she told Adrian.

He obeyed, and they entered an even rougher and wetter track than the original. But at last they were going in the right direction.

'Are we going to make it?' Chloe asked.

'So far.'

'What's your plan?'

'To get back to England.' Jessica wasn't in the mood for elaborating just then. She had quite a few ideas, but they would have to wait to be put into practice. Their first business was to evade any close pursuit.

They had driven for a further half an hour when Chloe, who had the sharpest hearing, again said, 'Choppers.'

The whirring became louder. 'Douse the lights and pull off,' Jessica said.

Once again they sought shelter beneath the trees at the side of the road. But the whirring came closer. 'They are following the track,' Encarna said. 'They know we are on it.'

But it was only one helicopter. Therefore, although Alonso must have told them that the fugitives were making for the border, they were obviously looking at other tracks as well. 'Just sit tight,' she said, and then added, 'Shit!' Because the aircraft had a searchlight, which was playing along the track. 'Nobody move.'

The beam came up to where they were, and then passed on. 'Whew!' Adrian commented.

'Don't count your chickens . . .'

'It's coming back,' Andrea said.

'Until they're hatched. Everybody out. Into the bush.'

They scrambled out of the jeep and into the undergrowth beside the road, and watched the light approaching, very slowly. The helicopter was hovering. Andrea stroked the barrel of her gun. 'We could take him out.'

'He'll be in communication with the others,' Jessica said. 'Better to hope he hasn't actually seen us.'

But a moment later the machine was directly overhead, the searchlight shining full on the jeep. 'That's it,' Jessica said. Until now, as far as she knew, they had not actually killed anybody, and she would have liked to keep it that way, but she could not doubt that the people above them intended to kill them. She aimed and fired. Andrea followed her lead, but as they did so, something plummeted down from the aircraft's doorway, following the beam to

199

land on the jeep. There was an explosion, and flames shot high in the air; the watchers had to crouch to avoid being knocked over.

'Bastard,' Andrea snapped, and fired twice more. But Jessica had already seen that their first bullets had struck home. Despite having had the time to drop the grenade, the helicopter was reeling. Andrea's shots finished the job. The aircraft slipped sideways and plunged into the trees with another great *whoosh!* of sound and smoke and fire.

'My God!' Adrian commented.

Miranda stared open-mouthed. Encarna crossed herself.

'Think there'll be any survivors?' Chloe asked.

'I doubt it. And even if there are, we can't have them with us. They'll have radioed for help – and, incidentally, pinpointed us.'

'So what do we do now?' Andrea asked.

Jessica got up. 'We walk.'

'Walk!' Miranda shrieked. 'Again?'

'I don't think it would be a good idea to stay here. As I said, those people will have pinpointed our position. Also, as they have been shot down, their playmates will know better than to present such a target next time. But if they have to call up ground support from sixty kilometres away, we have a couple of hours to move on.'

'But . . . move on where?' Adrian asked.

'I think, to begin with, just south of east. Half a mo, and I'll establish our position.' She used her GPS, and then Andrea and Chloe held the map for her and Encarna shone the torch while she located it. 'Right. Ten miles to the border, and then another forty to Uaruma.'

'But there's nothing in between,' Adrian said, peering at the map. 'No roads, no villages . . .'

'We don't really want to come across any villages on this side of the border, my lord. Ten to one they'll be in the pay of one of the drug barons. As for roads, they won't be a lot of help without the jeep.'

'But that's jungle! And those little green lines . . .'

'Are rivers. Or at least streams.'

'Do you reckon they'll have those . . . What are they called?' Chloe asked.

'Piranha,' Andrea said helpfully.

'That's it. I saw a programme on telly about them once. They can strip a man to his skeleton in ten seconds. I suppose they'd do a woman even quicker.'

Miranda burst into tears.

'Sergeant Jones,' Adrian said, becoming very formal. 'I do not think my sister is capable of making this trek.'

'Then tell us your alternative, my lord. Suppose we sit here and shoot it out when the drugs people catch up with us. What do you think will happen?'

'We'd be killed,' Chloe said.

'Well . . .' Adrian said.

'Okay. Supposing we sit here and when they turn up, we surrender. What do you think will happen then?'

'We will be killed,' Encarna said.

'So the piranha are better odds. And incidentally, sir – and milady – the proven cases of humans being eaten by piranha fish in any one year can be counted on the fingers of one hand.' She had no idea whether or not she was right, but the authority in her tone demolished the opposition. 'Right,' she said. 'Is there any food left?'

'It's all left.' Chloe held up the two bags. 'I brought them with me when I left the jeep.'

'Remind me to recommend you for the Queen's Police Medal. Let's go.'

Adrian had one last protest. 'Don't you think that we should at least wait for daylight?'

Jessica looked at her watch. 'One o'clock. What time does it get light around here, Encarna?'

'Maybe six o'clock. We are virtually on the equator.'

'So we can't wait for five hours, my lord. By then this place will be swarming with gunmen, who will know this bush much better than us. Come on.'

'I am so tired,' Miranda complained. 'And filthy. And just, well . . .'

'You can have a hot bath when we get to Rio,' Jessica promised.

'Rio? Is that where we're going? Rio?'

'That was our destination, remember?'

'But . . .' Adrian said. 'That's more than a thousand miles away.'

'I should think a whole lot more, from where we are now. So let's make a move. We can use the road for another hour.'

Even on the road progress remained very slow. They were exhausted from the day's adventures, except for Adrian and Encarna, and Jessica suspected that even Encarna was exhausted emotionally, while Adrian was clearly in a very nervous state. To make matters worse, after an hour it began to rain, exposing the hostess and Adrian to the wet. The other women at least had their ponchos, but their feet and legs were by then soaked in any event as they splashed through a succession of vast puddles.

After an hour Jessica called a halt. 'So far so good.'

They could hear nothing from behind them, but by now the rain was falling so heavily as to deaden all sound.

'Two thirty,' she said. 'What time would that be in England?'

'Seven thirty,' Andrea suggested.

'More like eight thirty,' Chloe argued.

'Time enough. Let's go under that tree, and you two hold out your ponchos over me.' She knelt at the foot of the tree, and they obliged. Sheltered as much as possible from the rain, she used her mobile. It rang several times before being answered.

'Yes?'

Jessica recognized the voice easily enough. 'Good morning, Mrs Adams. May I speak with the commander?'

'Who? Who is this?'

'Detective-Sergeant Jones.'

'You're very indistinct.'

'It's a poor line where I am. Is the commander about?'

'He's in the bathroom. Can he call you back?'

'I don't think that would be a very good idea, ma'am. It's quite urgent. I'll hold on.'

There was a grunting noise from the other end of the phone, but a few moments later Adams spoke. 'JJ? I do wish you'd call me at the office and not at home.'

'I apologize, sir. But I feel you might like to be brought up to date with the situation.'

'You mean you're back in England? What's that dreadful noise? I can hardly hear you.'

'I am in the middle of a rainstorm, sir.'

'You mean you are standing in the middle of a rainstorm to telephone me? At home? Really, JJ, have you been drinking?'

'No, sir. I am standing in the middle of a rainstorm because I have nowhere else to stand. I am not in England. I am in a place called Amazonia. It's on the border of Colombia and Brazil.'

'Good lord! Whatever are you doing there?'

'It's a long story, sir. However, it is a place from which my companions and I would like to be extracted as rapidly as possible. I should say that I have both Lord Lichton and Lady Miranda with me.'

'Good Lord!' Adams remarked again. 'I hope they are all right?'

'We are all very wet, very tired, and will soon be very hungry – supposing we are not very dead. I suspect that we are being hunted by every drug baron in South America. Now, sir, we are about five miles from the Brazilian border—'

'What is your nearest town?'

'On this side of the border there is no town we can risk. On the other side, about forty miles further on, there is a place called Uaruma. This is situated on the river Uaupés. This is our immediate destination. It is pretty rough country, so I reckon it will take us about four days to get there. It would be very helpful if we could be met there – or preferably before we get there, perhaps as soon as we are across the border – and, as I say, extracted.'

'You do land yourself in some impossible situations, JJ. I did say that you could expect no assistance on this mission.'

'I understand that, sir. But the mission has been completed. Now it is simply a matter of getting home. Or not.'

'Hm. You say Lord Lichton and his sister are with you? Let me speak with his lordship.'

Jessica held up the phone, and Adrian, who along with Miranda and Encarna had joined them under the tree, took it. 'Yes, Commander. Yes. Oh, indeed. Yes, she's been an absolute brick. What did they say about Wolfe, eh? Haw haw haw. Yes, old man, we should be most grateful.' He handed back the phone. 'He wants another word.'

'JJ? Give me your coordinates.'

'Our present position is . . .' She checked her GPS. 'Good heavens. We're exactly on the equator.'

'That must be pretty hot.'

'I'm sure it will be, sir, whenever it stops raining. We are also seventy degrees one minute thirty-four seconds West Longitude.'

'Wait a moment and I'll write that down.'

Jessica waited, rainwater running down her neck.

'Very good,' he said. 'Now, you will, as you say, proceed towards this place Ua—? . . . Well, you know where to find it. I will see what I can organize. You do understand that we are not on the closest of terms with the Brazilian government. But as I say, I will organize something. It will be a matter of finding out what the navy have in the Caribbean and obtaining over-flying rights, either from Venezuela or Guyana, and then getting some of our people out there. If anything can be done within four days, I will let you know. What you must do is keep moving towards this town you have identified, and keep in touch. Call my office every day with a position report so we can monitor the situation.'

'Yes, sir.'

'Well, then, good luck.'

Jessica restored the mobile in her bag. 'Let's go. We really want to be across the border by midday tomorrow. I mean, today.'

'Aren't we going to rest?' Miranda asked. 'I am absolutely exhausted. And my feet are blistered. I couldn't walk another step.'

'We'll rest when we're in Brazil,' Jessica said.

'Company,' Chloe remarked.

The Jungle

They could now all hear the chatter of the helicopter. But the noise was louder than before. 'Two of them,' Chloe said.

'Behind the tree,' Jessica snapped.

'They know this is the end of the track,' Encarna said. 'They will put down their people here.'

'Okay, so we withdraw into the bush.'

'Can't we take them out, like the last one?' Andrea asked.

'It's not yet self-defence. Our best bet is to avoid them, if we can.' Jessica checked her compass. 'That way. You first, my lord, with Lady Miranda. We'll cover you.'

Adrian hesitated for a moment, still reluctant to leave any fighting to the women, then held Miranda's arm and helped her up.

'But stay in sight,' Jessica said. 'If you get separated in this bush we may never find you again. Hang on to this.' She gave him her Sauer. 'But don't use it unless it's a matter of life and death; the noise will give away our position.' He thrust the pistol into his pocket, and then pushed Miranda into the bushes. 'Now we follow,' Jessica said. 'Slowly. Go.'

Andrea and Chloe crept away.

Now the noise was very close, and through the trees they could see the helicopters settle on to the ground and their passengers disembark. 'I make it about twenty men,' Jessica said.

'They will have Indian trackers with them,' Encarna whispered.

'They'll still be coming on our terms. And they don't know our firepower. Go.'

Encarna pushed into the bushes, muttering a curse in Spanish as her skirt snagged on a branch.

Jessica followed, every few seconds turning round to peer through the trees and listen to the chattering voices as the men hunted around for any signs of the fugitives – and from their exclamations it appeared they were finding a great deal. She muttered a curse herself when she realized that the rain was slackening, which would make it easier for the Indians to follow their trail.

She moved back as rapidly as she could, the poncho protecting her from the worst of the waiting thorns and bushes, and suddenly bumped into Encarna; she realized that the entire party had stopped. 'What are you waiting for?'

'There's this stream . . .' Adrian explained.

Jessica went forward to stand beside him and look at the tumbling water. Now the rain had stopped altogether, and above their heads the moon had broken through the clouds. 'We knew there was going to be a lot of water. And this one isn't very wide. I reckon about twenty yards. How deep do you think it is, Encarna?'

Encarna peered at the water. 'Only a metre.'

'If that's the biggest obstacle we meet, we're laughing. Will you cross, my lord? Those people are not very far behind us.'

'Ah . . . what about these piranha things?'

Jessica looked at Encarna.

'The water is running too fast for them,' Encarna said.

'There you go,' Jessica said encouragingly.

But then Encarna added, 'I think.'

'Ah. Can't we move along the stream?' Adrian asked.

'It will still have to be crossed, my lord. And those people are coming closer every moment . . . Oh, all right.' She drew a deep breath, and stepped into the water. It was cool, and came to her thighs, soaking her pants all over again. She refused to admit that she was afraid, but her heart was pounding as she wondered what it would feel like to have a mouthful of razor-sharp teeth sinking into her flesh. Suddenly the far bank seemed a lot further than the length of a cricket pitch.

She held the ArmaLite in front of her in both hands, arms extended, and stepped out vigorously, wishing she could see into the dark water, and then deciding it was probably best not to. Stones turned under her boots and once or twice she nearly fell, but then she was out the other side and standing on reasonably dry land. 'Piece of cake,' she said. 'Encarna.'

The hostess scooped her skirt to her waist and stepped in, giving a little shriek as her knickers were soaked, and then another as her foot slipped. 'Mind your step,' Jessica said, and then gave her a hand to help her out. 'Now you, milady.'

'I am not going into that water,' Miranda declared. 'No way. No, no, no.'

'My lord, will you bring your sister over, please. And ask her to be quiet.'

'Come along,' Adrian said. 'There really is no risk.'

'I am not . . . Put me down, you beast,' she demanded as he swept her from the ground and stepped into the stream.

'Quiet!' he told her.

'Mind your footing,' Jessica said. But as she spoke he slipped and sat down in the water, releasing Miranda, who uttered a piercing shriek.

'Shit!' Jessica muttered. Up till now their voices had been adequately concealed by the rushing of the stream, but anyone within half a mile would have heard that scream. 'Andie, Chloe, get across.'

The two policewomen splashed across while Adrian struggled back to his feet and retrieved Miranda, who had swallowed some water and was gasping and spitting. Jessica and Encarna were waiting to help them out. Now they could hear voices very clearly. 'We're going to have to stop them here,' Jessica said. 'And I mean *stop*. If we let them chase us into the bush, which they know so much better than us, they'll pick us off one by one. What's the ammo situation?'

'I have half a magazine,' Andrea said. 'And two spares.'

That would be roughly fifty rounds, Jessica calculated. She knew Andie had only used her pistol once or twice at the ranch; it also had two spare magazines, which made another fifty rounds. She was already on her second box for the ArmaLite, but she had one spare, and her Sauer, now in Adrian's pocket, was also unused. 'Chloe?'

Chloe checked. 'Half my box intact, and two spares.'

A further fifty rounds. 'Take these, my lord.' She gave Adrian her two spare boxes for the pistol. 'The magazine is full. Now, if you two ladies will take cover. I hate to ask you to do this, but you'd be safest lying on the ground.'

'I can shoot a gun,' Encarna said.

Jessica considered briefly, wondering how far the hostess could be trusted. Then she nodded: Encarna had burned her bridges by escaping with them. 'Okay. Andie, give Encarna your pistol and your spare magazines. Now, spread out and keep down. You come next to me, Encarna. Now listen. We're not short of ammo, but we can't afford to waste it; we don't know how many other shoot-outs we're going to have. Try to make every shot count: remember that we have to discourage these guys so much that they pack it in.'

'You mean you want us to actually kill somebody?' Adrian asked.

'*Every*body, if we can.'

'But I say, we can't just start shooting people, killing them. You said you only did that in self-defence.'

'My lord, I can assure you that they intend to kill us if they cannot capture us. And I'm afraid that I cannot contemplate myself, or any of my women, being captured by those thugs. We know what they can do. In my estimation this is a life-or-death situation, and we are entitled to defend ourselves by every means possible: that means hitting them before they hit us. Now, please remember: make your first shots count, as they will go to ground the moment we open up. But no one fire until I do.'

Adrian subsided, somewhat nervously fingering his weapon, and they crouched amidst the bushes, listening to the sound of the approaching people. Then a man appeared on the bank opposite, studying the ground. He gave a shout, and was rapidly joined by several others. 'Eight,' Jessica muttered. Not enough. But there was nothing for it now; they were too close for an immediate withdrawal. And, to her relief, they were all carrying weapons: pistols in their belts and machetes in their hands. She was not really into shooting unarmed men, however hostile.

She slid her hand up and down the barrel of the ArmaLite as the first man stepped into the water. Equally, and despite her determined words to Adrian, she also had no desire to kill anyone in cold blood. So she aimed at his machete, and fired. The bullet struck the steel with a tremendous *thwang!* and ricocheted into the trees. Instantly the men on the bank drew their pistols and began firing, but they had no targets and were immediately overwhelmed by the volley from the east bank. Four went down. The man in the water uttered a scream and turned back, but fell as another volley was fired. The remaining men had been seeking shelter, but the policewomen had anticipated that and lowered their sights. From the screams and groans every one of the opposition had been hit.

The man in the water slowly and painfully dragged himself on to dry land. Encarna levelled her pistol, but Jessica caught her hand. 'He won't be coming after us. Withdraw,' she commanded, and looked at Miranda, who was lying on the ground with her hands on her head. 'My lord, will you bring your sister.'

She reckoned they had earned a respite.

*   *   *

They kept going all the rest of the night, only occasionally pausing for a rest. They splashed through several more small streams, muttered curses as they were seized by trailing vines or struck by drooping branches or tripped by unseen bushes. With the ending of the rain they were also assailed by thousands of midges and mosquitoes; they sprayed themselves with citronella, to the accompaniment of complaints about the smell from Miranda. But by dawn Jessica reckoned they had covered a good five miles, and she was able to confirm this with her GPS. 'All right,' she said. 'Fall out and rest.'

They collapsed where they stood while she surveyed them. The three policewomen were now best off, their thick pants and ponchos having protected them from the worst of the flora, although they looked sufficiently bedraggled. But Miranda, if also protected above the thighs, had bleedings legs from the several cuts she had received; at least she was so exhausted she was no longer grumbling. Adrian's blazer was slashed and torn, and at some time during the night he had discarded his tie. Encarna had fared the worst, her uniform also torn and slashed, her stockings in rags, and her legs also bleeding. She had lost her sidecap, and her hair was a tangled soaking mess. But that went for all of them.

'Chloe, break out the grub,' Jessica commanded.

'I couldn't eat a thing,' Miranda groaned.

'You must. You have to keep up your strength.'

'I'm so thirsty.'

'Water water everywhere, and never a drop to drink when you need it,' Jessica agreed. 'Have you anything liquid in those bags, Chloe?'

Chloe investigated. 'Four cans of beer and two bottles of wine.'

'Forget the wine; that'll only make us thirstier. We'll share the beer.'

She sat down with a sigh, and Andrea gave her a can. She

took a swig and handed it back: it was warm, and there wasn't anywhere near enough of it. 'These streams we come to,' she asked Encarna, 'can we drink the water?'

'It is not good, but . . .'

'Better a case of dysentery than dying of thirst. OK, guys, as we can't hear any pursuit, we'll give ourselves three hours. But we'll have to keep a watch. Andie, Chloe, we'll do one hour each. I'll take the first hour; Chloe, you're next.'

'Here, I say,' Adrian protested, 'I'll take a watch.'

'You rest up, my lord. Your business is looking after your sister.' Who already appeared to be asleep. Andrea and Chloe also settled down as best they could beside each other on the still damp earth. 'You too, Encarna,' Jessica said.

'I would like to be of help.'

'You already have been, and I know you will again, because of your knowledge of the country. How do you know so much about it, anyway?'

'*Pouf.* I was born and raised in the country.'

'In Bolivia?'

'Oh, yes. I am Bolivian. I was born in a village called Araguey. My stepfather was the head man there. The *alcalde.* What you call the mayor. He is dead now, so now my stepbrother is *alcalde.* My real father was American, you see. That is why I speak the language so good.'

Jessica gulped, less interested in Encarna's apparently tangled history than . . . 'Your stepbrother's name isn't by any chance Santos?'

'Why, that is right, señorita. You have been to Araguey?'

'Briefly. Your brother was very kind. He rented us his truck.'

'That is good. I will tell him you say so when I go back.' Then her face fell. 'Will I go back?'

'Ah,' Jessica commented. 'We will have to discuss this when we get out of here.'

'If I cannot go back, I would like to go to England. I have heard it is very good there. This is true?'

'Yes. For most people. I'll see what I can do. Now you go and have a rest.'

Encarna hesitated. 'If they come, it will be very quietly.'

Jessica nodded. 'I am relying on that to slow them up.' But she was sure that the devastating firepower they had revealed had entirely discouraged the Colombians, who after all could only have become involved at the request of Ramon and not on their own account; she suspected they were taking their wounded to somewhere they could be treated while they waited for orders and no doubt more firepower of their own.

Encarna made a nest for herself, leaving Jessica to reflect what a small world it was, and also to make a mental note to tell the girls not to mention Araguey, as she felt rather despicable at the way she was using the mestiza woman after having robbed her village and wounded her brother. On the other hand, she reminded herself, the hostess had joined them of her own free will – but thank God for that!

Adrian sat beside her. 'I simply don't know how to tell you how much I appreciate all that you have done, and are doing.'

'Even if you don't approve of all of my methods?'

'Well, you see, in the army, it's been a long time since we've fought an all-out war; all our recent operations have been covered by things like rules of engagement, and it's very rare for those to include the right to shoot to kill. I suppose that doesn't apply in your profession.'

'Oh, it does. As I told you, we can only shoot to kill to protect our client, or if our own life is in danger. In this case, I reckon both those criteria apply. Tell me, my lord, who was this man Wolfe you and the commander were finding so amusing?'

'General Wolfe, don't you know. The chappie who captured Quebec in 1759.'

'I don't get the connection between him and us.'

'Oh, well, you see, the generals in London thought Wolfe was mad, but when they suggested this to George III, he said, "If Wolfe is mad, I wish he'd bite some of my other generals."'

'I see. You think I'm mad.'

'It was only a joke. And a compliment, you know. Wolfe was one of our greatest soldiers. Do you think we're going to come through? That your boss will be able to organize something?'

'Yes, on both counts. I believe I can get us out of Colombia and as far as this place Uaruma, and, if necessary, all the way to Rio, although that could take several weeks. But I also know that the commander can do practically anything he wants to, if he sets his mind to it.'

'As he respects yours. JJ, when this is over . . .'

'As I have said before, sir, I think it would be best if we considered what we should do when this is over.'

'Hm. Yes. I suppose you're right. Well, I'd better see how Mira is getting on. She's not really a bad sort, you know – just, at the moment, a little out of her depths.'

'I'm sure she is, sir.'

He glanced at her, and then looked at Andrea, lying flat on her back, legs outstretched. Her hair had flopped across her face, and moved gently as she breathed. Chloe, lying beside her, was on her side, curled into a ball.

'Quite a sight, aren't they?' Jessica asked.

His head jerked as he flushed. 'They're awfully good. And loyal.'

'They are. We've worked together before.'

'I'm sure. They seem very good friends.'

'They are. They share a flat.'

'Ah,' he commented, and went to join his sister.

She was feeling increasingly confident. There was still no sign of any further pursuit, and although she entirely accepted

Encarna's warning that if the Colombians were still following they would be doing so as stealthily as possible, she also stuck to her own conviction that even if they had been reinforced caution would slow up their pursuit irretrievably. Equally she would have supposed that, having to find them all over again, the Columbians would use helicopters to spot their trail, and there was no sign of those, either.

Her immediate concern was food; she would have to rely on Encarna for that.

She was relieved by Chloe. 'When do you think we can have a bath?'

'When we get to Brazil.'

She slept soundly, and was awakened by Andrea. 'All well?'

'Not a cloud in the sky.'

And she was right. The morning, now well advanced, was quite hot; even the bugs had disappeared for the time being.

'When do you think we can have a bath?'

'Keep dreaming,' Jessica said, and set about getting everyone moving.

First they ate the rest of the food, and drank the last of the beer. Jessica considered dumping the wine, but decided against it. One never knew. 'I reckon we've still got at least four days to go to reach Uaruma,' she told Encarna. 'What chance do we have of living off the country?'

'No problem,' Encarna said. 'You have knife, eh?'

'Ah . . . yes. But I didn't mean we'd live off each other.'

Encarna giggled. 'You give me the knife.'

Jessica did so, and they watched with interest as she selected the straightest thin branch of a tree she could find, cut it off, then trimmed it of all leaves and protuberances before shaving one end to a sharp point. 'You have matches?'

'Yes. You want to burn the end?'

'No, no. It is to cook the fish.'

'Ah . . . right. Which fish?'

'I will show you.'

They set off. Miranda was now limping very badly, and her sandals kept coming off. 'When do we stop walking?' she asked. 'I seem to have been walking forever.'

'You'll get used to it,' Jessica advised.

'My feet are a mass of blisters. They'll never be the same again.'

They came to another stream. 'Now, please to sit down,' Encarna said. 'And make no sounds, eh?'

They were happy to obey her. By now they had all taken off their ponchos, as it was very hot. Encarna removed her tattered jacket, pulled up her skirt and tucked it into her knickers, and then stepped into the water carrying her home-made spear. She chose a position almost in midstream, the water swirling about her thighs, and stood there, absolutely still, the spear poised.

A minute passed, then two, then five. 'How long?' Miranda whispered.

'Shhh,' her brother recommended.

Encarna suddenly moved, thrusting the spear down with tremendous speed and force before jerking it up and hurling it on to the bank; impaled on the point was an extremely large fish, flapping desperately.

'Lunch!' Chloe cried.

Encarna waded out. 'Is good?'

'You should be on telly,' Jessica told her. 'What is it?'

'We call it *lukunani*. Is very good.'

The hostess also showed them how to light a fire just sufficient to fry the fish but not to give away any tell-tale smoke or to set alight the entire jungle. Then she skinned and gutted the fish, wrapped it in leaves, and laid it on the glowing embers to produce a delicious meal. After they had eaten she carefully dragged earth and leaves over the place where the fire had been to hide the traces.

An hour after their late breakfast they came to their first

216

real river. Unlike the streams they had previously crossed, this flowed fairly slowly, and it was a good fifty yards wide. 'Gosh,' Andrea commented.

'How deep do you reckon that is?' Jessica asked.

Encarna pinched her lip. 'Four, maybe five metres.'

'How do we get across?' Chloe asked.

'We swim,' Jessica said. 'I thought you were desperate for a bath?' She checked her GPS. 'If it'll cheer you up, that is Brazil.'

'It is not good,' Encarna said.

'You don't want to go to Brazil?'

'Oh, yes. I think Brazil is good, for me and for you. But that water . . . There will be fish.'

'Piranha?'

'I think so, maybe.'

'Shit! Advice, please.'

'We're going to die,' Miranda moaned, sinking to her knees. 'I just know it. We're going to be eaten alive.'

'How accurate is she?' Jessica asked.

'Well . . . maybe there are no fish here.'

'Let's assume there are.'

'Well, they will only attack us if they can smell us, smell blood or something.'

'You have got to be kidding.'

Encarna looked at the cuts on her legs and Miranda's; the three policewomen and Adrian were also scratched and in places cut on their arms. 'You must make yourself smell bad,' Encarna said. 'But not rotten, eh? Just a big stink. You have something?'

Jessica snapped her fingers. 'Citronella.'

'It'll wash off in the water,' Adrian objected.

'Given time. But we're not going to hang about, right?'

'Who's going to go first?' Chloe asked.

Jessica looked around at their faces; even Andrea was clearly scared. 'Me,' Jessica said.

They watched her as she took off her boots and her trousers, and stuffed them into her shoulder bag; as this was waterproof, there was no risk to her GPS or mobile. Then she secured the bag round her shoulders and in the middle of her back, adding her rifle in the same fashion. Next she coated every inch of her legs and arms with the strong-smelling liquid; she also covered her face and even sprayed some on to her hair. 'How do I smell?'

'You wouldn't draw a crowd,' Andrea said.

'Great. Now . . .' She looked from face to face. 'I have no doubt I am going to make it, but just in case, Andie, you're in charge.'

'Oh, JJ . . .' Andrea looked ready to weep. 'What'll we do?'

'I have no idea. Keep your fingers crossed.'

Andrea and Chloe both embraced her, as did Encarna. Adrian looked embarrassed, and then shook her hand. Miranda merely looked embarrassed. 'Good luck.'

Jessica gave them the thumbs-up, walked to the edge of the river, and peered into the turgid depths. The water was brown but actually clearer than she'd expected, and she thought she could see fish flitting about, but she didn't want to think what they might be. 'Cover me for alligators,' she said. 'Or even caiman.'

Andrea nodded, and presented her rifle.

'Well . . . see you in the funnies.' She slid down the bank on her bottom, entering the water feet first as quietly as she could, as if that would make any difference; the piranha were attracted by smell rather than noise. The river was deep even against the bank and in a moment she was swimming, using an old-fashioned breast-stroke, which had the advantage of being virtually noiseless. Don't think, she told herself. Concentrate on that opposite bank. Don't think.

The rifle and shoulder bag seemed inordinately heavy – the waterproof bag, being filled with air, should have given her some support – and as she was already exhausted she tired very rapidly. Suddenly something brushed against her leg. She almost screamed, and certainly lost her breath as she recalled that people bitten by sharks apparently felt nothing more than a slight touch until they got ashore and discovered that they were short an arm or a leg. My God, she thought, if that applies to piranhas, I could be being eaten alive and not know it! But then she was against the far bank and dragging herself up, staying on her knees while she looked down at herself and feeling a rush of blood when she found no damage.

On the far side the rest of the team clapped.

Jessica put on her trousers and boots, and unslung her rifle. 'Who's next?' They had all coated themselves with citronella.

'I will come.' Encarna discarded her jacket, which was pretty well unwearable anyway, and slid into the water. She came across with a succession of powerful overarm strokes, and was beside Jessica in seconds.

'My lord?' Jessica invited. 'If you'd assist Lady Miranda.'

Adrian followed Encarna's lead and discarded his torn blazer, transferring his wallet from his inside breast pocket to the hip pocket of his pants and giving his pistol and spare magazines to Chloe to stow in her bag. Then he sat on the bank. 'Come along.'

'I can't,' Miranda said. 'I just can't. My God, to be eaten by a fish! A little fish!'

'Come *along*!' He seized her wrist and jerked her into the water.

'Aaagh!' she screamed. 'My shoes.'

Fortunately, the sandals floated, and Adrian was able to grab them. Then he struck out, using his legs as he towed Miranda behind him. Jessica and Encarna pulled them out, and they sat on the bank, dripping water. 'That's an experience I don't ever want to have to repeat,' Adrian said.

'You two coming together?' Jessica called.

The girls had already taken off their boots and pants and stowed them, Andrea revealing that she was indeed wearing her new thongs – was it really only two days ago that they had made plans in the comfort of their hotel bedroom? – which left virtually nothing to the imagination. Now they entered the water together, Andrea having followed Jessica's lead and strapped her rifle with the shoulder bag on her back, as had Chloe with her bag. Five minutes later they were on the far bank. 'Never felt so clean in my life,' Chloe said.

Jessica gave them the rest of the afternoon off. As the sky was clear and the sun was hot, the girls promptly stripped, both to dry their clothes and to sun themselves. Encarna regarded them for a few moments and then did likewise, no doubt determining that she should learn English customs as rapidly as possible. Miranda also stripped, with an apologetic glance at her brother. He undressed down to his underpants.

'What the hell,' Jessica said, and followed fashion. She suspected they were all, even Adrian, feeling a little hysterical. She understood that merely being on Brazilian soil did not mean they were home and dry; it did not even mean they were safe from pursuit, although it did appear that they had sufficiently discouraged the Colombians. It was merely that the traumatic events of the past two days seemed to have come to a climax in the successful passage of the river. Having triumphed over so much, none of them doubted they were going to reach Uaruma in safety.

And then? She called London. As it was mid-afternoon in western Brazil, she figured it would be about dusk in England, so she went for the commander at home as before, got through the invariable astonished reception from Mrs Adams, and reached the boss himself; he had just come in. 'I did ask you to use the office, JJ,' he complained.

'I know, sir, and I apologize. It's a bit difficult because of the time zones. I just wanted to let you know that we are now in Brazil, and on schedule.'

'Oh, jolly good. Any problems?'

'Ah . . . none we haven't been able to cope with.'

'Splendid. And the natives are cooperating?'

'We haven't actually encountered any Brazilians yet, sir.'

'Well, I'm sure they'll be eager to help. Now tell me, is Lady Miranda all right?'

Jessica looked at Miranda's long-limbed, golden-brown splendour stretched on the grass. 'I would say she is in the pink, sir.'

'Excellent. And his lordship?'

'Him too. Is there any prospect of us being extracted? Perhaps from Uaruma?'

'I'm working on it, JJ. Keep in touch.' The phone went dead.

Andrea, an even more compelling sight than Miranda, opened an eye. 'All well?'

'I suppose you could say that,' Jessica said.

They moved on for a couple of hours that afternoon, and then bivouacked for the night on the banks of a stream, from which Encarna extracted another fish for dinner. As they were not getting any greens, Jessica doled out vitamin pills. It rained during the night, heavily, and their clothes were soaked again. But no one seemed to mind; they were on the home straight.

'Where do you think Ramon is?' Miranda asked, walking beside Jessica as they pushed branches aside and forced their way through the undergrowth.

'Haven't a clue.'

'Do you think he's still in Colombia?'

'I don't think he was ever in Colombia, if only because he couldn't have got there before us.'

'But you said those men were working for him.'

'They were working for friends of his, who he managed to call up on the radio, or by mobile.'

'But we left him lost in the bush.'

'He was never lost in the bush. My bet is that he managed

221

to get back to that first village we found, where someone had a mobile. I should've let Chloe shoot him when she had the chance.'

'That's a terrible thing to say,' Miranda snapped. 'And now you want me to send him to gaol. I want to go to the loo.'

'All right. Everybody halt. Use those bushes over there.'

Miranda disappeared, and Adrian came over. 'Giving you a hard time?'

'Nothing I can't handle. My only worry is that she is going to freak out as a witness. That has to be *your* concern, my lord. Because if she does that, after all the mayhem we have created to get her out of Bolivia . . .'

'Don't worry. The family will sort her out.'

'Pity they didn't do that before she got married,' Jessica grouched, and then swung round as a piercing scream came from the bushes. 'Oh, my God!'

Chloe drew her pistol and dashed through the undergrowth. Andrea unslung her rifle and made to follow, when there was another terrified scream and a shout from Chloe. 'Goddammit!'

From the bushes there emerged a long thick body marked with orange and black diamonds. It was travelling at great speed, straight at them. Andrea got in a shot, but missed. Jessica fired twice at the head, smashing it to pieces. Then, to make sure, she fired twice more into the still wriggling body.

'I say, good shooting,' Adrian said. 'But Mira?'

Jessica looked at Encarna. 'What is it?'

'That is a bushmaster. Very dangerous.'

'Aaagh!' Miranda screamed again as she burst through the bushes.

'Help me!' Chloe shouted.

'Shit!' Andrea ran forward, rifle at the ready.

'It bit her!' Miranda gasped as she tripped and landed beside the dead snake. 'Aaagh!'

'It's dead,' her brother told her. 'Jessica shot it. Just relax. It didn't bite you, did it?'

'No, no. But Chloe . . .'

Jessica followed Andrea to stand above Chloe, who was writhing on the ground. Encarna joined her. 'The bushmaster's venom is fatal in a minute.'

'A minute?' Jessica shouted. 'Do something.'

Andrea dropped to her knees beside her partner.

Encarna knelt beside her. 'Give me your belt.'

Andrea pulled off her belt; her lips were quivering. Encarna unbuckled Chloe's pants and pulled them down. Chloe was groaning and still writhing. Now Jessica could see the punctures just above the knee; the fangs had penetrated the thick material and already the surrounding flesh seemed to be darkening.

Encarna passed the belt round Chloe's thigh, about six inches above the wound. Then she drew it tight, and passed it around the thigh again before tying it. Chloe screamed with pain. 'That will stop the poison from spreading too quickly,' Encarna said. 'Now give me your knife.'

Jessica handed over the clasp-knife.

Encarna opened it. 'Now strike a match,' she said.

Jessica obeyed. Encarna held the knife blade in the flame until the match burned down and Jessica had to drop it. 'Do you want another one?'

Encarna shook her head. 'Hold her legs. And you,' she told Andrea, 'hold her arms.'

Jessica grasped Chloe's ankles. 'What can you do?' By now Chloe seemed almost unconscious, but she was moaning and her breasts were heaving.

'We must get the poison out.' Encarna bent over the punctures.

'You're going to cut her?' Andrea was holding Chloe's wrists; her voice was high.

'It is the only way.' Carefully Encarna pressed the blade into the now blackened flesh. Blood seeped out.

'Oh, my God!' Andrea shouted.

'She is not feeling it,' Encarna assured her. 'When she screams in pain, we have won.'

Jessica watched the thin stream of blood issue from the wound, accompanied by a dark liquid; she was only dimly aware that Adrian and Miranda were standing above them, arms round each other in mutual support.

They watched Encarna make another incision across the first, which brought more liquid seeping out. Then she laid down the knife and put her lips to the wound, sucking hard before raising her head and spitting. Miranda made a strangled sound. Encarna lowered her head and sucked again before spitting again.

'How many times?' Jessica asked.

'Maybe several. Will you bring the wine?'

'I'll get it.' Adrian hurried off while Encarna sucked again. He returned with the wine, and she rinsed her mouth before resuming. Jessica looked up at Andrea's stricken face, and realized that at that moment all of them – even someone as experienced and, she supposed, hard-bitten as herself – were absolutely vulnerable.

Suddenly Chloe seemed to wake up, with a shudder and then a moan and then a scream of pain. 'Hold her!' Encarna shouted when Chloe tried to kick. 'Keep her still.'

'She's in agony,' Andrea protested.

'That is because she can feel,' Encarna said. 'We have won.' The wound was now bleeding freely. 'You have antiseptic?'

'I have iodine,' Jessica said. 'But you cannot put iodine on a deep cut like that. She'll go out of her mind.'

'Here in the jungle, infection is more dangerous than snake-bite. You must make the decision, but if the wound becomes infected, she will die. Or you will have to cut off the leg.'

I have to make the decision, Jessica thought. She looked up at Adrian, but he appeared to be petrified. Miranda was leaning against him, weeping. Then she looked at Andrea, who was looking back, her face a mask of misery. She

224

had to make the decision. 'Will you hold her legs, please, my lord?'

Adrian disengaged himself from his sister and took Jessica's place. She slipped her bag from her shoulder, found the first-aid box, and handed the bottle of iodine to Encarna. 'Give her wine to drink,' the hostess said.

Chloe's eyes were open and she was groaning and moaning. Andrea brought her arms in front and between them they raised her head. 'Help us,' Jessica told Miranda.

Miranda seemed to wake up, and knelt beside them to hold the wine bottle to Chloe's lips. Chloe gulped at the liquid and gave a sigh, and Encarna applied the iodine. Miranda whipped the wine bottle away just in time, as Chloe gave a convulsive jerk and uttered another scream. Jessica and Andrea and Adrian needed all of their strength to hold her down.

'Bandage,' Encarna said.

'In my bag,' Jessica told Miranda, who delved and brought out the roll and the lint.

Encarna expertly soaked the lint in more iodine and applied it to the wound, bringing another shriek and violent convulsion from Chloe, then wrapped the bandage round and round Chloe's thigh. 'Will the bleeding stop?' Jessica asked, seeing the white covering immediately turn pink.

'I think so. But she will be weak.'

'Will she live?' Andrea asked.

'I think so.'

Andrea burst into tears.

Jessica gave Chloe some codeine to swallow with the wine, and after a while she subsided into a deep sleep, breathing stertorously and occasionally tossing, but happily oblivious to her pain.

'When I think that could have been me . . .' Miranda said.

Andrea looked at her, and Jessica squeezed her hand.

'Oh, all right,' Miranda said. 'It's my fault. All I wanted was a pee.'

'It's nobody's fault,' Jessica told her. 'We happen to be trying to exist in a high-risk environment. But from now on no one is to be alone – at any time. No matter what you need to do, you must have a companion to keep watch. I'm sorry, my lord, but that applies to you, too.'

'Point taken.' He sat beside her. 'What are we going to do?'

'When will she be able to move?' Jessica asked Encarna.

'You mean walk? Not for many days.'

'Shit!' Jessica used her GPS. 'We're thirty-three miles from Uaruma. Travelling as fast as we can, I make that at least three days.'

'It would be best for her to rest for a few days,' Encarna said. 'And then she will have to be carried.'

Jessica chewed her lip. 'I'd better get instructions.' She called the office, as she reckoned it was still mid-afternoon in London.

'Ah, Sergeant Jones,' Mrs Norton said. 'You must be a long way away; your voice is very faint.'

'I am a long way away, Mrs Norton. Shall we say nine thousand miles? But the reason I am sounding faint is because my battery is just about flat. So would you please connect me with the commander.'

'I'm afraid the commander is in a meeting.'

'Mrs Norton, it is essential that I speak with the commander *now*. I do not know if, or when, I will be able to call again. And this is an emergency.'

'You are always in a state of emergency, Sergeant Jones. I will see if the commander can take your call.'

Adams was on the phone a few moments later. 'JJ? Have you reached that village? I'm afraid that was too quick for our arrangements.'

'We have not reached the village, sir. I have to report a serious case of snake-bite.'

226

'You have been bitten by a snake? Good lord! I hope it wasn't poisonous.'

'It was very poisonous, sir. One of the most poisonous in the world. And I have not been bitten. The casualty is Detective-Constable Allbright.'

'Good heavens! How did she manage to do that?'

'The snake attacked Lady Miranda, sir.'

'Oh, my God! Is she all right?'

'Yes, sir. DC Allbright managed to intervene.'

'And *she* is all right?'

'No, sir. As I said, she is seriously ill. We managed to get the poison out, but she is too weak to move, and will be unable to do so for some days.'

'Hm. And your situation? How long can you survive?'

'I think for a little while yet, sir. But it is urgent that we get DC Allbright to a hospital as quickly as possible.'

'Very good. Give me your coordinates.'

Jessica did so.

'Is that jungle, or open land?'

'It's mostly jungle, sir. But there are open areas.'

'Very good. How are Lord Lichton and his sister taking it?'

'As well as can be expected, sir. But they are anxious to get out.'

'Oh, quite. Now, JJ, there is a report coming out of La Paz about some tourists being involved in a gun battle on a ranch in the interior belonging to a man named Cuesta. Would this be our Cuesta?'

'Ah . . . I should think it is quite possible, sir.'

'Apparently the place was shot up by three heavily armed young women using assault rifles and rocket launchers. You wouldn't have had anything to do with that, I suppose?'

'Assault rifles? Rocket launchers? Those aren't standard departmental issue, sir. And if you will remember, sir, we were forbidden to take any arms.'

'That's true. And the local media are saying that the incident was drug-related. The trouble is, the tourists and the tour company have the names of these women: a widow, Jones, and a pair travelling together, Hutchins and Allbright.'

'What a remarkable thing. Up till now I never believed in coincidences.'

'You're denying that these three are you and your team.'

'How could it be me, sir? You know I'm not a widow.'

'That's true. And they don't appear to have identified them as policewomen. As I say, they are suggesting that the whole thing was drug-related, and seem quite keen to play it down. However, JJ, I am bound to say that someone with your weakness for walking on thin ice should bear in mind that some day the ice is bound to crack.'

'Yes, sir.'

'I would like to speak with him,' Adrian said.

'Lord Lichton would like a word, sir.'

'Oh. Ah. Well, you'd better put him on.'

Jessica handed him the phone.

'Commander Adams? Lichton here. Yes. Thank you. Well, not really. Conditions are extremely primitive and damned dangerous. My sister was all but bitten by a snake. Yes, I appreciate that. At the earliest possible moment. Very good. What I really wanted to speak with you about is the behaviour of your three women. No, no, they have been absolutely magnificent. Their devotion to duty is quite outstanding. I wish personally to recommend them all for promotion, and a medal. You don't give medals? A clandestine operation? Yes, I understand that, but I would like my commendation entered in their records. All of their records. Thank you, Commander. I look forward to seeing you again very soon.' He handed the phone back to Jessica.

'Will there be anything else, sir?'

'Yes, apart from remarking that as usual you have managed to wangle things so that you have landed squarely on your feet;

228

his lordship has actually made me very proud of you. Now listen. I wish you to move Allbright and your entire party to an open area. This is so we can get at you. As soon as you have established your camp, call me and give me your position.'

'Yes, sir. And thank you, sir.' She switched off the phone, and gazed at Adrian. 'Thank you, my lord. But I thought you weren't going to get involved?'

'Bugger that. If you're in trouble because of what you did, it's my business to sort it out. He's promised to extract us within forty-eight hours.'

'Providing we're somewhere accessible by air. So . . .' She looked around at the anxious faces. 'We have to move. Hopefully, only a short distance.' She spread her map. 'Where are we likely to find open ground, Encarna?' She prodded. 'We are here.'

Encarna studied the map. 'This river, here, is open.'

Jessica peered at it, then made a distance check. 'Three miles. Hm.'

'Can't we make some kind of stretcher?' Miranda asked. 'You know, sling her from a pole, like they do in the movies.'

'In the movies, milady, they usually have both the poles and the material for the stretcher arranged before they start shooting. We have neither.'

'I'll carry her,' Adrian said.

'Three miles? Through the bush?'

'You can clear a way for me.'

They packed up and set off. It was hard going, and they had to pause several times to rest while Encarna did some more fishing at the various streams they passed. It was dusk before they reached the river.

'I'm glad we don't have to cross that,' Miranda said.

Jessica agreed with her. This river – she reckoned it was the Uaupés – was all of a hundred yards wide, slow-moving and sinister. She went to where Adrian was carefully laying Chloe on the ground; big as he was, and strong as he was, he was exhausted. Andrea knelt beside him; she had stayed at his side throughout the march. 'She is bleeding again.'

'Only slowly,' Encarna said reassuringly. She used Andrea's first-aid box to re-dress the wound. 'If help comes soon she will be all right.'

Jessica's batteries were now quite flat. She used Andrea's phone to call London and give their coordinates, and tell him to use an amphibian. Adams wasn't there, so she spoke with Manley instead. 'Just stay put,' he told her. 'We'll get to you.'

They took turns at sitting beside Chloe all night, as well as keeping watch. But it appeared as if all pursuit had been abandoned, and it was just a matter of waiting for their rescue to arrive. And then? Jessica wondered if she could actually consider that, and decided that there were too many imponderables to think about until they were actually back in London.

She slept soundly when her watch was completed, soothed by the constant rustle of the river, and was awakened by a touch on the arm from Andrea. 'JJ,' she whispered.

Jessica's stared at her for a moment; it was just light, and she could tell from Andrea's expression that something had happened. 'Oh, my God!' she said. 'Not Chloe?'

'No,' Andrea said. 'Trouble.'

Jessica sat up, looking left and right, her hand instinctively closing on her rifle. But then she drew a sharp breath.

The six of them were entirely surrounded by at least twenty naked men, each armed with a spear and a blowpipe.

The Arrest

'What do we do?' Andrea asked. She also held her rifle. But they couldn't possibly kill twenty men without a very good reason. Equally, Jessica doubted that they could kill them all without taking return fire from the pipes. 'I think we had better negotiate. If we can.' She nudged Encarna. 'Do you reckon these are hostile?'

Encarna sat up and gazed at the men, clutching her throat. 'These are head-hunters. Look at their necks.'

Jessica looked as directed, and saw that each man wore a necklet of some kind of vine, from which, in the middle of his chest, there drooped a replica of a head.

'Those can't be real,' Andrea protested.

'Oh, they are real, señorita. They cut off the head, and then they shrink it.'

'Oh, my *God*!'

'You think they are interested in our heads?' Jessica asked.

'They will kill us first,' Encarna said unhelpfully. 'They will shoot us with their darts. The darts will be poisoned.'

'Not *wourali* again,' Andrea commented, having got her nerves back under control.

'That is the very thing. The poison will paralyse you, and then they will cut off your heads. *Our* heads.'

'While we're still alive? Holy shit!'

'Do you think they will speak Spanish?' Adrian was also awake, as was Miranda, who was clinging to her brother's arm.

231

'More likely Portuguese,' Jessica suggested. 'Do you speak it, Encarna?'

'No,' Encarna said.

Jessica watched the men, who continued to stare at them. She had a notion that they had seen a rifle before, although perhaps not an ArmaLite. 'Try them in Spanish,' she said. 'The languages are not very different, are they?'

'They are different in many ways.'

'Try them,' Jessica insisted. 'Tell them we are friends.'

Reluctantly Encarna stood up and addressed the Indians, using the word *amigo* several times, which they seemed to understand – not that there was any relaxation of the heavy features. But there was some movement. 'Looks to me like they mean to be nasty,' Adrian commented as he saw the pipes being fondled. 'Think we should withdraw into the bush?'

'No,' Jessica said. 'For three reasons. One is that our withdrawal would encourage them to begin hostilities, and two is that our strength would be reduced, as we – or *you* – would have to carry Chloe. The third is the most important: in the bush we wouldn't be able to see them, while they would be able to see us. I hate to say it, but we have to settle this business here and now. Encarna, I think they got the gist of what you said, even if they don't want to play ball. Now tell them that we wish them to clear off. Vamoose, eh? Tell them if they don't we are going to fire into them and kill them all. Now, would you all present your weapons in the most obvious manner. Lady Miranda, will you take Chloe's pistol.'

'I've never fired a gun in my life.'

'Just point it in the general direction of the enemy, and if we start shooting, you try squeezing the trigger. Now remember, if I shoot, we all shoot. And we shoot to kill, as many and as rapidly as possible. We have to wipe them out. My lord?'

Adrian licked his lips.

'It's that, or else you and milady may find your heads

hanging round one of those necks, suitably shrunk. Are you with me?'

'Yes,' Andrea said, very positively.

'Right. Tell them, Encarna. Draw your pistol first.'

Encarna obeyed. At the sight of the presented weapons a kind of ripple ran round the men.

'Andie, rear and left,' Jessica said. 'And you, my lord, rear and right. Encarna, front right. Milady, front left. Leave the centre to me. Okay, Encarna.'

Encarna drew a deep breath and spoke, while Jessica eyeballed the men facing her. She had no fears about the actual outcome of the coming conflict, if there was to be one. The Indians were about fifty feet away, which she reckoned was about maximum range for a blowpipe, although she couldn't be sure. But it was within murder range of an assault rifle, and in her magazine alone there were sufficient bullets to destroy all the men around them. But there remained the possibility that one of them would be hit, and they already had one casualty too many. Besides, as she really wasn't into murder, she prayed they would leave while Encarna was addressing them. They did not seem to be getting the message, however; even if they understood what she was saying, they obviously disbelieved her threat, and were shuffling their feet and preparing their pipes. 'Stand by,' Jessica said – and from above her there came a loud whirring noise.

The Indians looked up at the large helicopter dropping out of the sky, gave a collective shout of alarm, and melted into the trees.

'Do you think it's Cuesta?' Adrian asked.

'No,' Jessica said. 'It has floats.'

The helicopter settled on to the river, then taxied to the bank. A crewman wearing naval uniform leapt out with a rope to fasten it, followed by four armed men; these were wearing bush kit. 'Well, hi,' Tom said. 'Am I glad to see you.'

'You know something?' Jessica replied. 'Snap.'

*   *   *

'Ah, JJ,' the commander said. 'Welcome home. Did you have a pleasant voyage?'

'We were well looked after, sir.'

'Splendid. Having read your report, I won't ask you if you had a pleasant visit to Bolivia. At least it was a successful one from our point of view, even if there are quite a few questions to be answered. I mean to say, these expenses . . .' He flicked the papers on his desk. 'One hundred pounds for the rent of a truck, for three hours? How do you explain that?'

'Inflation, sir.'

'I think you were had. I would have thought someone with your experience would know when she was being robbed. You do give me some problems.' He raised his head. 'What is the matter with your face? Those marks.'

'Mosquito bites, sir. They got to other parts of me as well.'

'Ah.'

'But I am assured that they will fade quite rapidly. In fact, they have already done so over the past week.'

'I'm sure. You'll be pleased to know that I have had a note from Lord Lichton, repeating his praise of you and your, ah . . . young ladies.'

'His lordship is very kind, sir.'

'Yes,' Adams agreed, somewhat drily. 'You do understand that I cannot implement any of his recommendations, at least not at this time. This operation must remain top secret, until and unless Cuesta is brought to trial.'

'I quite understand, sir. Is he going to be brought to trial?'

'We certainly hope so.'

'And Lady Miranda will give the required evidence?'

'She's being interviewed by our drugs people. I gather she had quite a horrendous experience.'

'She shared our experience, yes, sir.'

'Oh, quite. What is the report on Allbright?'

234

'She is very sick, sir. She lost a lot of blood while we were trying to extract the poison. And it was two days after the incident before we could get her to the transfusion unit on board the warship. Despite our efforts, some of the poison got into her system, and in her weakened condition it acted the more potently.'

'What are you trying to tell me?'

'The doctor was indicating that she may be unable to return to duty, sir. At least in an active capacity.'

'Damn. How is Hutchins taking it?'

'I don't really know. She's at the hospital now. I shall be seeing her shortly.'

'Well, it's a damned shame. We shall have to see what we can do. In the meantime, JJ, take a week off. That goes for Hutchins, too.'

'Thank you, sir. May I ask what is the situation with Miss Santos?'

'She is being treated like any other illegal immigrant.'

'With respect, sir, she is not an illegal immigrant. She entered this country as our guest. Without her I do not think we could have survived.'

'She still has no right to be here.'

'If she is returned to Bolivia, sir, she could well face execution.'

'But not by her government. I don't think being chased by a drug baron comes into quite the same category as political asylum. However, don't worry about it. The Earl of Clandine is taking it up at the request of both Lady Miranda and Lord Adrian, and I believe she may be released into his custody as a domestic until her case is sorted out.'

'A domestic? Isn't that rather patronizing? She's an airline hostess. And, may I say, a highly qualified backwoodswoman.'

'I am sure the earl has that in mind. Not that I believe there is a great call for backwoodswomen in this country, however highly qualified. Calling her a domestic is a temporary expedient. Now, for God's sake go home and relax. You've carried out your mission very successfully – if, shall I say, a trifle overenthusiastically. My congratulations.'

Tom was waiting downstairs. 'The fatted calf?'

'You have got to be joking. If Lord Lichton hadn't put in a word for me, it would have been the cloven hoof.'

'Well, it's in all the papers. Ordeal of British holidaymakers caught in drug battle and that sort of thing. One of them even claims to have had what he calls a close relationship with the leader of the baddies. I thought she was a cute little blonde, he says, and suddenly she produces a Kalashnikov from her knickers. Would you care to comment on that?'

'Only that he doesn't know a damn thing about guns.'

'And close relationships?'

'Those neither.'

'Where would you like to go now? The pub?'

'No. Home. And a hot bath.'

'You had one this morning, before we left the ship.'

'So? I intend to have two a day for the foreseeable future.'

She soaked in the tub. It was so good to be home.

Not that she was the slightest bit relaxed. Apart from the various bites, scratches and bruises, which were aggravated by the hot water and the bath salts, and her feeling of black despair at what had happened to Chloe, she was terribly aware of unfinished business. To think that all she had put herself and the girls through, with such a sad outcome, could be rendered a waste of time by that silly little girl's refusal to testify . . .

And there remained the Tom situation. He was doing his best to pretend their quarrel had never happened. On board the warship during the voyage home he had been a perfect gentleman, and she had shared a cabin with Andrea – they had both been too exhausted and worried about Chloe to do more than sleep and occasionally weep in each other's arms, while for most of the voyage she had been prostrated with sea-sickness – she had never been a good sailor. Now he had brought her home, and she had observed that his clothes were still in the wardrobe. So, was she going to throw them – and him – out, as she had threatened to do? Or was that dependent on more unfinished business, such as Adrian Lichton? Or even Andie. But Adrian had made no effort to arrange a get-together. Did that mean she had imagined the whole thing, at least on an emotional scale, or that she had frightened him off by her ruthlessness? While Andie, poor Andie, was obviously going to be in an emotional mess herself . . .

No, she was going to have to take whatever decisions were needed. She washed her hair while reflecting that she was far more capable of coping with alligators, snakes and hostile Indians than with her own private life.

Tom came in. 'There's an e-mail.'

Jessica tossed wet hair from her eyes. 'From whom?'

'Ah . . .' He studied the printout. 'The Earl of Clandine.'

'Give me that!'

She snatched the paper from his hand, hoping that her pounding heart wasn't giving away too much of a flush.

Dear Sergeant Jones, or may I call you JJ, even though we have never met: I feel I know you so well already. My wife and I wish to express our most sincere appreciation of all that you have done – at, I am informed, great personal risk – to return Miranda to us, and also to convey our concern and condolences for the unfortunate accident to your colleague, Miss Allbright. We would be very pleased if you and your other colleague, Miss Hutchins, could join us for dinner at Claridge's on Saturday week. Adrian and Miranda, as well as our younger son, Thomas, will be with us. Shall we say eight o'clock for nine? There is no necessity to dress. With every good wish, Clandine.

'Talk about moving in high society,' Tom remarked. 'I note that partners are not included.'

'Chloe happens to be in hospital.'

'I'm not in hospital.'

'I don't think the earl knows that you exist.' Jessica brooded at the sheet of paper. She would have expected, and she would have preferred, to have received the invitation from Adrian personally. But no doubt they did things differently in the aristocracy.

The doorbell rang.

'That'll be Andie,' she said. 'Let her in, will you?'

Tom used the entry phone. 'It's not Andie. Some fellow named Smart. Says he knows you, and that it is most important that he speaks with you.'

'Joe!' She scrambled out of the bath, scattering water. 'Tell him to come up.'

She towelled herself vigorously, ran a comb through her wet hair, pulled on a dressing gown . . . and checked. What the hell was Joe Smart doing in England? Nicolette had suggested that they might be coming over, but not in a couple of weeks. And she had never quite trusted him.

She heard Tom opening the door. 'Mr Smart? Jessica seems to know you. Come in. She'll be out in a moment.'

Jessica opened her drawer and took out the Skorpion, checking to make sure it was loaded, and put it in the pocket of her dressing gown. Then she went into the lounge. 'Joe! You caught me with my pants down, quite literally. I'm still trying to wash Amazonia out of my system. But how good to see you.' She embraced him and kissed him on the cheek. 'There's nothing wrong?'

'I'm hoping you'll tell me that, JJ.'

'Explain.'

He glanced at Tom.

'Oh, don't mind him. He's a policeman too. Sit down. Drink?'

'Scotch?'

'Of course. Will you pour, Tom. This is Tom Lawson, by the way. We live together. And Tom, this is Joe Smart. He's a friend of the Lichtons. He was most helpful to us in La Paz.'

Tom shook hands, then went to the sideboard. 'You?'

'Just a glass of wine. Red. Do sit down, Joe.' She sat beside him on the settee, pulling the dressing gown across her knees. 'Is Nicolette with you?'

'She's in England, yes.'

Tom brought the drink, and she touched glasses. 'Now, what is it you wish me to tell you?'

'Where Cuesta is. And whether he's dead.'

Jessica frowned at him. 'He's not dead, at least as far as I know.'

'Didn't he follow you into the bush?'

'He had us landed in Colombia to be dealt with by his pals, if that's what you mean. But I would say he stayed at his ranch. There were a certain amount of repairs necessary.'

'He's not at Cuesta Ranch. In fact, so far as I can find out, he's not in Bolivia. There's a bit of a stink going on, you see, with tourists involved in a gun battle, which everyone is assuming was drug-related. Well, I suppose it was. So there is a strong suggestion that if the DEA comes up with a warrant for his arrest, no one in Bolivia is going to stop them serving it.'

'So he's done a runner. I wonder where. But . . . why does it matter so much to you?'

Smart finished his whisky and handed Tom the glass. Jessica realized that he was in a highly nervous state. 'He knows I . . . well, if I say so myself, I did rather organize the whole thing, from arming you to arranging your escape.'

'That wasn't too successful,' Jessica reminded him.

'That bastard Alonso. I had no idea he was in Cuesta's pay. He had worked for me for several years.'

'Ferrying freight for you. May I ask what this freight was?'

239

'Well . . .' Smart flushed.

'I see. You and Cuesta are business rivals. That explains an awful lot. Does the DEA know about this?'

He took his refreshed glass from Tom. 'I do not grow cocaine,' he said with some dignity. 'I am an agent for certain businessmen in Bolivia and the United States.'

'Just like Sprightly, in fact.'

'He was one of our people, yes.'

'I see. And it was your friends who provided the hardware for us.'

'Well . . . I did try to dissuade you, remember? But when it became obvious that you were going in regardless, I realized that there was a golden opportunity to blow Cuesta off his perch.'

'Being afraid to do so yourselves.'

'Well, we couldn't do it ourselves. That would have involved open warfare. Then the government would have had to intervene, and the whole business would have gone up in smoke.'

'But if three crazy and over-armed English policewomen were to go in and take Cuesta Ranch apart, you could raise your hands to heaven and declare your innocence of any involvement – before rubbing them together in glee at the outcome. Whether or not we managed to get ourselves killed was no concern of yours.'

'I did warn you that you were committing suicide,' he insisted. 'And you weren't killed.'

'No thanks to you. And now it has all blown up in your face, has it?'

'Because you didn't get Cuesta.'

'It was not our remit, and you knew that.'

'I knew he would never let you take Miranda off the ranch.'

'He wasn't too keen, I'll agree. OK, so we didn't do the job as you would have liked. We certainly put him out of business for a while. And it's going to be a long while. I can promise you that he's going to have too much to worry about for the foreseeable future to come gunning for you.'

'You don't understand,' Smart said, finishing his second drink. 'My associates are unhappy. I told them that we were getting rid of Cuesta. Permanently. That hasn't happened. In our business, only success matters.'

'Ah,' Jessica said. 'So you have been told to get the job finished. Or . . .?'

'These are tough people, JJ. You know that.'

Tom had been listening to the conversation. Now he remarked, 'Seems to me you've dug yourself a bit of a hole.'

'They're going to kill me. And Nicolette . . .'

'They don't usually go after wives.'

'Perhaps not. But without me . . . JJ, I'm begging for your help. OK, so Alonso pulled a dirty one. I didn't know about that. But without my help you wouldn't have got anywhere.'

'Whatever your motives,' Jessica remarked thoughtfully, 'I understand your problem, Joe, and I'd help if I could, but I'm afraid I don't have a clue where Cuesta is. Have you tried the Lichtons?'

'I came to you first. They're not likely to know.'

'Miranda might have some ideas.'

'Yes. Well . . .'

'You don't want them to know you're in the business yourself. Cambridge and all that.'

His head drooped. 'I had hoped to be able to retire to England in a couple of years. Sort of set myself up . . .'

'But if it gets on to the social grapevine that you're a retired drug dealer, you won't get into the best clubs. How sad.'

'All right. I suppose you're entitled to your pound of flesh. Listen, is there any chance of police protection until Cuesta is caught? I can't go back to Bolivia before then. And if it doesn't happen soon enough, they're liable to come after me here.'

'You have got to be joking,' Jessica said. 'I'm bending the

rules as it is, simply because you did help us, by not taking you in now for questioning. You have just confessed to being a drug dealer.'

'Well . . .'

The entry phone buzzed.

'Does Nicolette know you're here?'

'No, no. She knows nothing about the situation.'

'Then it'll be Andie,' Jessica said. 'Tell her to come up, will you, please, Tom.'

Tom picked up the phone. 'Yes. Come on up.' He released the door. 'She sounds agitated.'

'She *is* agitated, with Chloe in the condition she is. Something else for which it is possible to hold you responsible, Joe. You'd better leave.'

Smart stood up. 'But you won't help me.'

'I cannot help you. My advice is to lie very low until we catch up with Cuesta. We will, very shortly.'

His shoulders slumped, and he turned to the door, which opened at that moment to admit Andrea, who, thrust violently from behind, staggered across the room and fell over the settee.

'What the . . .' Jessica turned to help her, then turned back to look at the door – and the three people standing there: Ramon, Duarte, and Felicity. Immediately her hand dropped to her dressing-gown pocket, but she was too late. Each of the intruders was armed with a silenced pistol. Facing them, Smart had already drawn a weapon, only to be hit in the chest by Duarte's bullet. He fell over backwards and struck the floor with a crash; Jessica estimated that he had died instantly. The other two guns were pointed at her and Tom, and she knew she would be dead long before she could draw the Skorpion, but since the dressing gown was made of heavy brocade, there was every chance that they would not suspect the gun was there.

Ramon closed the door. 'Up,' he said.

Jessica and Tom both raised their hands. Andrea rolled over and sat up. As she was wearing a short dress and knee boots, she hastily adjusted the dress, then pushed hair from her eyes. 'JJ,' she said. 'I'm so sorry. I was utterly careless. I just didn't think anything more could happen.'

'Don't blame yourself,' Ramon said magnanimously. 'You were taken by surprise. We had to gain admittance, you see.'

'Am I allowed to look at him?' Jessica pointed at Smart.

Ramon shrugged. 'If you wish. I do not think it will do him any good. Take his gun, Duarte.'

Duarte took the gun from Smart's lifeless fingers. Jessica knelt beside him, but as she had suspected, he was dead. 'How the hell did you know he was here?' she asked.

'Oh, your flat has been under surveillance for some days. We were waiting for you to get back. And then, as I say, we had to wait for someone trusted by you to request admittance. We saw that carrion come in, but we were not sure he would be acceptable. This beautiful young lady, now . . . well, I remembered her.'

Felicity made a remark in Spanish, and Andrea muttered, 'My God!'

Jessica raised her head.

'Of course,' Ramon said. 'You speak Spanish. Tell her what Felicity said, Miss Hutchins.'

Andrea licked her lips. 'She said when can she have you, to *cut*,' she whispered.

Jessica looked at Felicity. There was a jagged scar down her cheek. 'I'm sorry about that,' she said. 'But you did bring it on yourself. I'm sure a good plastic surgeon will be able to work wonders.'

Felicity switched to English. 'I am going to cut off your tits and cook them before your eyes and then make you eat them,' she said.

'It's her Indian blood, you see,' Ramon explained. 'An

Indian never forgets an injury. I know this. I have Indian blood myself.'

'Now look here,' Tom said, having recovered from the shock of the invasion.

'Who are you?' Ramon inquired.

'He is my lover,' Jessica said.

'How interesting. Do you think he will still love you when Felicity is finished with you?'

'If you lay a finger on her, you slimy little bastard . . .' Tom said.

'For that,' Ramon said, 'I am going to give you also to Felicity. She will make you eat your own balls.'

Andrea gave a groan, and fainted. Her knees gave way and she collapsed on to the settee again. Jessica knew she hadn't fainted – Andie had never fainted in her life. But she didn't know what her sidekick was trying to achieve; as she wasn't on duty she wasn't carrying her shoulder bag and was therefore unarmed. 'She is mine,' Duarte said, dropping his pistol into his coat pocket.

'Help yourself. But be careful. These people are trained in unarmed combat. Now you, my little friend, I am going to make Felicity wait while I have you myself. This is something I have been promising myself. If this lout moves, shoot him,' he told Felicity, who pointed her gun at an impotent and angry Tom. 'Now, let's see, I know all about your skills.' Ramon presented his pistol to Jessica's head. 'Untie your dressing-gown cord.'

Slowly Jessica released the cord. She knew she could still not risk attempting to draw her Skorpion without getting a bullet in the head. But if she let him tie her wrists she was done. Out of the corner of her eye she saw Duarte roll Andrea on to her back and lift her skirt to her waist. Now, she prayed. Oh, now, Andie! Now!

Andrea might have heard her. As Duarte lowered his head to pull down her thongs, she opened her eyes and in the same moment brought her hands together over Duarte's ears, as Jessica had done to Tom before she had left for South America. But Jessica had intended to do nothing more than get him off her; Andrea meant to hurt, and gave the clapping hands all the strength she possessed. Duarte gave a shriek of the most utter agony, reared off her, and fell to the floor.

Ramon, his attention already caught by the sight of Jessica's body as the dressing gown fell open, was further distracted by the scream. Jessica acted with the greatest speed, sweeping his hand aside so that the bullet he fired crashed into the wall and drawing her own weapon at the same time, firing into Ramon's thigh. He uttered a shriek to match Duarte's, and went down. Jessica stepped on his wrist, and when he released his pistol, she kicked it away.

Then she could turn her attention to Felicity. But she was too late. When the women had gone into action, Tom had leapt at her, but she had cut him down before he could reach her, and he was on his knees, streaming blood. Felicity was swinging the gun towards Jessica, but Andrea stooped beside Duarte, pulled his pistol from his pocket, and fired in the same instant. Struck in the chest like Smart, Felicity crashed backwards against the wall. Again like Smart, she was dead before she reached the floor.

'Call Superintendent Manley, an ambulance, and CID,' Jessica snapped.

Andrea ran to the phone.

'Help me,' Ramon shouted. 'I am bleeding to death.'

Duarte was still rolling on the floor, moaning; blood dribbled from his punctured eardrums.

'You'll have to wait your turns,' Jessica told them, and knelt beside Tom. 'Bad?'

'I don't know.'

His shirt-front was covered in blood, but there was none coming from his mouth as he breathed. She helped him up and laid him on the settee, and tore open his shirt to find the wound. He was bleeding heavily, but again, the blood wasn't pumping out.

'I think you've lost a rib.' She dashed into the bedroom, collected the spare first-aid kit, and returned to bind him up.

'They're all on their way,' Andrea said. 'What do we do about him?' She nudged the moaning Duarte with her toe.

'Haven't a clue. He'll have to suffer until the ambulance gets here. But put a bandage on his nibs.'

'Bitches,' Ramon moaned. 'Bitches. You are bitches from hell.'

'You'd better believe it,' Andrea told him.

Jessica picked up the phone, punched the numbers. 'Commander? I'm sorry to bother you again so soon. But I have Ramon Cuesta.'

'You have arrested Cuesta? My God! But we have no evidence against him yet. If you've blown this, JJ . . .'

'I'm charging him and his associate with murder, attempted murder, grievous bodily harm, attempted rape and unlawful entry. He's not in very good shape, I'm afraid. But he'll be able to stand trial – with the aid of a pair of crutches.'

Andrea was waiting for her in the lobby when Jessica came down from the office. 'How'd it go?'

'I think the old buzzard was actually pleased. There's to be a commendation. For you and Chloe, too.'

'Oh, great. That'll cheer her up.'

'I never had the chance to ask you how she is.'

'Let's say she knows her police days are done. At least on active service. That's depressed her. You know, obviously I am going to have a new partner, and, well . . .'

'Tricky,' Jessica agreed. 'How do you feel about it?'

'Well . . .' Andrea blushed. 'You won't believe this, but Adrian, Lord Lichton, has asked me out to dinner.'

Jessica gazed at her. 'Not at Claridge's, Saturday week?'

'No, no. This is tomorrow night. At the Savoy. He left the

message on my answerphone, and I haven't replied yet. Do you think I should accept? I mean, there's Chloe, and . . .' She gazed at Jessica with enormous eyes.

Ships that pass in the night, Jessica thought. Dreams ditto. 'I think you should accept,' she said. 'And I wish you all the success in the world.'

Jessica sat beside Tom's hospital bed. 'I reckon you saved my life.'

'All in the line of duty.'

'I'm not going to forget it. The downside is that we are going to have to move. Complaints from the neighbours, etcetera, etcetera.'

'We?'

'Well, your clothes are still there.'

'About that shirt . . .'

'I think that is something we *should* forget.'

'Right. You know . . .' He picked up her hand. 'When those thugs broke in, you told them I was your lover. Did you mean that?'

'Why not?' she said. 'Beggars can't be choosers.'